A MATTER OF TIME

Themah Carolle-Casey

A MATTER OF TIME

Copyright © Themah Carolle-Casey 2014

Themah Carolle-Casey asserts her moral right to be identified as the author of this work in accordance with the Copyright, Designs and Patents Act 1988:

This is a work of fiction. Names characters, places and incidents either are the product of the author's imagination or are used fictitiously, and any resemblance to actual persons, living or dead, business establishments, events or locales is entirely coincidental.

All rights reserved. No part of this publication may be reproduced, stored in or introduced into a retrieval system, or transmitted, in any form or by any means (electronic, mechanical, photocopying, recording or otherwise), without the prior permission of the publisher.

ISBN-13:978-1502412218

Cover Design: Themah Carolle-Casey

For my mother who dreamed of writing and my daughter who is a constant inspiration.

Without freedom from the past, there is no freedom at all, because the mind is never new, fresh, innocent.
                                        Krishnamurti

In the darkness she felt her way along the wall in search of an opening, a way in. As her mind moved over the cold, hard surface, a whispered thought offered a mere suggestion as to the length of time the wall had been there and the resistance necessary to create a thing of such density. She brushed the thought away as if flicking an irritant hair from her eye and continued with her search.

The wall had not always been there, she knew that, but it was a long time since she'd had access to whatever lay on the other side. She decided it had been there long enough; it was time for it to come down. There were times when her mind explored the wall, she felt unsure how and why it was there. Was it to keep something in or something out? She expected to come across a door that would require a key, a word, an image or a symbol which, like magic, would open the door to a torrent of bright light and it would collapse, disintegrate.

The very thought created a strange feeling within her head. She saw a little girl rushing towards her with open arms, full of joy and playfulness. The little girl wanted to take her by the hand and eagerly show her what pleasures lie in wait for her. As suddenly as she had appeared the child was gone and she was left facing the stone wall again that now appeared more icy and unmoving than before.

"Doubt. It's doubt that will do it every time. You must believe." Where did that come from? She turned inside herself to see but the thought had gone. "If you believe, anything is possible. Give your doubt to the wind and walk through the wall." She observed the solidity of the dark cold wall.

"You have created it and are therefore one with it. Walk through it." Her chest tightened and she felt she would never breathe again. Is that what it is? Fear? A wall of fear? She caught a fleeting glimpse of the child with her arms reaching towards her, only to be replaced again by the wall, the tightness, unable to move, frozen in time.

The stirring of a memory crept from deep within her mind. Words from a book.

"Remember," there was the voice again, "you must focus. Become one with the wall and move through." Slowly, she felt a strength stir, a belief in the seemingly impossible and she took a small step towards the wall.

"Keep your focus." Taking a deep breath she stepped forward and realised the wall was not solid at all. The atoms separated in front of her and she moved between them, like walking into a strong grey wind. Before she could breathe out the wind dropped and she gazed in awe at the bright colour filled landscape. Shock, relief, amazement washed over and through her.

"I did it!"

London, ENGLAND

The alarm grew louder as she surfaced from her dream, dragging her consciousness with her as she reached towards the clock, silenced it and slipped from the bed. She fumbled for her robe and made her way to the bathroom. Looking in the mirror at her dishevelled reflection, the result of yet another disturbed night, she tried to shake off the exhaustion that wanted to seduce her back to the oblivion of sleep. It was always the same; the forest, the house, the wall, impervious, the same feelings of fear and inevitability. No doubt a therapist would be able to explain these dreams but she didn't have time for that now. There were people to see and deadlines to meet. She showered and dressed, still haunted by leftover emotions that hung on the edge of her consciousness, remnants begging resolution.

It was two weeks now since the dreams started, not every night, but frequent enough to disturb her usual equilibrium and encroach into her daily life.

Downstairs in the kitchen she prepared breakfast. Unhelpfully her mind sought out the dream wanting to make sense of it, re-engaging the fearful emotions. "No!" she screamed silently, "Not now". She could feel the pressure of the day's commitments close in around her. Okay. She would do something about it, but later. She would call James, meet him for a drink after work. Maybe he could help her make sense of it all.

She grabbed her jacket, after all it was only mid-May and the temperature could be so unpredictable. She checked her briefcase and, closing the front door behind her, determined to get on with the day.

Elegant and petite, inherited from her Italian mother, she hailed a taxi and told the driver her destination. Leaning back into the seat, Lucia closed her eyes and mentally went over the details for her first meeting. Despite some early misgivings she was in fact excited by the project. As an art journalist she had secured a much coveted interview with Giacomo Martinelli to discuss his family's prestigious art collection. First she was to meet with a representative here in London who would make the arrangements for her visit to the Martinelli villa just outside Florence where the collection was housed. As the taxi pulled up outside the hotel, Lucia felt the adrenalin rise and any other residual feelings dissolve into the shadows.

Newly opened and still trying hard to impress the hotel was not to Lucia's taste. Light reflected from the abundant shiny surfaces as she made her way to the lounge with its bright red seating and mirrored tables.

Antonio Martinelli stood and walked towards her, offering his hand in greeting.

"Signorina Walker, *buongiorno*" he smiled. "*Sono* Antonio Martinelli."

"*Piacere*," she responded shaking his hand, a little disconcerted. She had not expected the representative to be Signor Martinelli's elder son. He reminded her of someone but there wasn't time for her memory to explore it as she was directed to a seat and coffee ordered.

The next hour passed quickly and arrangements were discussed and confirmed for Lucia to fly to Florence the day after tomorrow, Wednesday. She would be collected at the airport and taken to a hotel nearby the Villa Martinelli. She would meet with Signor Martinelli for lunch on Thursday followed by a tour of the gallery and the interview. It was made clear she was to focus only on the art collection and not the family's personal lives.

"It was a pleasure to meet with you Signorina Walker and I hope you will enjoy your stay in Italy. Any problems please do let me know You have my number." Antonio Martinelli smiled as he stood and offered his hand again, this time to finalise the meeting. Again Lucia felt a sense of recognition, a cobweb brushing across her mind and quickly lost in their goodbyes.

She left the hotel satisfied the meeting had gone well and then realised she would be leaving for Italy in 48 hours. She felt the panic surge to her throat and her breathing constrict as the thought sank and lodged itself at the forefront of her mind.

"Ok, ok," she breathed deeply, *"Calma, calma."* A phrase remembered from childhood, used by her grandmother in times of stress and one where she now sought comfort.

She had a day and a half to prepare for the interview and her visit to Florence. As she tried to focus on the day ahead she felt remnants of the dream seeping through. She shook her head to clear the unsettling images and, returning to the present, called James. They arranged to meet at six.

"Si, si, va bene." How many times must he say so, he thought, as he ended the call to his father. Antonio Martinelli knew very well that his father was used to having his own way and getting what he wanted.

There had been much speculation recently about Antonio's younger brother, Lorenzo and his connection to some dubious business dealings. Did his father think he could deflect any negative publicity by giving this rare interview about the family's art collection? He had been emphatic, and repeatedly so, that there were to be no questions about the family's personal lives. It had been Antonio's job to find an art journalist not only with integrity but one who also understood Italian culture. And what did he mean by that – someone not only appreciative of the valuable collection but also aware of the Italian need to maintain *la bella figura* and would not pry below the surface? He had approached the task with some trepidation. As an Italian, he understood the culture only too well. Also, the world of journalism was not necessarily known for its sensitivity.

Antonio tugged at the cuffs of his shirt and buttoned his jacket. Immaculate in a beautifully tailored suit he glanced in the long mirror. "Hmm ... *la bella figura*", he thought ruefully and quietly smiled.

His work at his father's gallery in the centre of Florence and independent of the collection that was housed at the villa, had brought him into contact with artists, collectors, gallery owners and journalists around the world and although he had been reluctant to become part of his father's business, he had discovered early on that his opportunities were limited if he wanted to stay in Florence. He had studied art hoping that one day he would become a successful artist and had found this required more than he was willing to invest. Florence was full of aspiring artists and it turned out that his love for Florence was stronger than his dream of being an artist. Uncomfortable with such strong competition Antonio soon realised his path would be better paved by joining his father at the gallery. A mixture of youthful naivety and arrogant charm Antonio quickly found the success he desired. Now in his early thirties, experience had tempered the arrogance and, with a little maturity, he had gained a quiet confidence.

Like many unmarried Italian men Antonio lived in the family home but often used the small apartment above the gallery. He loved Florence, and was happy he had not made the compromise made by many of his peers of moving away from the city to find work. Somewhat oblivious to his own good fortune of being born into a wealthy and successful family, he took for granted a lifestyle to which many in Italy could only aspire.

So, here he was in London having fulfilled his father's very specific wishes.

"Just find someone," his father had said. "And make it clear, they are to ask about the collection only – our private lives are not to be discussed!"

"But..."

"*Basta!* I do not wish to discuss it. Please," he added gently, "just do as I ask".

Antonio knew when not to press him.

Returning to the present, he remembered the

meeting earlier with Lucia Walker. What was it about her? He was sure that they had not met before but he felt as if he already knew her, there was a feeling of familiarity that he could not explain. Anyway, he thought, dismissing any further musings, she was the perfect choice, fulfilling the criteria so adamantly set by his father. Satisfied that he had done his job well he made arrangements to return to Florence as quickly as possible.

Meanwhile, not far from Antonio's hotel, Lucia was making her own arrangements to travel to Florence. She had booked her flight online for the following day from Gatwick, and decided that she would stay on a few more days after the interview so she could catch up with her aunt and cousins. She loved Chiara, her maternal aunt, and thought this would be a wonderful opportunity to spend time with her. She had only managed to see Chiara once in the last two years when she had visited London on business and that had been more rushed and fleeting than either would have wished.

Ah, the time! There was still another meeting to attend and she then had to go to the office to tie up loose ends there before meeting James.

On and off throughout the day James had pondered on his sister's words and her uncharacteristic behaviour. Always calm, some may say controlled, he had never heard her sound so flustered and, well yes, emotional. It wasn't that she was unemotional, just that he'd heard something in her voice, something he hadn't heard before. Fear, that was it, fear. He tried not to dwell on these thoughts too much and told himself that she would make sense of it all when he saw her later, unaware that it was Lucia who was expecting him to make sense of her irrational feelings.

As the eldest, James had always felt responsible for his younger sisters despite them now being adults and perfectly capable of taking care of their own lives. Whilst he did not intrude in their lives he, inexplicably, worried about them and their ability to make good choices even though experience told him otherwise. Maybe it was a trait carried by many first born children. How many times had he been told by his mother "....look after your sisters" or "...... watch your little sisters, won't you". It was like an inbuilt password protected computer programme which he could not access to modify.

As for himself, James, now in his mid-thirties, was a successful businessman. As the director of an Italian food and wine company, he travelled frequently between London and Italy. Through his business he had maintained strong ties with his mother's family there and visited them whenever time allowed. He had initially studied law with dreams of becoming an international lawyer and, as often happens, life had other ideas for the young James. After gaining a training contract with a top London law firm he quickly became disillusioned and when his father died he had taken leave to help his mother tie up the estate. He had also kept the business going while his mother decided whether to keep it on and put in a manager or to sell it. His father had created a moderately successful, if somewhat outdated, business importing fine wines from Italy and had met James' mother during a business trip to Tuscany many years earlier.

James soon found he enjoyed running the business far more than being a lawyer and quickly became inspired with new ideas. It was not long before he introduced some carefully sourced foods to complement the wines and discovered to his surprise that he had found a niche market that proved to be very profitable. Relieved to find her son was a natural entrepreneur, James' mother happily handed over the business, content it would remain within the family domain for at least another generation.

As his working day came to an end, James' thoughts returned to his sister.

"Well Luci, what's this all about? You sounded flustered on the phone."

"Oh, probably nothing really. How are you? How's the business?" she feigned interest in James' life in an attempt to avoid the irrational feelings of rising panic.

"Luci. What's going on?"

She took a gulp of wine and watched the pale golden liquid settle in the glass as she put it down on the table.

"It's just that.... you remember ..." Lucia faltered over the words, and avoiding James' eyes, breathed deeply as if about to dive into a deep pool. "You remember when we were little and used to go to *nonna's* for the holidays and we'd walk through the forest to that house? Well, I've been having this dream, the same one, for about two weeks." She felt her breath catch high in her chest as she spoke. She went on before the air ran out, "and there's a wall and.... and.. I'm sure it's there, and......"

"*Calma, calma,* Luci," James watched his sister with concern, "this is not like you."

"And …. and I fly to Italy the day after tomorrow." Lucia looked at her brother with an intensity he found unsettling.

"Luci, Luci, what are you trying to say?" James said gently.

"Oh, I'm not sure. It's just that now that I'm going to Italy the dream seems to have taken on …... er, it seems more real. And the feelings – they're so strong, and, ... visceral. I was scared, James. I am scared and I don't understand why". Lucia took another gulp of wine then said in a calmer tone, "James, you know me, I'm not exactly known for falling apart".

James smiled, "True, Luci", he said.

"Oh, maybe I'm being silly. You know, reading, feeling too much into it. I've been so busy recently that I don't have time to think, outside of work that is." Lucia gave James a faint attempt at a smile. Another sip of wine and she felt some of the stress from the day slip away as she was able to relax a little in the safety of her brother's presence. "It's good to see you. Thanks for coming."

"*Niente*," James said, it's nothing. "How about we get something to eat, if it's not too early for you."

"Yes, no, that's a good idea" Lucia paused for another sip of wine, before adding, "We can eat here or go to the Italian round the corner."

"Let's go to the Italian – get you in the mood." As soon as the words were out James regretted them as he watched Lucia's expression darken. "Sorry Luci, I didn't mean to …... look let's go somewhere where we can sit quietly, have some good food and talk this through."

Relenting, Lucia smiled faintly and said, "It's okay James, the Italian's fine. Sorry if I'm a bit edgy. Let's finish our drinks and go."

They came out into the already cool evening air and walked the hundred odd yards to the restaurant. Thankfully, James thought, it was Monday evening and early enough to get a table without a prior reservation. They were greeted enthusiastically by the owner, Alberto.

" *Buona sera, buona sera ...... certo, certo*", he sang and led them to a corner table by the window.

After the usual pleasantries and perusals of the menus they ordered their food and some wine. James looked thoughtfully at Lucia searching for words that would not startle her and cause her to retreat behind her usual confident mask.

"Don't worry James", she said, jolting him from his reverie with her sharp intuition, "I do want to talk about it, it's just that I don't know how to explain it, but I will try".

She unfolded the napkin on the table in front of her and placing it on her lap curled a corner round her finger, her eyes focussed on the table cloth where the napkin had sat. Searching her mind for a beginning and the right words, she took a deep breath in an attempt to speak calmly and clearly. Whilst she appreciated James' patience Lucia was not sure she had that much patience with her own ability to relate something that was still beyond her comprehension.

As she spoke she slowly raised her eyes to look at James. She trusted James more than anyone she knew. Despite any disagreements they may have had, he had always been there, supported her and when necessary, been honest with her. He had an easy openness that she often struggled to find within herself. Maybe she was less tolerant and forgiving of the flaws she saw in others and in herself.

"It began a couple of weeks ago and at first I gave it little thought. It was just another dream. You know how it is, fragmented, half remembered. Then a night or two later it happened again, the same dream. I still didn't pay it that much attention until it happened a third and then a fourth time. Each time my memory of it became clearer and the feelings I experienced on waking were more intense." Lucia paused for a sip of wine aware that the bottle had arrived at the table and her glass filled without her realising.

"Go on," James encouraged in a quiet voice.

Finding safety in his attentiveness she continued, "I don't know if I can make sense of it really, and now I have to put it into words it sounds silly. Anyway, remember when we were little and went to stay with *nonna*? I loved it there. The sun was always shining, we explored the woods, swam in the river and every day brought a new adventure. Then one day we found that old house, the *casetta*; it was empty, the owners up and gone long ago like so many places in Tuscany. Remember when we got back and told *nonna,* she seemed angry and said that it was dangerous and not to go there again? I think she said something about vipers and that was enough to dull any curiosity I had after that. Anyway.... the dream. I'm alone in the woods and there's a house. At first I didn't recognise it, or maybe it changed, you know how it is in dreams. So the house, with each dream, became more familiar and I began to explore more of it. Then one night I came across this wall and I was drawn to it. I can't explain it. I know it sounds like nothing but this feeling of fear and inevitability intensified more each time and now I'm waking up drenched in sweat and filled with panic. James it's exhausting and I don't know what to do. Should I go there since I'll be close by or …. oh, I don't know!" Lucia threw her hands up in exasperation at the same moment as her food arrived and nearly sent the plate flying from the waiter's hand.

"*O dio! Mi dispiace,* I'm so sorry!" Lucia fell back into her chair while the waiter put the plate down on the table in front of her and safely retreated.

James looked quizzically at his sister, "Luci, what do you...."

Before James could finish his sentence, Lucia cut in, "That's it, it doesn't make sense! That's what I don't understand. I remember the house, it was quite sweet and looked so small in the shadow of those cypress trees standing round it, protecting it. No, it's more to do with the sense of the place. It draws me in and the magnetism increases with each dream, as if something is about to happen, something inevitable and I'm involved in whatever it is in some way. Oh James," Lucia sighed, "I hoped you might remember something or, I don't know, see something I can't."

Now she'd tried to communicate it, Lucia felt a little foolish about the whole thing and smiling, said, "Maybe I'm more stressed about this interview than I thought. Let's eat."

She held her glass out towards James who reciprocated, "*Salute!*" they said in unison.

"Luci, I wish I could remember something, I only

vaguely remember the house. Didn't we go there two or three times before we told *nonna* about it? I don't remember anything unusual though. Maybe Chiara will know something. Have you spoken to *mamma*?"

"No, no, no. You're the only one I've mentioned it to. I just hoped you'd be able to make some sense of it that's all." Lucia smiled. "You're right, I'll talk to Chiara. I don't want to worry *mamma* with it." She felt better now, for having said it, shared it with someone; it somehow diffused the intensity of it and she relaxed a little more.

"It's so good to see you James. I feel better just talking to you, thank you. Tell me, what's happening with you?"

"Oh, you know how it is." James leaned back into his chair. "The business takes up most of my time. It's doing well. Better than expected so far this year, in fact. I'm going to have a look at some new oils and wines in a couple of weeks – shame we won't be there at the same time. There's a place on the edge of the Chianti hills that I've heard about. One of those old family estates that are finding they need to expand beyond Italy if they are to survive. They've won awards for their oil and their wine so I'm hopeful it will make a good addition to our range if negotiations go well." James paused to drink some wine, "Mind you, this wine's not bad, what do you think?"

"Er, yes", Lucia said, aware she was beginning to drift again and quickly brought herself back to the present. "I've been here a few times and always enjoyed it. Also they do an excellent *spaghetti alle vongole*, which I love."

They continued their meal interspersed with

conversation about each other's work and lives, or lack of them, and after they had finished their coffees, James signalled to the waiter to bring the bill.

"My treat, Luci. Let's do it again soon. How about when you get back and before I go?" He handed his card with the bill to the waiter and waited for him to return with the payment machine. "*Cara*, let me know how it goes. You know if you need anything you only have to give me a call." Content he no longer needed to worry and that his sister was probably just more stressed than she realised and it was playing out in these dreams, James paid the bill.

"*Andiamo.*" Let's go. They said their goodbyes to Alberto and promised to return soon then stepped out into the street where they hugged and said their goodbyes.

"*Ciao cara, a presto."* James said.

"*Ciao James, e grazie,"* and Lucia gave her brother one last squeeze and set off in the opposite direction towards home.

Tuesday passed without incident for Lucia as she continued to finalise her research and preparations for the interview with Giacomo Martinelli. James had sent her a text that morning to wish her well and *buon viaggio.* She had managed to have a dreamless sleep the previous night, and now that her fears had dissolved into the past she felt somewhat embarrassed by her recent reactions to them. Comforted by the thought that in a couple of days the interview would be out of the way and she would be able to enjoy some much needed time with Chiara and her grandmother, Lucia sent James a text to thank him for being there and that she was already feeling better about it all. As she pressed the send button Lucia felt a whisper of fear tinge the moment. She brushed it aside telling herself she was being silly and carried on ticking the items on her check-list. Finally, she put her neatly packed case by the door and made herself a chamomile tea before settling down on the sofa to relax with the still unread Sunday papers.

It was, of course, ridiculous – this dream thing, she thought as she flicked through one of the magazines hardly taking in the headlines. Nothing more than a bit of stress. It's just been so busy and …… well, and I suppose I only have myself to blame for taking on too much.

"Is that so?" she thought she heard a soft voice say in her head and, dismissing it, put it down to a mixture of imagination and stress.

"Well, it couldn't be anything else – I'm on my own; I mean, there's no one else here." Lucia said out loud in an attempt to convince herself that was the case. Finishing her tea, she took the cup to the kitchen and got ready for bed noting that she must do something about it as soon as she got back from Italy. Or maybe, she would speak to Chiara and ask her for a remedy.

Exhausted, and relaxed by the tea, Lucia fell into a deep sleep as soon as her head touched the pillow. She was shocked to be woken by her alarm and the realisation that she had slept through the night. Vestiges of dreams danced across her memory, too flimsy to grasp yet she was aware of fragile, kaleidoscopic images – the house, the wall, but this time too distant and diaphanous to hold their usual emotional charge.

She switched off the alarm, leapt out of bed as she realised she had a plane to catch and went straight to the shower where she let the water wash away the remains of the night. Refreshed, she made coffee and grabbed a croissant before getting dressed and doing a final check that she had everything she needed for the trip. She heard the taxi pull up outside to take her to the station and with a deep breath and one last look round the apartment, picked up her case and stepped out into a fresh spring morning.

Victoria station was at its busiest and negotiating her way against the tide of people heading out from the platforms on their way to work, Lucia eventually boarded the Gatwick Express with only a few minutes to spare. She found a window seat and was aware of an anxious fluttering in her solar plexus. She put it down to the anticipation of travelling and took out the book she had brought with her for the journey. As the train pulled away from the station the anxiety increased, rising towards her heart then upwards and catching in her throat. She took a deep breath and looked out of the window as the train passed the old Battersea Power Station.

I must concentrate on the interview and not let these other silly thoughts get in the way. She reminded herself how lucky she was to have been asked to meet Giacomo Martinelli and that this was the first interview he had agreed to give for many years. She was well aware that he had made it a condition that any questions about the Martinelli family were strictly forbidden yet, like any good journalist her curiosity was strong and she hoped there would be an opportunity to touch on something of a more personal nature beyond the art collection itself. She had done her research and found that whilst the art collection was well documented anything else to do with the family was not. Oh, the family's support of the arts, particularly in Florence, was well known as was the small part they played within Florentine society but whenever she had tried to scratch beneath the surface, there was nothing to be found. That was, until recently and the fiasco and rumours surrounding the younger son, Lorenzo Martinelli.

Hm, Lucia thought and smiled, a crack appears in the family portrait. She reminded herself to buy a newspaper when she got to Florence and ensure she hadn't missed any fresh news to do with the Martinellli family. A flicker of excitement rose in her at the thought of an afternoon and evening alone in the city she loved, that was the home of her family.

The train sped past the stations without stopping until it finally arrived at Gatwick. With a little more confidence than when she had left London, Lucia gathered her belongings and alighted from the train to a busy platform. She looked around to get her bearings and headed towards the departure desk to check in.

Relieved of her case, Lucia turned from the desk towards the concourse in search of a cup of coffee. On second thoughts she would be in Florence in a couple of hours or so and maybe it would be best to wait and have a real Italian coffee rather than waste her caffeine quota here.

Once through the security checks and passport control, she went to the departure gate and had time to make a final check of her mobile for any emails before the boarding light came on and the gate was opened.

A few minutes later she settled into her window seat, adjusted and fastened her seatbelt and, feeling more relaxed now that she was actually on the plane, waited for the last of the passengers to board and the take-off procedure to begin. She felt a rush of adrenaline as the plane lifted from the runway and soared upwards. She smiled and enjoyed the thought of being unavailable – no mobile, no emails, nothing for at least two or so hours. Ignoring the flight attendant's display of safety instructions, she looked out of the window to see the London suburbs give way to a green and brown patchwork as they headed towards the English Channel. It was not long before the white cliffs of Dover were left behind and the open countryside of France came into view.

The plane climbed above the cloud line and Lucia's spirit rose as the sun's rays sent beams of light into the cabin. Such a different light to the grey mist she had left behind at Gatwick. She mused on the quality of light she had experienced on her travels and like a magnet her thoughts were drawn to her destination; Florence, Italy. A mixture of emotions stirred within her as she contemplated the next few days. Of course, there was the joy and excitement at the prospect of seeing her aunt and grandmother, yet she was aware of an underlying disquiet. No more than a whisper until given attention, it then clung to her consciousness, grappling to take hold and Lucia, once again, became aware of an anxiety deep within, still unexplained.

Attempting to brush away such thoughts she concentrated her mind on the interview with Signor Martinelli. She was looking forward to meeting this man who had become an enigma over the years and she wondered whether this was by design or merely his own nature.

Giacomo Martinelli was the head of an old Italian family whose ancestors had arrived in Florence in the sixteenth century. Having fled from Cortona they had managed to preserve valuable works of art that now formed part of the famous Martinelli collection. Once settled in Florence they soon became a presence in Florentine society. She mused that the upper echelons of Florentine society are still a closed circle today and their walls not easily breached and wondered if much had changed from the time of the Medici and their hold on the city in the 15th and 16th centuries. How the renaissance had changed the city and indeed beyond, with its far reaching influence.

She brought her thoughts back to Signor Martinelli, and, in particular, the son Lorenzo. His father cannot have been happy that his recent escapades had gained attention from the press. Again, the phrase came into her mind *"la bella figura"* and she thought how fragile that veneer becomes once cracked.

Would the family be able to smooth this over, she wondered, or was this only the beginning of far deeper cracks? She was well aware of the complex politics within such families and gave thanks for the comparative simplicity of her own family.

Florence, ITALY

WEDNESDAY
Mercoledi

Of all the seasons Chiara loved spring most. Everything was at its best. The temperature was equable, the sky was blue more than not and everywhere nature sang its beauty like an operatic aria. A naturally elegant woman, she gave grace to the most mundane clothes, which she did now dressed in a pair of old grey jeans and faded pink sweatshirt. "Ah, what's the point of dressing well only to get dirty in the garden," she could often be heard saying. And this was a time of year when she could be found in her garden tending and nurturing the plants and herbs that had become not only her business but her life's joy. She frequently gave thanks for her good fortune, feeling blessed beyond her expectations.

Her family had not been wealthy in a conventional way. Their home was small but adequate for herself, her sister Daniela and their *mamma,* Isabella. Their father had died when they were children and notwithstanding any sadness this caused, Chiara's childhood memories were happy ones, filled with laughter, adventures and sunlight. Memories of her mother and grandmother often visited her as she worked in the garden, their voices advising her, recommending this and that – "this plant will do better here" or "now is the best time to transplant this one", and so on.

Her grandmother, Rosa, had been the local healer and often people would go to her for advice before, or instead of, visiting the doctor. To Chiara, Rosa knew all there was to know about herbs and plants and curing sickness, not only of the body but also the mind. She and Daniela spent many hours with their *Nonna* Rosa who would care for them after school and during the holidays while Isabella was busy building her own business based on Rosa's teachings. Isabella had found a small shop in one of the quiet little streets in Florence near the Duomo where she sold the creams and potions she had made based on her mother's recipes and knowledge. She had used some of the money her father, Pietro, had left for her in the hope of providing an income and future for herself and her daughters.

Having grown up before and during the war, Isabella knew how to make the most of limited resources. Their house in the forest in the foothills of the Pratomagna gave not only the family protection but also members of the resistance, who hid in the harsh terrain leading to the summit. Isabella would tell Chiara and Daniela how Rosa would give her baskets of food to take to these courageous men caught between their conscience and their families.

Aware of the increasing bureaucracy, Chiara had

trained as a chemist. She knew that if she wanted to expand the shop and use the knowledge passed on to her from her mother and *Nonna* Rosa she must have the necessary qualifications required by Italian law. Once qualified she was able to extend the range of products she already offered. It was not long before the business flourished and they had to move to a larger shop and an already faithful clientele grew to include some of Florence's wealthiest families. Chiara often wondered how she ever managed to find the time to marry and be the mother of two, now adult, children.

Surfacing from her reverie of gratitude, Chiara's thoughts returned to the present and her niece's visit. Franco was away and she didn't expect him to be home for at least ten days which meant she would be able to give Lucia her full attention. She knew Isabella was also looking forward to seeing her granddaughter and that she needed to allow space for them to spend time together, aware how limited that time may be for each of them.

The plane gained altitude as the Alps came into view and another surge of adrenaline caught Lucia by surprise as she realised she would soon be in Florence.

Damn, what is this! Annoyed by the intrusion, she affirmed, this is not going to get the better of me. However, her body spoke a different story as the adrenaline turned into panic and rose upwards to her throat leaving her mouth dry and wondering where the next breath would come from.

Ridiculous! she thought, and breathed as deeply as she could. She felt her heartbeat increase and vibrate through her body. Why is this happening to me?

Her immediate surroundings faded into the background and she found herself in a misty light and muffled silence.

"You will come" a quiet female voice said without inflection. Confused by the ambiguity of the words, Lucia was unable to discern whether it was a statement or a question. She stopped breathing as she remembered the voice from the previous evening that she had summarily dismissed as her imagination but was stopped from following the thought further.

"S*ignora, va bene?*" the stewardess leaned towards her asking if she was alright. Disorientated, Lucia looked up realising that her face was damp and felt drained of any colour. She was shaking.

"*Si, si, grazie,*" Lucia managed to thank the stewardess, took a deep breath and through the shock wondered what had just taken place. She was speechless, even in her own mind. There was no context, no experience where she could find an explanation.

How can this happen? There, then not there ..... how ..... what ..... what is happening to me?

Another voice broke in as the captain announced they would be landing shortly and that the temperature in Florence was a warm 24 degrees and it was not long before the plane was taxi-ing along the runway to the applause of the Italian passengers on board.

Still shaken by her momentary loss of control, Lucia took her time leaving the plane and when she did step outside was immediately hit by the warm air and bright sunlight. She made her way to the baggage hall and waited for the carousel to start churning out cases. Turning on her mobile, she breathed a sigh of relief to see there were no messages that needed her immediate attention.

It wasn't long before she had retrieved her case and was wheeling it through customs and the arrivals gate to be greeted by a sea of faces seeking recognition and maybe reunion. Lucia scanned the barrier for someone holding a sign with her name on it and caught her breath to see Antonio Martinelli look directly at her and smile.

"*Signorina Lucia, benvenuto*" he said as she approached him, "I hope you had a pleasant flight."

"Yes, thank you," Lucia replied, "Er, I wasn't expecting you to ….." the question tailed off as Lucia regained her composure and continued, "what I mean to say is I wasn't expecting you personally."

"Ah, I was at the airport to oversee a shipment so, it is perfect."

"Oh," was all Lucia could manage, followed by a cough in an attempt to cover up her loss of control.

"The car is not far, in the car park. It is not possible to park outside as we once did." another smile showed perfect teeth, white against deep olive skin. "Shall we?" Antonio led the way to his car.

Once outside the airport building Lucia was struck by the cacophony of noise, both aural and visual. She had forgotten how the volume seemed to be turned up a few degrees here and the plethora of hoardings and signs assaulted the eyes.

They left the airport and headed east towards Fiesole where the Martinelli villa nestled in the hills above Florence. The road snaked up from the city, in places edged by walls of magnificent jasmine hedges hiding palatial villas from prying eyes.

"I hope you will enjoy your stay with us. I believe you are staying on for a few days to spend time with your family."

Again Lucia's breath caught in her throat as she wondered how he could know this. Before she was able to respond and as if reading her thoughts Antonio continued, "My mother knows your aunt and you know how Florence is ...." he shrugged, splaying an upturned right hand in a gesture of unspoken words.

Another, "Oh," was all Lucia could manage before Antonio interceded saying how much his father was looking forward to meeting her.

Lucia's mind started to race over the past few weeks searching for something in the process of how she had been chosen for this interview. She felt at a disadvantage in some way. There was a discomfort she couldn't explain. In fact, there was so much that seemed inexplicable right now!

"It's not far now. You will be staying in our garden apartment which has become available. So, if you'd like to settle in, have something to eat – Maria has prepared some food for you - I could pick you up in a couple of hours and show you the gardens."

"Thank you," Lucia replied, and, with apprehension, wondered what other surprises lay in wait for her, then added, "I would like that."

The car pulled up outside ornate iron gates and Antonio took the remote control from a recess in the dashboard, pressed the button and, as the gates slowly opened, he drove through to the cypress lined approach to the Villa Martinelli. Ahead was the impressive villa where it had stood since the 15^h century. A grand and imposing façade with symmetrical steps sweeping to a large central arched door, Lucia took in the aged grandeur and beauty of what was before her eyes. She had heard and read about such villas, many dating back to, and some built by, the influential Medici family that had held court over Florence for some three hundred years. Antonio drove to the back of the villa and into a barn-like outbuilding that she thought must have originally housed carriages or horses and was now where the family garaged their cars. Amazingly, despite the renovations, swallows swooped and dived in and out of the open doorway which, Antonio explained, they had been doing for hundreds of years, returning each spring to nest and leaving again at the onset of autumn.

As she stepped into the large courtyard she was stunned by the panoramic view over Florence, its famous *duomo,* and to the mountains beyond.

Taking Lucia's case, Antonio led her round to the west side of the house, through an archway to a walled garden with a small pool, and the apartment where she would be staying.

"*Allora*," Antonio deposited her case inside the door, "please make yourself at home – is how you say in English? And, I will see you, shall we say, at 4 o'clock?"

"*Grazie mille,"* Lucia thanked him, looking forward to some time on her own so she could make sense of the last few hours. "See you then."

Although not a large apartment, high arched windows and glass doors leading to a loggia gave a sense of spaciousness that belied its actual dimensions. A hallway led to the living room that was simply decorated with whitewashed walls. Contemporary paintings added colour as did the ceiling's old chestnut beams and the richly coloured, decorative cushions and throws scattered over a white sofa and chairs. Well-worn terracotta tiles covered the floors in a diamond pattern and Lucia smiled in appreciation that these had not been removed to make way for a more modern flooring such as marble. An archway led to the *cucina*, the kitchen, which was well-equipped and large enough to comfortably take a table and four chairs.

Further down the hall, the only bedroom had a double bed with crisp white cotton bedding, and a white mosquito net draped from the ceiling, which all contrasted against the deep colour of the terracotta floor tiles. Smaller windows with half closed north facing shutters created a welcoming coolness. Another door at the far end led to a marble tiled bathroom comprising of both a shower cubicle and bath.

Lucia was on her way to the living room when there was a knock at the door. A middle aged woman introduced herself as Maria and explained that she had prepared lunch for Lucia. Behind her, a trolley boasted various antipasti, salad, bread and fresh fruit.

"I can make pasta too, if you wish?" Maria offered.

"*Grazie, non*. This is fine, thank you." Lucia replied, suddenly realising that it had been a long time since her early breakfast. She had declined to eat on the flight and was now very hungry. Maria went to wheel the trolley into the kitchen. Lucia stopped her saying, "It's ok, I think I'll eat outside. *Grazie*."

Maria wheeled the trolley on to the loggia and when Lucia said she would serve herself, Maria left saying she would collect it later.

As food now took priority, Lucia helped herself to the wonderful variety of food in front of her. There was *prosciutto, carciofi, olives, mozarella, pecorino,* and much more; fresh bread still slightly warm, a carafe of red wine and a bottle of water. After a mouthful or two of food she relaxed a little into her surroundings, poured herself a glass of wine and made a decision to enjoy her short stay here. Where the wall became lower beyond the entrance, the west facing view from the loggia was breath-taking.

She had discovered in her research that it was not only the art collection that the family were known for but also their gardens. Dating back to the 15th century they had been restored many times over the years always attempting to maintain and preserve their original design and beauty. Only outshone by the famous gardens at nearby Villa Gamberaia at Settignano, the Martinelli gardens were reported to be 'a feast for the eyes that brought harmony to the soul'. Lucia looked forward to her tour later that afternoon.

Refreshed and sustained by her lunch, Lucia set off to explore the small garden that enclosed the apartment. Red geraniums and blue plumbago plants tumbled profusely from old stone urns and wisteria carpeted the loggia roof with a waterfall of flowers giving much needed shade from the afternoon sun. Below the west facing wall, terraces of olive trees gave way to row upon row of vines. Sentinels of cypress trees stood on guard nearby and statuesque umbrella pines gave a sense of majesty as their dark green needles contrasted against the cobalt sky.

To the south the land dropped steeply away from the wall that then gained height as it bordered the pool to meet the apartment on the east side. Tempted as she was to enjoy a swim, Lucia decided that maybe she could do it later and now she would shower and change ready for her tour of the gardens with the curious Antonio Martinelli.

She went inside and unpacked her case. Even though she was only there for one night, she hung her clothes in the wardrobe and emptied her toiletries and cosmetics into the bathroom cupboards. She slipped out of her clothes, turned on the shower and stood under the water, allowing it to wash away the confusions of the day. The water pressure was strong and Lucia left the shower feeling cleansed and refreshed. She dressed in trousers and a light sweater thinking that the temperature could easily drop while they were walking round, especially up here in the hills. She picked up a pashmina for her shoulders, just in case.

As she walked through to the sitting room she heard the muffled ring of her mobile coming from her bag and was happy to see her aunt's name displayed in the screen, *"Ciao Chiara, come stai?"*

"Ciao amore, va bene. E te?" Chiara's words sounded like a song and they danced between English and Italian as Lucia confirmed she'd had a good journey and was now staying in an apartment at the villa and would be interviewing Signor Martinelli the following day. Sharing their excitement at the prospect of seeing each other, Lucia agreed to call Chiara after the interview when they would arrange for Chiara to collect her from the villa. Lucia had always referred to her aunt as Chiara, her being more than ten years younger than

Lucia's mother and therefore not much more than a child when Lucia was born.

Energised by the conversation with her aunt, Lucia went to sit outside and waited for her escort. It was almost four o'clock and, as she was thinking how much she was looking forward to seeing Chiara, she heard the gate click signalling Antonio Martinelli's arrival. She rose from her seat as he walked towards her. He was dressed casually in cream trousers and a pale green open necked shirt. Lucia admitted to herself that, whilst he was not her type, he was good looking and she imagined he must have many admirers.

"*Buona sera, Lucia,*" he smiled. "May I call you Lucia ...... and, please, do call me Antonio."

"*Buona sera,*" Lucia returned his smile, adding, "and yes, of course you may."

"*Va bene, andiamo*"

She followed Antonio to the gate and he led the way to the gardens that were terraced below as the land fell away from the villa descending the hillside towards Florence. Four or five steps led down to the first level where the garden was divided into quadrants by box hedging and pathways designed around a large central pond and fountain. Each quadrant was filled with geometrically designed flower beds of roses and box topiary. On either side it was edged with lemon trees and roses growing abundantly from aged terracotta pots. Beyond a stone wall the next level was stepped in terraces and a central water channel flowed down to a pond at the far end. Slender cypress trees edged either side. More terracotta pots overflowed with geraniums and plumbago edging the paths on both sides. A mulberry tree in the far right corner broke the symmetry as it arched over a curved stone seat.

As they walked Antonio explained that the garden was very old and how, over the generations, the Martinelli family had tried to preserve the original nature of its design.

"I think they have introduced more flowers than would have been here before. In the beginning it may have been more green. I prefer the colour of the flowers."

"It's very beautiful. So peaceful." Lucia commented, aware of a precision that reigned over chaos to give this effect. "It must need constant attention," she added.

"Yes, I believe the symmetry is important and the design is intended to create harmony." As they walked Antonio spoke of the Medici's influence on the design of the gardens, how they might have looked then and how they had changed over the centuries.

They walked down to the next level and Antonio said, "If you would follow me, I can show you the secret garden," and he indicated in the direction of an arched gate in the wall behind the cypress trees. Easily missed if you didn't know it was there.

Enclosed by a stone wall and a mix of high jasmine and honeysuckle hedging, the garden appeared to be a perfect square. To the south, the hedging gave way to stone arches allowing a divided view over Florence yet still enclosed in this private space. Stone seats and statues interrupted the hedging and wall and more curved seating formed part of a circular central design where an effusion of colour and scent filled the air.

Lavender hedging and roses produced a softer impression, irises and, "oh, I'd forgotten how pretty it can be – *i capperi!*" exclaimed Lucia as she saw the wall covered with the delicate white flowers against the dark green leaves of the caper plant.

"Yes, they have come out early this year."

"Ah, I remember them as a child when we came for holidays ...." Lucia tailed off aware of a sudden rise of nostalgia and the conversation entering more personal territory. Unsure of whether she wanted to continue in this vein, she asked, "Was this part of the original design or was it added later?"

"I believe it was added in the 18th century. It is beautiful, *no*?" Antonio asked as they walked to the far end to take in the breath-taking landscape offered beyond the arches.

"As you can see, there is Florence and to the south east the mountains of the Pratomagna."

Lucia felt a sudden chill, as if someone had walked over her grave as she looked in the direction of the mountains, shivered and wrapped her pashmina round her shoulders.

"Oh, you are cold. The temperature can still drop quickly at this time of year. We can walk back through the vegetable garden to the villa. If you like to join us for a drink on the terrace, my father would very much like to meet you."

Lucia had not thought beyond the tour of the gardens, apart from the interview tomorrow. Again, the goal posts were moving and, ignoring a slight churning in her solar plexus, Lucia acquiesced, "Thank you. I also look forward to meeting your father."

"Good," Antonio smiled, "let's make our way

back."

In the northern corner of the hedged wall was an arched door which led to the kitchen garden where vegetables stood to attention in neat rows. The far side was bordered by elegant cypress trees and an avenue of umbrella pines led to another villa which Antonio explained was mainly used as a hunting lodge. Beyond the villa lay the forest where, from September to January, in accordance with Italian law, they were allowed to hunt the wild boar. Lucia was aware that *la caccia* was an important tradition here as was hunting the elusive and valued truffles in the autumn. In fact, Lucia remembered hearing from her grandmother that the competition was such that some men would put down poison for other men's truffle hounds so as to prevent them finding these rare and highly valued *funghi*.

Antonio walked with Lucia up the steps to the terrace that stretched the length of the villa's back elevation. The view, again, was stunning and Lucia took in and savoured the beauty of the tall, dark cypress trees silhouetted against the soft green of the rolling hills framed by the deep mauve mountains on either side. Florence sat like a misty jewel in the centre.

"Can I get you a drink, Lucia? An *aperitivo* perhaps, or some wine, a glass of *Prosecco*? Please sit down and be comfortable." Antonio indicated to a table and chairs on the terrace carefully placed so they could still feel the remaining warmth of the sun's rays.

"Thank you, *Prosecco* would be lovely," she replied, reminding herself that she must not drink too much or be seduced by the beauty of the place. It had been a long day and she needed to be rested and fully focussed for the interview tomorrow.

She sat down and waited while Antonio attended to the drinks. Her thoughts were interrupted as she heard approaching footsteps and she turned to see Maria carrying a tray. She was followed by Antonio and an elegant, middle-aged woman whom he introduced as his mother, Luisa Martinelli. After the usual Italian pleasantries, Signora Martinelli explained that her husband sent his sincere apologies for not being there but he had been called out to an urgent appointment and she hoped Lucia would eat an early supper with herself and Antonio.

"Thank you, Signora, it would be a pleasure," Lucia responded, relieved that it would not be a late evening.

Although friendly, the formality of the conversations with Antonio and Signora Martinelli were tiring and Lucia longed to be able to relax.

"Please, call me Luisa. Antonio," she smiled at him as she sat at the table, waving a graceful arm across the glasses, "would you mind pouring the wine?"

"Of course," Antonio filled the glasses, sat down and raised his glass in a toast, "*Salute*". Both Luisa and Lucia reciprocated in unison.

The evening passed amiably. It was agreed they would eat on the terrace. Luisa asked Lucia about her family and their connections to Florence, briefly mentioning her friendship with Chiara. They talked generally about art and touched on the history of the villa, Luisa saying she was sure her husband would go into far more detail tomorrow.

Antonio said little, just adding a comment here and there to Luisa's account of life in Florence. However, Lucia felt observed and more than once caught his eyes focussed on her even though she was not speaking at the time. The disquiet she had felt at their first meeting began to gnaw at her again and she was relieved when coffee was served bringing the evening to an end and allowing her to say *buona notte*. It had been agreed that they would meet on the terrace for lunch at 12.30 pm, which would give her the whole morning to herself.

She returned to the apartment, wrapping the pashmina around her against a chill that filled the air when she walked into the more shaded path that led to the arched gate in the garden wall. It was nearly 8.30pm and the sun had gone down leaving a turquoise and azure sky punctuated by small, diamond-like stars. Breathing in the jasmine's heady perfume she thought how good it was to be out of the city, not only Florence but also London. Where she lived in Holland Park was fairly quiet but there was always the background noise of nearby busy roads and at night, the glare of lights from a multitude of sources. Here, the sky was high, open and clear.

Once in the apartment, Lucia noticed the light on her mobile phone indicating there was an unread message. She opened it to find it was from James to say that he hoped it was all going well, and this little bit of support gave her a feeling of warmth that helped her relax. She made a chamomile tea, found her book and stretched out on the sofa with her feet up.

Her thoughts revisited the earlier part of the evening at the villa with Antonio and Luisa. What is it about him, she wondered, that makes me feel ..... feel what? Unable to find words to adequately describe it she returned her attention to her book. It's not that I'm uncomfortable with him .... it's just ..... it's not even .... it's as if we should know or do know each other and yet as far as I'm aware we've never met, well not before a couple of days ago anyway. It just doesn't make sense!

Restless again, Lucia opened the door to the garden and went outside. The moon was almost full, sharing its soft, silver light in the night sky. She curled up on one of the seats hugging her knees to her chest aware of the anxiety within her. She thought she could compartmentalise the different aspects of her life and was now realising that they were overflowing into each other beyond her control.

I just have to get through tomorrow, the lunch, the interview .... then, I'll see Chiara and ..... oh! she leapt up from the seat throwing up her hands in frustration. She went inside, thinking the coffee had been a bad idea and, annoyed at her lack of willpower, refreshed her chamomile tea with hot water and took it through to the bedroom. She found her book and climbed into bed.

Shortly after midnight when the villa was sleeping, one person was wide awake. His arrogance belied any fear as he walked through the hermetically sealed gallery. He kept the lights low and his footsteps soft as he moved through the rooms, searching. His eyes scanned the paintings as he passed them until finally pausing in the early renaissance room. As always, he was drawn like a magnet to the familiar portrait of a woman set in a Tuscan landscape. The painting itself was not remarkable yet it had disturbed him as long as he could remember. A whisper of fear was instantly dismissed as he continued his search.

He eventually selected and photographed four paintings. The high megapixel professional camera was heavy due to the large lens but necessary for the detailed reproduction he required. Satisfied he had what he needed, he retraced his steps to the slumbering silence of the villa, poured a small glass of *grappa* and returned to his room.

THURSDAY
Giovedi

Despite thinking that she would not be able to sleep, Lucia slept for at least nine hours straight through. As she leisurely stretched diagonally across the bed, relishing the thought of having the morning to herself, she put it down to a combination of exhaustion and a peaceful environment. If it wasn't for this interview, she thought, I could almost be on holiday.

She was rudely awakened from her reverie by a knock on the door. She grabbed a robe and, as she made her way there, another knock came, this time more urgent. Lucia opened the door to find Antonio breathless and clearly stressed.

"My apologies for disturbing you so early, Lucia. We have an emergency at the house, it's my father; he is unwell and my mother has gone with him to the hospital. We have to postpone the interview, I am sorry. My mother has arranged for a car to take you to your aunt's home when you are ready. Please, take your time, have some breakfast and let Maria know when you would like to leave. I must go now."

As Lucia tried to digest his words, Antonio turned to head towards the gate.

"Of course. Please let me know how he is – if there is anything I can do ….." her words petered out as Lucia felt their futility.

"Thank you, I'll call." And he was gone.

The place felt suddenly empty and Lucia fell on to the sofa wondering what to do next. There was now no reason for her to be there and despite Antonio's polite invitation to take her time, Lucia decided she would have breakfast, pack and leave as soon as possible. She picked up her mobile, found Chiara's number and pressed the call button. She explained what had happened and once Chiara confirmed that she would be at home all morning, she agreed to go over as soon as she was ready.

She headed to the kitchen to make coffee. She found fresh bread on the table and butter, jam, cold meats, fresh fruits and yoghurt. Absent-mindedly Lucia cut some bread, made coffee then sat down at the table, still shaken by the turn of events. Her mind fast-forwarded to possible future scenarios in a hopeless attempt to collect herself and find some solid ground on which to stand.

Okay, she thought, I still have a few days in Italy. I shall go to Chiara's and then ….. then what? I'll have to wait until I hear from Antonio, I suppose - whether or not the interview will be possible or, if it will have to be cancelled. She began to feel marginally better now she had the threads of a plan.

She had finished her breakfast, showered, dressed and packed by ten o'clock and was about to go up to the villa to find Maria when there was a gentle knock at the door. It was Maria to see if there was anything she needed. Lucia assured her that she had everything and was ready to leave. Maria told her she would ask the driver to come round to the gate in about five minutes.

"And if you are sure there is nothing else .... " Maria hesitated as if trying to find the correct words, "I say goodbye."

"Thank you, Maria. *Arrivederci*," Lucia smiled and Maria made her way back to the villa.

She was wondering why she had not asked Maria about Signor Martinelli when she heard the car tyres scrunching the gravel outside. She took her case, made one last check of the apartment and left.

"Antonio! Antonio!" Luisa called for her son. "Antonio, come quickly!"

"*Mamma*, what's wrong?" Antonio took the steps from the garden two at a time, and arrived breathless in the long hallway trying to locate his mother's voice.

"Antonio, I'm here, in the bedroom!" Luisa called out.

"What is it *mamma*?"

"It's Giacomo. I've called for an ambulance. They should be here any minute. I don't know what happened. When we got up he said he didn't feel too well and then when I came out of the shower he had passed out. I found him on the floor, here. Please stay with him, I must get dressed."

Antonio entered the bedroom and saw his father lying on the floor. "B ..but.... " he stuttered, unable to find any words.

Luisa returned, now dressed and talking into the

phone, "Yes, if you could take Signorina Walker to her aunt when she is ready to leave. You know the place, near Bagno a Ripoli. Thank you, Guido"

They heard the ambulance arrive and Antonio ran down the steps to meet them and show them the way. When they arrived in the room Luisa told her son to follow her to the hospital once he had spoken to Lucia and that he should tell her as little as possible. Guido would drive her to her aunt's when she was ready to leave and they would call her there.

"Yes, *mamma*, but …."

"Antonio, he will be alright. Don't worry. Follow me to the hospital and we can talk there."

Giacomo was carried, still unconscious, on a stretcher to the ambulance and Luisa travelled with him while Antonio watched them drive away wondering what he was going to say to Lucia.

Not wanting to waste time, Antonio ran down the steps from the terrace and round to the garden apartment. He was breathless by the time he reached the door. He knocked and waited for Lucia to answer then said the few words his mother had directed him to say as politely as possible. He was relieved that Lucia did not question him and he was able to leave immediately.

When he arrived at the hospital, his mother was talking with one of the doctors.

"Ah, Antonio, *vieni.*" Luisa beckoned her son to join them. "This is Dr. Giannini. He is looking after your father."

The two men shook hands and exchanged polite greetings.

"I was just explaining to your mother that I believe

he will be fine. It is not clear exactly what happened, we will know more when we have done some tests. I would like him to stay here for a few days until we get the results of the tests and also so he can rest."

"But do you have any idea what is wrong?" asked Antonio.

"I will know more when we have the test results and in the meantime I prefer not to speculate."

Antonio looked at his mother, then returned his attention to Dr Giannini and thanked him.

"I will call you as soon as I know more," the doctor said. "Please try not to worry."

Luisa linked arms with her son and gently said, "Come, let's see him."

They entered the room where Giacomo was lying in bed sleeping and various tubes and wires attached him to a machine at his bedside. Antonio was shocked by the fragility of the scene in front of him. His father appeared to be sleeping and the machine next to him was beeping a regular rhythm.

"Why don't you sit with him for a while, maybe he'll wake up soon? I'll get some coffee."

"*Mamma*....." Antonio began, "no, it doesn't matter. Coffee would be good."

Stripped of his usual confidence Antonio felt lost and unable yet to navigate this new territory. He sat in one of the two chairs at the side of the bed. The room seemed claustrophobic as if he was trapped and unable to go beyond the door. His father appeared so different to the man he knew. A powerful man who usually commanded everything before him with ease, he now lay weakened and helpless.

Luisa returned with two coffees.

"The doctor says he may sleep for some time. They have sedated him so he can rest. Some of the tests should be back this afternoon and the rest may take a few days. I will stay here but if you want to go I can call you as soon as there is any news."

"No, *mamma*, I'll wait." Antonio said wanting to support his mother. He looked at his father as if searching for the man he knew, expecting him to suddenly reappear.

Once in the car Lucia put all thoughts of the last few days out of her mind and absorbed the beauty of the Tuscan landscape. Although she was still disconcerted by the morning's events, she was happy to be on her way to her aunt's home the other side of Florence, thinking how beautiful it looked in spring, new life bursting forth in all directions. Blossom and buds everywhere, provided a contrast to the ever upward reaching dark green cypress trees.

Then, for a brief moment, her immediate surroundings became blurred as they had done on the plane and in her head Lucia heard the soft voice again, "It is almost time".

Her heart racing, she felt chilled despite the warmth of the sun's rays radiating through the car windows. So many thoughts raced through her mind simultaneously.

What is happening to me?

What does it mean?

So, the dreams have stopped and now I hear voices?

Am I going mad?

I must pull myself together before I see Chiara.

She leaned back in the seat and breathed as deeply as she could against the fear that coursed through her body sending her adrenals into overdrive. As she looked out of the car window she began to recognise the odd landmark and found some comfort in knowing that they were approaching her aunt's home. She took a mirror from her bag and checked her face and hair and was surprised to see that even though she felt spun out and shocked by the last few minutes, she looked remarkably normal.

Thank god for that, she thought, at least I won't have to go into lengthy explanations the minute I arrive.

Her mind momentarily returned to the morning's events and she wondered how Giacomo Martinelli was and the likelihood of getting an interview with him within the next few days. She was irritated by the thought of having to return to London without seeing him. She'd put in hours of research and didn't like the thought of it going to waste. Immediately she remembered a phrase her *nonna* would say, that nothing is wasted.

The car turned off the road and made its way slowly along the winding unmade road to Chiara's home. She smiled at the familiar beauty of the avenue of slender cypress trees and statuesque umbrella pines so iconic of Tuscany that led the way to the villa.

Finally they drove through the gate to where her aunt was already waiting. Rushing to the car, Chiara opened the door for her and before Lucia was fully out of the car Chiara was hugging her, kissing her head and saying in her melodious voice, "*Amore, amore,* at last, it's so good to see you," as if Lucia were still twelve years old.

Lucia soon relaxed into Chiara's welcome and only just remembered her case which the driver had deposited by the front door. She turned and thanked the driver who merely smiled politely, returned to his car and drove off. Chiara and Lucia linked arms and went through the heavy wooden doors to the villa as Chiara continued to effuse at seeing her niece.

As with most Tuscan villas the ground floor, *la cantina*, was reserved for the storing of wine, logs and other such things and the living quarters were on the upper floors.

"*Cara, mamma* is so looking forward to seeing you but I have to tell you she may not be as you remember her. She is a bit forgetful and she tires easily. Please be patient with her."

"Of course," Lucia said as Chiara placed her hand over hers.

"*Eh,* I'm sorry to hear about Signor Martinelli. I hope he will be alright. Do you know what happened?"

"No, not really, only that he was taken to the hospital."

"Mmm, maybe I'll call Luisa later and see if there is any news. *Allora,* how about some coffee?" Chiara said as she led her into the kitchen.

"Ooo, yes please," Lucia replied as she walked over to the large window and took in another panoramic view of Florence, this time from the south.

"Beautiful, isn't it. I never tire of it." Chiara watched her niece and thought how she had grown since she had last seen her. Not physically, but she seemed more self-contained and to have matured a little. Yet, there was something else that Chiara had not seen in her niece before, a tension, a tautness that seemed at the same time fragile. "How long can you stay?"

"Well, I'm due back the middle of next week, if you'll have me 'til then. Of course, there's the interview with Signor Martinelli, if he's well enough and ....." Lucia turned to face Chiara and smiled, "..... it's so good to be here."

"Come, *cara,* sit down," Chiara touched the back of a chair, "we'll have coffee and then I'll show you your room. And later, while you relax, I'll prepare lunch. *Va bene*?"

In the presence of such warmth Lucia melted into the chair surrendering to Chiara's ministrations. It had been a long time since she had been on the receiving end of such loving attention and she felt a sudden wave of exhaustion drift over her and a knowing that she was in the right place.

Chiara brought a pot of coffee and two small espresso cups to the table. Lucia asked if she could have a little milk as she found black coffee too harsh. Chiara fetched a small jug of milk and smiling said, "*Eh*, so English *cara*, the milk in the coffee." She sat down opposite Lucia observing her momentarily before saying, "*Allora,* tell me all your news. How is everyone? What is happening in your life?"

Lucia looked up from the coffee cup that had her undivided attention to her aunt's open face wondering where to begin.

"Well, *mamma* is much the same. I haven't seen her for a while as work has been so demanding and even though it's not that far, it's the time it takes to get out of London that makes it difficult. I speak to her now and then on the phone and she always seems to be busy with one thing or another. I saw James just before I left and he sends his love and hopes to visit very soon. As for Gabriella, she was somewhere in Asia the last I heard, on her way to Australia, I think, quite the little adventurer. And you, Chiara, how are things here? You said Franco was away – will he be back before I go?"

"*Eh,* I'm fine. Like you, work is demanding – the business takes so much of my time these days, but I have managed to make arrangements so I can spend some time with you over the next few days. I may have to go in to the shop for a short time tomorrow. If you'd like to, you can come with me and spend some time in Florence – just let me know. As for Franco, I don't expect him back until the end of next week so you probably won't see him. In fact, I see very little of him myself these days," Chiara laughed, "that's probably why we get on so well."

Lucia wondered if now was a good time to talk to Chiara about the recent events that had been troubling her or if she should wait until later. She was so happy to see her, to be here, that she didn't want to spoil it, so decided to wait,.

"Come, let me show you your room and then you can tell me all about the Martinelli's over lunch – how does that sound?"

"Great," Lucia said relieved not to have to deal with anything just yet.

As was common in Tuscan villas the main rooms were on the first floor with a square central tower above. It was to the tower that Chiara now led Lucia. It had been converted to offer a good sized room with large windows through which Lucia could see the marvellous view over Florence. The room was simply decorated; the walls were traditionally whitewashed and stark against the dark chestnut beams. Rich autumn colours in the rugs and furnishings brought depth and warmth. There was a sumptuous double bed, a sofa and chair, a small table and a separate bathroom tiled in pale marble.

"I hope you like it. We thought it nice for guests to have some privacy."

"Oh, it's beautiful Chiara. Thank you."

"*Allora*, I'll leave you to unpack, make yourself comfortable and come down when you are ready. I'll be in the kitchen." Chiara turned to her niece and gave her a hug "It really is good to see you, *amore*."

"Me too," Lucia reciprocated her hug and smiled as they parted, "See you shortly."

Left alone, Lucia opened her case and found homes for the clothes and toiletries. Chiara seemed to have thought of everything. There were the usual requisites such as towels and soaps in the bathroom but she had added essential oils for the bath, pots of creams and potions for all skin types and soft fluffy robes in white and charcoal grey. In the main room itself, Lucia found the latest fashion magazines on the small table, as well as writing paper, pens and pencils and a well stocked bookcase.

She opened one of the doors that led out to a narrow terrace and she breathed deeply, taking in the air and the beauty that surrounded her. She looked out towards Florence and the iconic duomo, much as she had from the Martinelli villa, only here it was closer, more immediate. As she did so she couldn't help wondering what she was doing here, here being Italy, and Florence in particular. Yes, it was her familial home, well on her mother's side anyway. But why here, why now? Not wanting to stir up unwanted feelings, she returned to the room and made her way down to the kitchen where she found Chiara preparing lunch.

"Ah, *amore*, did you find everything you need?"

"Yes, thanks. You've done a wonderful job, Chiara. It's beautiful. I remember the last time I was here, you'd only just started the renovations."

"Oh, but that was nearly five years ago. Has it really been that long? *Eh,* I saw you for a short time when I came to London the year before last, *no*? As for the renovations, you know how long everything takes here – all the plans, the permissions and then you have to do everything about twenty times. It was finally signed off a couple of months ago."

"Mmm, I didn't realise it had been that long. Time seems to disappear so quickly these days and ...... oh well," Lucia sighed, not wanting to continue the thought, "anyway, it's great to be here with you now."

"Yes, it is and we'll have a wonderful time." Chiara put some water in a pan to boil for the pasta, and turned to Lucia saying "In the refrigerator is a bottle of Prosecco – would you open it please? Let's celebrate! The glasses are on the table."

Lucia took a cloth and carefully turned the cork until there was a gentle pop of released air. She poured a little wine into each glass and placed the bottle in a cooler on the table. The table was a delight, a display of colourful salads and *antipasti.*

"Come, *cara,* let's eat while we wait for the water

to boil. They sat at the table and raised their glasses in a toast, "*Salute*," they echoed in unison. "Now," Chiara said intently, "tell me about your visit to the Martinelli villa."

As Lucia thought about it she realised there was very little to say. "Well, I wasn't there that long. The villa is very old and grand and the gardens are beautiful. The elder son, Antonio, gave me a tour of the gardens yesterday just after we arrived."

"And what did you think of him?" Chiara interrupted.

"Oh he's very charming and, er, I don't know – impeccable, I suppose. His clothes, his manners .... and very self-assured." Lucia smiled and looked directly at Chiara, "and not my type!"

Chiara poured more wine into their glasses and got up from the table to put the spaghetti into the pan of now boiling water. "I didn't mean ...... "

"Okay, yes he is good looking and all but .... mmm ..... I don't know what it is, there's something not quite right," Lucia continued, "I can't explain it .... "

"Maybe you don't need to, *cara*. Sometimes we just have feelings about these things without knowing why until later, and sometimes we may never know. *E cosi*." Chiara shrugged.

"The pasta is ready." She said as she strained the spaghetti, mixed in a tomato and garlic sauce that she had already prepared and shared it between two plates. "*Ecco – buon apetito*!" She said, putting one plate on the table in front of Lucia and the other in her place before sitting down. "*Formaggio*?" Chiara asked handing a bowl of grated parmesan to Lucia.

"*Grazie*." Lucia thanked her and sprinkled some

cheese on the pasta before continuing. "I didn't get to see inside the villa as we had an early supper on the terrace with his mother, Luisa. She said her husband had been called away and wouldn't be joining us. Afterwards I went straight back to the garden apartment where I was staying. Actually, it was all a bit disconcerting because it had been arranged that I would stay in a local hotel and then have lunch with them today followed by the interview. It wasn't until Antonio met me at the airport that he told me I would be staying at the villa. Not that it matters now, but ...."

"Ah, I see." Chiara waved a hand dismissively. "*Allora,* you know how it is here."

"Yes, I suppose I'd forgotten how quickly things can change and yet somehow nothing happens. I remember how frustrated *babbo* used to get on visits here." An image of her father floated into Lucia's mind with a sadness that he was no longer there to shake his head in a certain way at the idiosyncrasies of Italian culture.

"This sauce is good."

"*Grazie, cara* it's very simple." Chiara smiled mischievously, "I have some *stracchino,* remember how you loved it with a pear when you were little?"

"Oh Chiara, yes. I'd love some. I haven't had any for ages!" exclaimed Lucia at the thought of the soft, creamy cheese she had so loved as a child.

"*Va bene*, the pears are grown here and later, if you like, I can show you what I've done here, unless, of course, you are tired and would prefer to rest?"

"Oh no, I want to see everything. You've done so much since I was last here and I want to see it all," Lucia enthused.

"Bene, I'll show you where I grow the herbs and other plants first and then we can go to the lab where I make the lotions and remedies. By that time *mamma* will have had her siesta and we can surprise her. How does that sound?"

"Perfect."

Lucia was just about to suggest making coffee when she heard the muted ring of her mobile in her bag. She didn't recognise the number and pressed a button to answer, "Hello."

"Buona sera, sono Antonio. I am sorry I had to rush off and leave you this morning. I wonder if you would be free to come to the villa tomorrow? Maybe your aunt would like to join us and we can have lunch – say, 12.30?"

"Er, thank you. May I call you back in a few minutes? I will check with my aunt whether or not she is free then." Lucia played for time to allow her to take in what was happening.

"Va bene. If you could please let me know as soon as possible. Thank you." And before Lucia could ask after his father the line went dead.

"What is it, *cara?"* Chiara asked. "What is it you will check with me?"

"That was Antonio, he's invited us to lunch tomorrow at 12.30. Are you free?" said Lucia, praying her aunt's reply would be affirmative.

"Well, I have to go to the shop at some point tomorrow. We could go into Florence together in the morning and then go on to the villa."

"Okay," relieved, Lucia called Antonio to confirm that they would both be at the villa at 12.30. Again, the call was brief and Antonio ended it before Lucia was able to ask any questions.

"Are you alright, *cara*? You seem a little, how do you say, flustered?"

"I'm fine," Lucia replied, attempting not to show how disconcerted she really felt. "It was just unexpected, that's all."

"Yes, of course. Let's have coffee and then enjoy the rest of the afternoon." Chiara said encouragingly.

Again, she verged on telling Chiara about her dream and her fears but somehow the words wouldn't form in her suddenly dry mouth. She finished the wine in her glass hoping to stem the panic that was now beginning to rise again. She didn't want to spoil the afternoon and decided that it could wait until later.

Chiara returned to the table with two cups of coffee and a small jug of milk for Lucia. "See, I remembered the milk."

"Thank you." Lucia smiled, satisfied that the moment had passed and she was able to breathe easily again. "Tell me, what else have you been doing? How's the new skin care range going? I read about it not long ago in one of the glossies."

"Yes. I met this young man, oh, it must be several months ago now, and he's re-done the whole website, given it a completely different feel; more commercial, or maybe more stylish I suppose. His mother has been coming into the shop for years and he came in to buy a gift for her and we got talking and, well, you know how it is. It seems he's not only a technological wizard but he also understands about herbs and plants. Anyway, there's been so much more interest in the products and I've had to take on more help to deal with the orders. Of course, the shop continues much as it's always done, a mixture of regular clients and tourists. You'll see tomorrow. Are you ready? *Andiamo.*"

Lucia followed Chiara from the villa into the grounds. Just below the terrace was the herb garden set out in a medieval design. She remembered how as a child she would walk through another garden and the woods with her grandmother who would tell her stories of the herbs and plants as she picked them, and explain their uses.

It was beautifully laid out and Chiara was explaining how, that now the demand had increased, she had to grow the herbs further down in a larger plot that had been specially cleared though Lucia barely heard her, caught in her own reverie. A strong smell of rosemary brought her back to the present as Chiara pushed a sprig under her nose, "Smell, *cara*, is it not beautiful?"

"Ah, yes. I remember *nonna* telling me to use it when I was revising for exams as it's good for remembering."

"*Si, si, anch'io,*" Chiara said as she stopped walking and turned to look at Lucia. "Lucia, are you alright? You seem as if part of you is somewhere else."

"Oh sorry, Chiara. The last few days have been stressful and now all these changes .... I suppose it's unsettled me a bit."

Chiara looked at her again, trying to see beyond the words. "Of course, it's only natural but if you want to talk, you know I'm here, *cara*"

"Thank you," Lucia smiled at her aunt and said, "Let's not spoil the afternoon with my nonsense. I want to see the rest. I want to see everything!"

The two women continued their walk round the gardens, Chiara explaining the different plots, what was growing and how she used them in her products. Both dark haired, slim and with a natural elegance, there was a strong familial likeness and they looked as if they could be sisters. As they made their way back in the direction of the villa, Chiara linked her arm through Lucia's, "Come, *mamma* should be ready to see us now. She has a small *casetta* by the villa and is so longing to see you."

Lucia, warmed by the afternoon sun and the enjoyment of her aunt's company, was, at last, feeling more relaxed and beginning to wish that she did not still have work to do here. They were nearing the villa when Chiara led them on to an old track and after about fifty metres they came to her mother's cottage set back in the shade of three cypress trees. Chiara opened the gate and walked up the path that divided the front garden in two to the loggia where Lucia could see someone sitting at a table strewn with plants. Lucia's breath caught in her chest with a feeling of apprehension. She had not seen her grandmother for a few years and remembered Chiara's words from earlier. She followed Chiara along the path and suddenly there were familiar, melodious sounds of greeting from mother to daughter and then Isabella saw her granddaughter and the volume increased.

"*Allora, amore, amore, vieni qui! Come stai?*" With outstretched arms she moved slowly forwards to Lucia and embraced her saying, "*Bene,* you have come."

Lucia felt a momentary chill at the words she heard then was lost in the warmth of the welcome and joy at seeing her grandmother.

"Yes," she said, "it's wonderful to be here and to see you at last. It's been far too long."

Isabella held Lucia at arm's length. "Let me see you. You've grown – inside as well as outside, *eh*?"

Chiara put her arms round Isabella and Lucia, "Come let's go inside and sit down. You two can catch up and I'll get something for us to drink."

Isabella looked up at her daughter from her diminutive height and said enthusiastically, "*Si, si,* there's Prosecco in the fridge .... "

"But *mamma,*" Chiara interrupted, "you know ...."

"*Eh,* Isabella said waving her arm dismissively, "this is a celebration, *vai, vai,* go, go!"

Turning her attention to Lucia, Isabella took her arm, "Come, we can sit in here," and led her to a sun-filled room at the back of the house. "I like to follow the sun as it moves round."

They sat down by the window and Lucia began to understand Chiara's words as she realised how frail Isabella had become. Always small and slim she had also been strong and wiry, even robust, but now there was a fragility that Lucia had not seen before.

"Now tell me what you've been doing. Last time I saw you was, *o dio,* how many years now? *Allora,* my memory escapes me these days," Isabella said with a smile that creased her face with joy.

"About five years, I think, *nonna*. You were in the other house."

"Ah, yes," Isabella paused, lost in the memory for a moment.

"*Nonna?*" Lucia began and was interrupted as Chiara entered the room with the drinks.

"*Ecco.*" Chiara said as she put the tray on a table and passed glasses to Lucia and Isabella.

"*Eh*, let us toast!" exclaimed Isabella. "To Lucia being here and us all being here together."

They each raised and clinked their glasses. "*Salute.*"

The next hour passed quickly as Lucia spoke about the last few years of her life. She noticed that sometimes Isabella didn't seem to be listening and wondered if this lack of attention was also part of what Chiara had been talking about. As if her mind had drifted off somewhere else. It only happened a couple of times but it was enough to concern Lucia.

"*Mamma*, we must go now and you must be tired." Chiara said. "We can come by tomorrow if you like, about the same time?"

"Yes, yes, and look after our precious Lucia. We can talk more tomorrow." Isabella got up to walk to the door with them and hugged them each in turn.

For a moment Lucia felt like a child again. As they were walking back along the track, Lucia asked Chiara what had happened to her mother.

"I'm not sure when it started but you know how *mamma* can be. She was always a bit scattered. Then a few years ago she was ill with what we thought was influenza but it seemed to go on and on. She was so weak and we were worried that it might be something serious. The doctors did tests, well as much as *mamma* would allow – she was not the easiest of patients as you can imagine. Anyway, the results of the tests were clear but then when I visited I noticed that she would just drift off in the middle of a conversation. Not often but enough to cause concern. As you know she lived the other side of the valley and I couldn't visit as often as I would have liked, but at the time *mamma* would not discuss moving; she was adamant that she had lived in her house for years and was not leaving it.

Then I went over one day and I just knew there was something wrong. There was a smell of gas and I found *mamma* asleep in the chair in the *cucina*. It seemed she'd turned on the stove and not lit it. Fortunately the gas bottle was almost empty and therefore it was not as bad as it could have been. However, whether it was the influenza, the gas, or a combination of the two, it seems her lungs were weakened and she began to find it difficult to do even simple daily chores. So, we did up the little cottage for her and she came to live here about two years ago. Although she's weaker than she was, most of the time she's fine and at least I can see her nearly every day."

"Did she mind moving here?"

"Surprisingly, no. After all the earlier arguments she somehow thought she was helping me by moving here so I went along with that. I didn't want to say too much before as most of the time she's fine. It's just that, well, you can see ... "

"I'm sorry, Chiara," Lucia touched her aunt's arm.

Chiara covered Lucia's hand with her own, "I know."

They walked back to the house in silence. Not an awkward one, more a reverent silence.

After a simple supper of risotto, fish and green vegetables, Chiara and Lucia moved from the *cucina* to the living room.

"You must be tired, *cara*. So much in one day."

"Mmm... I suppose I am," Lucia responded, stretching languidly along the sofa. "I wonder what tomorrow will bring."

"Ah, I think it is sometimes best not to wonder for fear of what you might invite." Chiara's voice held a touch of irony as she smiled and raised an eyebrow.

"What do you mean?"

"Well, just that it is best to let things unfold naturally. Often when we visit the future with our mind all we do is project our fears and ..... *pero,* I like to keep an open mind."

"You mean we create what we fear?" Lucia frowned as she explored Chiara's words.

"Si, I think that is possible."

"I hadn't thought of it that way before or, in fact, given much thought to it at all." Lucia said, as her dream drifted into her present and she wondered what her own fears might be creating. Thankfully, the wine was having a soporific affect and her usually reactive adrenals remained calm. She heard her name and looked up to see Chiara leaning forward in her chair.

"Lucia, *cara*, are you alright?"

"Si, si, it must be the wine and maybe I'm more tired than I thought."

"Of course, would you like a chamomile *tisana*?"

"Thank you, no I think I'll just go straight to bed." Lucia got up and headed for the door but first turned round to say, "It's so good to be here, *buona notte."*

"Anche te, dormi bene," Chiara wished Lucia to sleep well.

It was already afternoon and Signor Martinelli slept on. Antonio spent the time between the café, where he drank numerous cups of coffee, and his father's bedside. He felt overwhelmed by questions to which he had no real answers. And where was Lorenzo? He'd left copious messages for him but to no avail. What was he playing at?

"*Mamma*, what are we to do?" he turned to his mother, frustrated by her seeming lack of concern.

She calmly turned towards Antonio from the other side of the bed where she held her husband's hand, "I think we should invite the *signorina*, what is her name, Lucia Walker, and her aunt for lunch tomorrow. Things will be clearer by then."

"And if they are not?"

"Then we will deal with that when the time comes." Luisa felt drained of energy but as always showed a calm exterior that belied what was going on behind the façade. "Maybe you could try Lorenzo again, *per favore*?"

As always Antonio felt caught in the middle. He knew it unlikely that Lorenzo would answer his calls and he could not tell his mother the truth as, in any event, she would not hear anything negative said about her younger son. And what was he to say to Lucia? Since there was no point in trying to discuss this with his mother, he called Lucia and invited her and Chiara to lunch the following day. Thankfully, she agreed and he was able to keep the call brief before she could ask any awkward questions.

"I need some air. I'll be back in a few minutes. Can I get you anything?" he asked.

"No, I'm fine thanks."

He wondered what it was that his mother was not telling him. There was usually something lurking unsaid beneath the calm she portrayed to the world. He believed it was more to do with his father and his obsession for privacy than any cunning on his mother's part. She clearly adored Giacomo and blindly supported him, and it was this that had given Antonio cause for concern on several occasions.

In an odd reflective way he also had found it necessary to keep his reservations to himself. His father would not be interested and he had no wish to betray his mother and then there was Lorenzo. Yes, he was young and irresponsible, with his lack of boundaries and indiscriminate relationships, the opposite of his father. This latest problem was not going to be easy to deal with let alone the possible repercussions on the family. Lorenzo just didn't seem to care and he certainly wasn't going to take advice from his elder brother.

Antonio's thoughts turned to Lucia and wondered what his mother was thinking when she asked him to invite her to lunch. He hoped she was right and it would all be clear by then.

He had decided he liked Lucia. She was a very attractive woman and he appreciated her directness which he found refreshing. He hoped the invitation wasn't going to involve her in one of his family's dramas. For some strange reason that he didn't understand, he felt protective towards her.

Brushing these thoughts to one side, he was about to, yet again, call Lorenzo but decided against it and went back to his father's room. As he approached the door he heard voices and recognised the defiant tone of Lorenzo and his mother's futile attempts to soothe and calm.

"*Tranquilla, amore*," she said, "let's not disturb your father. We can discuss this later."

"*Ciao*, Lorenzo," Antonio greeted him as he entered the room, making no mention of the numerous attempts to contact him.

The air was thick with unspoken words. Luisa seemed unaware of the atmosphere or, if she was, showed no signs of it. Antonio, as always, wished he could be elsewhere.

"So, *mamma*, what happened? Maria told me he'd collapsed."

Luisa related the morning's events to Lorenzo in a calm, unhurried, almost detached way. Antonio often wondered if his mother ever felt anything these days or even allowed herself that opportunity. Even though she always appeared self-contained, controlled, Antonio had realised in recent years that his mother protected an inner fragility that, in his opinion, was more to do with her husband's paranoia than any personal insecurity on her part.

"We'll know more later when some of the test results are back and the sedation should have worn off by then also."

"*Va bene*. I have to go, *mamma*, mi dispiace," Lorenzo said apologising to his mother, and then turned to Antonio, "You'll call me if there's any news?"

"*Certo, certo*" was all Antonio could manage without mentioning the number of times he'd already called him, knowing that would only exacerbate a difficult situation.

Lorenzo left as abruptly as he had arrived.

"*Mamma*, why……" he began and was interrupted by his mother.

Luisa gently said through frayed edges, "Antonio, please, just leave it."

After a few minutes of silence the door opened. It was the doctor Luisa had spoken to earlier. The expression on his face gave no indication of what he was about to say.

"*Buona sera,* Signora, Signor. We have the first set of results and they are a little puzzling. We would have hoped he would have come round by now, however, we should know more when we get the remaining results in a few days' time. In the meantime we will monitor his progress and will let you know immediately there is any change. I am sorry I'm not able to tell you more at the moment."

Luisa calmly thanked the doctor and they exchanged the usual polite pleasantries before saying goodbye for the time being.

Turning to Antonio, Luisa said that she would remain at the hospital in case there was any change. For the first time since his father's collapse Antonio thought he caught a glimpse of fear in his mother's demeanour, almost like a crack appearing in a mirror before it shatters.

"*Mamma*, why don't you take a break, get some food, you haven't had anything today."

Resisting his concern, Luisa said she was fine and suggested he go home and wait for her there. Not to be put off Antonio said he would get some food and bring it to her, adding that he didn't want to have to deal with another collapse.

Giving a faint smile Luisa turned towards her husband and Antonio went to the hospital café to see what food he could organise for his mother.

The café was on the ground floor with views over the hospital garden. Antonio breathed a sigh of relief at seeing blue sky, trees and plants through the wall of windows on one side of the café. He thought how claustrophobic hospitals were with their closed in corridors and small rooms with shuttered windows.

After a few minutes he returned to where his mother was sitting holding her husband's hand.

"*Ecco, mamma.* Please try to eat this," he said handing her the tray with a plate of *spaghetti pomodoro* on it. "There's cheese as well if you'd like some."

"Oh, *grazie, amore.*" Luisa stood up and took the tray. Sitting down again, she looked at the food.

"Please, *mamma.*"

Luisa looked at her son, sighed, picked up the fork and slowly twirled the pasta. She managed to force a few mouthfuls before putting the plate to one side and returning to hold her husband's hand.

The doctor's words had felt like a physical blow that left her winded. She had been so sure it wasn't serious and that her husband would be well enough to go home with her today. How foolish she had been. How could she have been so wrong? She wondered how many other things she had misjudged. She was jerked from her self-berating reverie by a groan from her husband as his hand moved slightly in hers.

"Antonio, Antonio! Call the doctor! He's coming round!"

"Lu.....Lu.....i.....sa," Giacomo slowly stuttered her name as Antonio ran down the corridor to the nurses' station to tell them to alert the doctor.

"I'm here, *caro*. Don't try to talk. The doctor is on his way." Luisa looked closely at her husband and stroked his hand.

FRIDAY
Venerdi

Despite her exhaustion, Lucia did not sleep well. Maybe it was the strangeness of the place, but then she had slept well the previous night. No, it wasn't that, she thought as she lay wide awake at 4am. It was the third, or was it the fourth time she had woken from a fitful sleep strewn with strange images of people and places, at once familiar yet no-one and nowhere she recognised or could remember.

This last time she had woken in a cold sweat, clammy and with a feeling of apprehension. Well, at least it wasn't that dream again she thought in an effort to comfort herself.

She went over the last two days in her mind, attempting to find a semblance of order. Maybe she should have spoken to Chiara, sure she would have allayed her fears with some rational explanation, but even though she had wanted to, the words had stayed locked inside unable to find release.

She drifted in and out of sleep until about 8 o'clock

when she decided she could stay in bed no longer. Opening the shutters, she was greeted by a high, clear blue sky and the beauty of the light as it washed over the Tuscan landscape gently infused her with a sense of hope. She took a long shower, as if the water would cleanse and refresh more than her body. Once dressed and her dark hair shining and dry, she went down to the kitchen where Chiara greeted her with coffee and warm bread.

"*Buongiorno amore. Che bella giornata! Dormi bene?*" Lucia agreed it was a beautiful day and lied saying that she had slept well, hoping her aunt's perceptive gaze would not pierce the illusion.

Chiara suggested they leave about ten o'clock for Florence so she could then go to the shop to do what she needed to do and Lucia could spend an hour or so exploring the environs nearby.

"*Perfetto.*" Lucia agreed, thinking it would be good to familiarise herself with Florence once again and looked forward to some leisurely window shopping and maybe a coffee in a nearby bar.

Cheered by a sense of purpose, she was able to deflect any anxiety she was feeling about the rest of the day to the back of her mind where she hoped it would stay. She was determined to enjoy the short time with Chiara and briefly convinced herself that she was just being silly and if only she could relax, everything would be alright.

They did not have to leave for over an hour and Chiara brought her up to date with what else had been happening in her life and those of the children. Lucia absorbed it all and wished she could spend more time with them here in Italy. It was as if a part of her had been asleep and was now waking up. She thought how much her life in London was overshadowed by work and, as much as she loved her job, it demanded nearly all her time.

"How do you do it, Chiara? How do you manage a business and a family?"

"Oh, *cara*, I'm not sure I do. I have learned with the business that the only way I can survive is to delegate and I'm very lucky to have some good people working for me. As for the family… well, I don't think they would say I do it very well. What about you? Is there anyone special?"

"No, no, I simply don't have time. I was just thinking how consuming my work is and wondering what I can do about it."

"Well, I think you have to decide what is important for you and make those things a priority."

"If only it were that simple," Lucia said weakly.

"It is, *cara*." Chiara said gently with compassion. "Only you can make the choices you need to make." Then with a smile and an upturned hand and slight shrug of her shoulders, "Maybe you should spend more time here?"

"Oh, I wish I could," Lucia said surprising herself by the amount of feeling she had instilled in those few words.

"Maybe you can."

Lucia saw Chiara's mouth move but the voice she heard was not hers. She recognised it immediately. It was the voice she had heard before; in London and on the plane. She felt as if she was collapsing into herself and fell back into the chair.

Chiara rushed round to the other side of the table

and put her arm around Lucia's shoulders, looking into her face with concern.

"*Amore*, what happened? You've gone so pale. Did I say something …. I didn't mean to upset you in any way?"

Lucia looked around her and at Chiara.

"No, no. I don't know what happened. I'm alright now." She said as she gathered herself. "Please, can we talk about it later, when we come back after lunch?"

"*Si, si, certo*" relieved to see the colour return to her niece's face, and thinking it best not to push her for an explanation.

"Thank you," Lucia paused, "I promise, I will explain later. I'm fine now so let's enjoy the day."

Although disturbed by hearing the voice again, she was determined that it would not impinge on her day and once she had recovered, Lucia resolved to talk to Chiara later. Relieved that she had not pressed her for an explanation she got up from the table to pour another coffee.

"More coffee?" she asked Chiara.

"*Si, grazie,*" Chiara held out her cup.

Lucia poured another coffee and returned to the table. She told Chiara that she had met James before she left and that he would be visiting in a couple of weeks.

"Wouldn't it be wonderful if we were all here together?"

"Of course, maybe you could stay on, or come back with James?" Chiara suggested.

"Oh Chiara, I wish I could but I have to be back next week – with or without the interview."

"*Che pecatto,*" Chiara said, what a shame.

Lucia suddenly felt excluded and alone; weighed down by a restriction that prevented her from being part of something – her family. In that second her mind whirled from Italy to London and back again trying to make sense of what she was feeling. Unable to shake it off, she simply smiled.

Chiara, sensing her niece's discomfort, reached out and placed her hand over Lucia's, "*Mi dispiace*, of course you have other commitments, some other time. *Allora*, we had better get ready to leave."

Half an hour later they were ready to leave the villa and head for the centre of Florence.

"*Andiamo*," Chiara said, let's go. "I usually take the little car, the Smart, when I go into town, *va bene*?"

"*Si, certo.*" Lucia's spirit rose at the prospect of movement and the opportunity to spend some time in Florence. Even though the city would probably be full of tourists she still found a beauty there and felt a deep connection to the place.

The car approached the centre following the road that ran alongside the River Arno. Lucia could see the famous Ponte Vecchio in the distance and shortly before they reached it Chiara turned right, taking the preceding bridge over the Arno and manoeuvred the little car along the narrow streets around the Uffizi. Eventually she turned through an archway with large open gates into a courtyard where she parked.

"My friend, she lets me use her space here," Chiara explained, "and it's close to the shop."

She guided Lucia through a nearby alleyway that led to the street next to the one they wanted. Down another narrow cobbled street they came out about fifty metres from the shop.

"*Allora*, you think you will be able to find your way?" Chiara asked as they stopped outside.

"Yes, I remember where we are now, no worries."

"*Va bene,* see you in a couple of hours then?"

"Okay," and they kissed cheeks and parted company.

Lucia wandered in and out of narrow streets until she came out on the Piazza della Republicca, edged on either side by the famous Café Gilli and Giubbe Rosso, where the rich and famous had once whiled away the hours over wine and coffee and, of course, perfected the art of being seen. These days frequented by tourists maybe hoping to taste a sense of how it might have been.

Ah, but coffee is a good idea and she found a small bar nearby that was not so much on public view.

"*Un cappuccino, per favore.*" At least it was still morning and therefore acceptable to order a *cappuccino* without instantly being recognised as a tourist – after noon it was derisible for an Italian to drink anything other than an espresso.

"*Grazie,*" she decided to sit at a table even though it would inflate the price of the coffee than if she had stood at the bar and contemplated how to spend the next two hours. She didn't have long so decided not to do too much as she wanted to be as relaxed as possible before going up to the Villa Martinelli.

"Santa Croce," the voice sounded in her head.

"I don't know if I'll have time," came her automatic response before she realised that she was still sitting at the table in the bar; there was no dizziness, no fading, it all seemed quite normal apart from the voice in her head.

"There's time, *andiamo*," the voice was gentle yet commanding.

Lucia feeling surprisingly calm, got up, paid for her coffee and, a little confused by how normal it felt, made her way to Santa Croce. In a way she was happy to go there as she had always preferred it to the duomo where most visitors to Florence flocked like sheep.

Once inside the church, Lucia was immediately aware of the timelessness of the place and the strong presence of the Renaissance in the many paintings and sculptures of the artists of that period. Dante, Machiavelli, Gallileo and the seemingly omnipresent Medici family, well known for their patronage of the arts over generations and also of their interest in alchemy, were also there.

Drawn by a pattern in the floor tiles, Lucia was pondering on the power of the Medici family and its exclusivity, when she felt as if she had been struck hard by something that left her winded and disorientated. She thought she had been thrown several feet and was surprised to find her feet had not moved, in fact, her body was perfectly still, in the same place next to the tiles that had caught her attention.

Now what! she thought, shaken and at the same time irritated, by this sudden disturbance. Conflicting thoughts flitted in and out of her mind as she tried to make sense of it. She shook her head in an attempt to clear the confusion and looked around wondering if anyone else had seen anything. She instantly knew there was nothing for anyone to see; this much she had understood.

She carried on with her tour of the main body of the church before going to the room dedicated to St Francis of Assisi by which time her breathing had returned to normal. After a glance at the *della Robbia* ceramics displayed at the end of the corridor, she headed outside to the museum. Here she sought out the angel she had seen on her last visit a few years ago.

She had come to Florence with her then partner, Ben. She rarely thought of him, having become adept in the art of deflection. It seemed such a distant world now – from coupledom to singularity, from a love-filled life to a life filled with work. Devastated by the dissolution of her future with Ben, Lucia had thrown herself into her career leaving little, if any, time for anything else. Odd dates, usually arranged by well-meaning friends, had come to nothing and she had created a self-contained, controlled life for herself. Even friends had drifted away from lack of contact.

The exhibits had been moved to different rooms and it took her a while to locate the angel. Then, there it was, a plaster copy of an angel on the front façade with the beatific smile that had caught Lucia's attention the first time she had seen it. It was a smile that held a secret, a knowing, with such gentle beauty that it surpassed her deflections and lodged itself firmly in her memory of the good and allowable.

She stood in front of the statue determined to capture the enigmatic smile with her camera. The quality of the statue, or lack of it, did not matter to her, it was the simple beauty of the expression that, for some reason, touched her deeply.

Once satisfied she had enough images, she made her way to the exit and out into the piazza. Retracing her footsteps she headed back towards her aunt's shop. As she walked her mind returned to the strange incident in the church and she wondered whether she should mention it to Chiara. She had already decided to talk to her later about the 'voice' and maybe it would be better to get through that first.

She arrived at the shop and was eagerly greeted by Chiara even though it was less than two hours since they had last seen each other and was introduced with enthusiasm to the two women who worked there. She then answered the profusion of questions about how she had spent the intervening time as she looked around the beautiful displays of her aunt's products. There were creams and lotions for every type of skin, all made from natural ingredients and the herbs that Chiara grew on the estate. Expensive French perfumes left lingering scents in the air as did the artisan soaps and bath and shower products made with pure essential oils.

"Oh Chiara, it all smells so wonderful!"

"*Grazie, cara*," she thanked Lucia. "I will be ready in five minutes, please sit down."

Lucia saw an armchair in the corner and sat down while Chiara ensured everything was in order before she left for the day.

"*Allora, andiamo.*" They both said their goodbyes and went out into the street to make their way back to the car.

Chiara drove out of the city as Lucia wondered what the purpose of this lunch could be. She imagined Giacomo Martinelli must still be in hospital and whether Antonio and his mother were merely being polite or ……… Lucia stopped her thoughts there seeing the futility of such speculation and decided to enjoy the scenery as they left the city.

"Penny for them?" Chiara broke the silence.

"Oh, I don't know. I'm just curious about this lunch I suppose."

"*Eh,* you know how it is. They probably just want things to appear normal – which they are not."

"I suppose," though Lucia did not sound convinced. She was contemplating the luxury of self-deceit and the Italian obsession with *la bella figura* when they drove through the high gates and along the cypress-lined drive leading to the villa.

Chiara parked the car and turned off the engine as Antonio walked towards them to greet them.

"Lucia, Chiara, *buongiorno,*" he smiled at them in turn, "it is good of you to come."

Chiara responded quickly, "*Buongiorno, Antonio.* I was sorry to hear about Giacomo, how is he?"

"As well as can be expected. He needs to rest, which is not easy for him, as you can imagine. We will know more in a few days. Let us join my mother and we can talk some more." He stood to one side holding out his arm in the direction of the steps leading to the terrace where Lucia had had supper the night before last.

Following his direction they went up to the terrace where a table had been set for lunch under the shade of a large umbrella to protect them from the sun which, even in May, could be strong.

Luisa appeared through one of the terrace doors. Lucia thought she looked worn and tired despite her make-up and elegant outfit, though to be expected given the circumstances of the last 24 hours or so.

"*Buongiorno,*" Luisa smiled and greeted them both with kisses to each cheek in turn. "Thank you both so much for coming."

"Luisa," again it was Chiara who led the conversation, "how are you? It must have been such a shock. If there is anything we can do?"

"*No grazie.* It doesn't seem to be terribly serious, though we will know more when we have the test results in a few days. It seems my husband needs to rest, which, as you can imagine, does not come easily to him."

"*Eh,* I know what you mean. Franco is the same. I hardly see him these days, he is so busy."

"And Lucia, you are married?" Luisa enquired.

"No, I'm not" Lucia replied, then diverting attention from her singular state, added, "I am sorry not to be able to meet your husband, *Signora.*"

At that moment Maria arrived with a tray of plates filled with various antipasti which she transferred to the table. There was *schiaccia,* similar to the Italian bread sold in England as *focaccia,* bowls of salad and bottles of red and white wine, the white wine in an ice bucket to keep it cool.

"Please, let us sit down." Luisa indicated towards the table. Once seated she turned to Lucia, "Lucia, call me Luisa; there is no need for formality here. Do you prefer red or white wine? Antonio, please, would you pour the wine?" And for about half an hour Luisa barely paused as she chatted to Chiara about her business and to Lucia about her work as a journalist. Apart from an odd comment here and there, Antonio was quiet.

They finished the antipasti and Maria deposited a large bowl of *spaghetti alle vongole* on the table, much to Lucia's delight.

"*Allora*, Lucia, I am wondering how long you are able to stay in Florence."

"Well, I'm due to return to London next Wednesday," she replied.

"*Bene*. As I said earlier, my husband is under strict orders to rest and we are to wait for the test results also, but he does hope to be home by the beginning of the week. If you are here then he would still like to do the interview. I hope that will be possible for you."

"Of course, I would like that very much. Perhaps you could keep me informed of his progress and if necessary I can make arrangements to stay an extra day or two."

"*Grazie mille*. I would appreciate that as I know it means a great deal to him."

Lucia turned towards Chiara but before she could say anything, Chiara gave her a big smile, "You can stay as long as you like, *cara*, you know that."

Lucia suddenly felt as if she had lost control of something though was not sure what it was. The ground beneath her feet began to feel unstable and she dismissed a moment of dizziness as more to do with a glass of wine at lunch than anything else. She smiled at Chiara and thanked her before asking to be excused so she could go to the bathroom.

She entered the villa through a door leading directly into a hallway and found the bathroom door. Once inside she stood in front of a large mirror set in marble tiles and looked at her reflection almost in askance of her own existence. Then, like a whisper, another face seemed to overlay her own and, before she could even form a thought, it was gone. Her first thought was to dismiss it as a trick of the light, but she knew that was not the case and, easy as it could be to deceive herself, she also knew this was not the time to do that.

She took a deep breath in an attempt to quell the rising anxiety. She told herself that she just had to get through this lunch and she would then at least be able to talk to Chiara whom she felt sure would have a rational explanation for all the strange things that had been happening. As always, Lucia, adept at hiding her true feelings, managed to return to the table without showing a hint of the inner turmoil she was experiencing, or so she thought.

Chiara's eagle eyes and innate sensitivity to the moods of others soon picked up that all was not as well as it seemed with her niece. She decided not to mention anything in front of the others but rather stored it away to be discussed when they were alone.

"Ah, Lucia, Antonio was just telling me a little about the art collection and has offered to give you a viewing after lunch. What do you think?"

"Oh," Lucia said, taken by surprise by such an unexpected offer, "that would be wonderful. Thank you Antonio, that is very generous."

"*Eh, niente,*" he shrugged. "You have come all this way; it is the least I can do."

They continued with the meal and as always, being Italy, there were several courses, interspersed with conversation, mainly led by Luisa with occasional contributions from Antonio. Lucia noticed that neither spoke of anything remotely personal and by the time they had finished their coffees Antonio suggested taking Lucia to the gallery while Luisa and Chiara remained on the terrace to continue their conversation.

The gallery had been built on to the east side of the villa and every care had been taken, and no expense spared, to maintain an optimum atmosphere for the conservation of the works of art. Double automatic doors at the entrance created a vacuum to minimise pollution and maintain an even temperature.

Once inside Lucia was aware of a silence and stillness rarely experienced in her busy city life, and felt even her breath would cause too great a disturbance.

The paintings and sculptures were arranged in such a way that they did not compete for space and light, and the observer was able to contemplate each piece without distraction. What a luxury, Lucia thought, to be able to appreciate such beauty so privately and without interruption. Antonio merely introduced her to the different sections of the gallery then retired to a corner so she could fully enjoy the experience, but remained close by should she have any questions.

Some of the paintings were familiar to her, others she had not seen before and one or two were a complete surprise, in particular a Giotto and another that appeared to be an unfinished piece by Leonardo da Vinci.

Then, one painting caught her attention. It was an early portrait of a man painted on wood panel, showing the typical Florentine profile set in a Tuscan landscape. The details gave the artist as 'unknown' and she thought it fairly nondescript, yet there was something about it that was having a profound effect upon her. She felt a sense of recognition ….. that she knew the man. But that's impossible, she thought, as she tried to disengage from it. Still the painting held her attention and she searched for the source of its fascination. There was something familiar and as she looked with more care she noticed his ring and it sent a chill down her spine. Hypnotised and unable to move, for a second it was as if the world of the painting and the gallery merged, her present environment receding into shadow. It was then that she heard the voice in her head.

"Remember me. Help me." Then silence.

Lucia stood still, immobilised. As she became aware of the gallery again, she realised she was trembling and her face felt cool and damp. Antonio was by her side.

"Lucia, Lucia, you are unwell? Can I get you something? Please, come and sit down."

"Erm …. thank you, no. I'll be alright. Probably the combination of too much wine and sun," she said trying to brush aside his concern. "Maybe we should return to join your mother and Chiara."

"Of course," he responded, though did not sound convinced.

"Thank you for this," she said waving her arm to indicate the works of art. "It is wonderful to see so much beauty in one place." Her voice was still wavering a little and she hoped he would not question her further. There was still so much she did not understand herself.

As they returned to the terrace the afternoon sun felt hot after the ambient temperature of the gallery and

Lucia was quick to regale Luisa and Chiara with her appreciation of and enthusiasm for the gallery as they prepared to leave.

"I am pleased you were able to see it and I apologise for the inconvenience to your plans. I hope we will see you again very soon." Luisa smiled.

"Oh no, please there is no need to apologise." Lucia responded, with a little more gravitas to her voice. "I hope your husband recovers soon. Please give him my best wishes. And thank you for your kind hospitality and a wonderful lunch."

"You are very kind and understanding, and we will be in touch as soon as there is any news."

"Luisa, *grazie*. It's good to see you again. *A presto*." Chiara said, thanking Luisa, until the next time.

They all said their goodbyes and Antonio escorted them down the terrace steps to the car. After another exchange of thank yous and goodbyes, the two women got into the car and drove out of the courtyard.

"Well, that was interesting," observed Chiara. "Don't you think it strange that they hardly mentioned Giacomo, other than when we did?"

"Oh, I suppose so. Why, do you think they're hiding something?"

Ah, always the journalist," said Chiara smiling. "Although I suspect they're not the only ones. You seem somewhat preoccupied yourself."

"What do you mean?"

"I'm not sure, *cara*. It's just a feeling. Is there something worrying you?"

Again, Lucia chose to dismiss the opportunity to talk to her aunt and blamed the combination of the sun and wine as she had done earlier to Antonio. She knew, however, that she would not be able to shield herself much longer from Chiara's acute perception, nor did she really want to. She was well aware of the stress she caused herself by these attempts to maintain an illusion of well-being; her agitated solar plexus was clear evidence of this.

"*Va bene.* Let's call in on *mamma* on the way home." Chiara suggested and wondered what it was her niece was trying to hide. It was clear to her that Lucia had been edgy since her arrival and she had decided not to press her earlier as she did not want her to shut her out. She remembered when Lucia was young how she would retreat into herself if pressed too hard to talk about something she preferred to keep to herself. She could go for days without speaking. Whilst she had not known Lucia behave in this way as an adult she wanted them to enjoy this short time together and hoped Lucia would talk to her when she was ready.

"Yes, that would be lovely," Lucia responded, relieved not to have to explain further.

It was not long before they pulled up outside Isabella's cottage. The afternoon sun was losing its intensity and the earlier heat had become a gentle warmth. Chiara hoped they would not be disturbing Isabella's siesta but her concern was soon dismissed as Isabella came out to greet them.

"Ah, Chiara, Lucia, how lovely," Isabella said, exchanging kisses with each of them in turn.

"Mamma, we are not disturbing you?"

"No, of course not. *Vieni, vieni,*" Isabella said inviting them into the cottage. "Come, tell me what you've been doing. You would like some tea?"

"No thank you, *nonna*, we've just come from having lunch. In fact, a glass of water would be good."

"And you, Chiara, you also would like water?" Isabella said at the same time screwing up her nose in distaste.

"Yes, thank you *mamma*."

Isabella went to the kitchen and returned with two glasses of water to which she had added a slice of lemon and a sprig of lemon verbena.

"*Ecco*," she smiled, "enjoy."

Amid their sounds of gratitude, Isabella sat down attentive for their news.

"So, how was lunch? Was this at the Martinelli villa?"

"Yes, but we don't know much more than we did yesterday, only that Luisa and Antonio hoped he would be well enough to do the interview in the next few days."

"*Eh*, these people. There is more to this than they say."

"Why do you say that *mamma*?"

"Only that all is not what it seems with them. Remember my house? Well, I would sometimes see Giacomo in the village and there was talk that he was looking to buy a property there. It made no sense – it was a ruin with a bit of *bosco* not far from my house. There was no hunting in the woodland, not even *funghi*. You will both remember it – you used to play there a long time ago and I warned you of the vipers. I used to go there sometimes to collect my herbs.

Lucia suddenly felt faint and went cold. Not only did she remember the little house in the woods, it was also the house in her dream.

"Lucia, *amore*, what is wrong? You look as if you've seen a ghost."

Lucia remained silent and Isabella looked towards Chiara for an answer.

"I don't know, *mamma*. I'm sure Lucia will tell us in her own time."

"Lucia?" Isabella turned to her again.

"Er…" Lucia tried to speak but the words became like clay in her mouth. She looked at her aunt and grandmother and collapsed inside herself holding her head in her hands.

"*Amore, amore,* what is it?" Chiara was at her side and as she put her arm round her shoulders, Lucia dissolved into tears.

"Ah, I think we need something a bit stronger than water," and Isabella got up, went over to the cabinet and poured three small glasses of *vin santo*. "Well, not too strong," and handed one to Chiara to give to Lucia.

Chiara waited for the sobs to die down before handing the glass to Lucia. "Here, *cara*, when you're ready maybe you can tell us what is going on."

Lucia took a sip from the glass and felt the golden liquid's warmth spread through her body. She looked at the other two women and wondered where or how to start. It was clear that she was not going to be able to continue to avoid this as she had been doing.

Taking another sip she took a deep breath and tried to explain the strange events of the last few days and the recurring dream of the last week or so. She recounted her fragmented memories of the dream and the voice she had first heard in London asking her for help. How she had heard the same voice again on the plane, then in Florence guiding her to Sante Croce and again at the villa earlier that day. Finally she said, "You see, that's the house, I'm sure of it, the one in my dream."

Isabella was the first to speak. "This voice, you have heard it before you started to have this dream?"

"No, never."

"It's alright, *amore*, it is not that unusual to hear voices. We just need to understand who it is and why."

"Well, I'd like it to just stop and go away!"

"*Amore*," Isabella said very gently, "for some reason this voice has chosen you as someone who is able to help. Is it familiar to you in any way?"

"No. It means nothing to me at all. Am I going mad?"

"*Cara*, of course you're not." It was Chiara who spoke now. "It seems to me that you have a gift and only need to understand it."

"Lucia, she is right." Isabella tried to reassure her. "Maybe Chiara will know someone who can help you. Chiara?"

"I will do what I can, *mamma*. In the meantime I will make a remedy for you, and then we shall see if we can find out why this is happening."

Lucia, now a little calmer, looked at Isabella and said, "What happened to the house?"

"I don't know. It's still there as far as I know. I remember they could not trace the owners, like so many of these abandoned places, so Giacomo was not able to buy it. I believe he had spent a lot of money trying to acquire it and was furious when he had to walk away from it. It was a very odd business."

"What do you mean *nonna*?"

"*Allora*, I seem to remember that at the time he went round the village asking people questions about the little house and its history. More than you would ask if you were simply trying to find the owners. *Eh*, why would anyone want to spend so much money on a ruin!"

"I see, *mamma*. But what has this to do with Lucia?"

"I don't know, Chiara. Lucia, can you tell me more about this dream?"

Lucia, looking intermittently at Isabella and her hands tightly holding each other on her lap, recounted the dream again and this time included as much detail as she could remember.

"*Ecco*! There it is. Chiara, you must know someone who can help this child unlock the mystery of her dream."

"Well, there is someone who just came to my mind. I'll call him and see if he can come over." Chiara paused and turned to Lucia, "If that is alright with you, *cara*?"

There was a pause as Lucia continued to look at her hands before looking up, her eyes red and cheeks tear stained. "Of course, anything if it will make it all go away," she said in a quiet, exhausted voice.

"I can't promise that, *cara*, but we may be able find some answers as to what is happening and how you can deal with it."

"*Va bene*. Lucia, *amore*, I know it is not easy but I am happy you have told us. Now we can do something. You will let me know how you get on?" Always one to create order when needed, Isabella smiled gently at her granddaughter, suddenly remembering how stubbornly private she used to be as a child. "Mmmm …." She said almost to herself. "*Si, si,* let me know, won't you?"

"She is a strange one, this Signorina Lucia. Don't you think Antonio?" Luisa asked as she relaxed on the terrace before returning to the hospital.

"I think she is a little tired and maybe a bit stressed. Although she did behave a little oddly when we were in the gallery. I thought for a moment that she would faint. Probably the effect of the sun and wine as she said." He shrugged.

"What do you mean?"

"*Allora.* I stepped back so she could have a private experience of the artworks and I could not see well what was happening. She seemed quite happy, then as she stood in front of one of the paintings, she became still and the colour left her face. She looked very weak, I don't know, as if she had seen a ghost."

"Oh. Which painting?"

"Er, the portrait of…, oh, what was his name? The one with Florence in the background, a *di Credi* I think. No, no it wasn't that one. It was an earlier portrait with a Tuscan landscape. We don't know the artist. Why?"

"I see. I must go. Will you join me later?" Luisa did not wait for an answer but got up to gather her handbag, a jacket and car keys before heading towards the car.

Antonio watched his mother descend the steps from the terrace to the courtyard. He was used to her erratic behaviour, which often bordered on rudeness, and paid no attention to her brusque departure.

As she drove to the hospital Luisa mused on Lucia and

the painting that seemed to have had such a profound effect on her. She had not involved herself too much with the gallery and its contents, leaving any matters concerning it to her husband. She had learned early on in their marriage how secretive he could be especially concerning matters relating to his family and their history. She knew there were links going back to the Medici but Giacomo had always avoided any questions relating to this in his dismissive, yet finite, way. Anyway, she had plenty to occupy her with running the villa and maintaining a busy social life, little of which involved her husband but centred mainly on the groups and charities she had become involved in over the years.

Arriving at the hospital she parked the car and made her way down the long corridors to the room where Giacomo greeted her with a smile and "*ciao bella.*"

Luisa thought that he must be feeling better and walked over to the bed to lightly kiss him on the cheek avoiding the tubes that still attached him to a monitor.

Ignoring the usual pleasantries Giacomo straightaway asked, "How was lunch with the Signorina?"

"It went well. She says she will still see you for the interview and try to extend her stay if necessary."

"*Bene*. Did Antonio show her the gallery?"

"*Si, si.* As I said it went well. There's nothing you need to worry yourself with apart from getting well, *caro.*" She knew the *caro* sounded like an afterthought in an attempt to ameliorate her frustration with his questions, but Giacomo seemed not to have noticed.

Before Giacomo could continue, Dr Giannini

entered the room.

"Ah, Signora Martinelli, *buona sera*. I am happy to find you here. Signor Martinelli, *buona sera*."

They both returned the greeting.

"I have received some of the test results. They arrived more quickly than I thought. Anyway, the news is not all bad. It's still not entirely clear what caused you to collapse. It may be that when you fell you hit your head and the resulting trauma interrupted the blood supply to your brain momentarily. There is no evidence of any damage but I would like to carry on monitoring you until the rest of the results come in. I would also like to repeat some of the tests in a day or two as you become more stable. That way we will have more true and accurate readings." Dr Giannini paused, half expecting objections from his patient and when none came he continued.

"Now, to other matters. Your tests show that your cholesterol is high and I have arranged for a nutritionist to talk to you about your diet. Also, once I am satisfied you have recovered I think it would be a good idea to devise a gradual exercise programme for you. It may be that it is a matter of genetics in which case I will recommend statins to keep it under control. Have you any close relatives that have had heart problems?"

Giacomo Martinelli shook his head.

It was Luisa who spoke next to ask when her husband would be able to come home.

"As I said, I would like to keep an eye on him. You can't be too careful in these matters but if all is well I should think you can have him back early next week." Dr Giannini smiled only to find his small attempt at humour fell into a void. "Very well, I will see you again tomorrow. Signor, Signora, *buona sera."* And, he turned and left the room.

"Now, *caro*, will you tell me what happened?" Luisa said with a firm insistence.

"*Eh,* you heard the doctor, it is nothing. I must have hit my head when I fell. Now, get me out of here!"

"What do you mean? You heard what the doctor said …."

Before she could finish Giacomo was saying, "I don't care what the doctor said, I'm not staying here. Now, where are my clothes?"

With her hand on his, Luisa leaned forward and looked her husband directly and carefully in the eyes.

"And, I don't care for what you are saying. You will do as you are told and stay here until the doctor is satisfied you are well enough to leave."

Giacomo fidgeted under her hand to free himself and in doing so the beeping emitted from the monitor increased and almost immediately a nurse was in the room to investigate the reason for the change.

"Pah!" he exclaimed. "I'm fine. Look, look, it's going down again."

The nurse still insisted on checking everything and told him he was to stay calm and not become agitated.

Luisa returned to his side and smiled, "*Allora,* it's no good fighting it. Now what is so important that it cannot wait another day or so?"

Giacomo grunted at his enforced capitulation. "Where's Lorenzo? I want to see him. And Antonio, did he not come with you?"

"I'm sure they'll be here," Luisa said calmly as she thought, yes, Antonio may follow her to the hospital but as for Lorenzo, she had no idea where he was or when he would return.

Luisa worried about Lorenzo, so headstrong and unpredictable. At least with Antonio she knew where she was; they may not always agree but he was responsive rather than reactive. Or maybe she was being unfair. Antonio was at least ten years older than Lorenzo but no, it was not just that, their characters were completely different. Lorenzo had expectations that Antonio had never expressed. Yes, he'd been arrogant in his youth but not in the demanding way that Lorenzo displayed for all to see. Well, she didn't want to think about it now and she didn't want him turning up again and upsetting his father.

"*Caro*, I think you should rest now. If there's nothing I can get you, I'll say goodnight and see you again in the morning."

Giacomo looked at his wife and for the first time noticed the exhaustion in her eyes and a tenderness briefly passed between them which dissolved the words he was about to say demanding she find their son.

"*Grazie cara.* No there's nothing. You must also rest. *A domani,* see you tomorrow."

Luisa kissed his forehead and gently pressed his hand before leaving the room.

By the time they had returned to the villa Lucia seemed calmer though Chiara was not convinced by her quiet demeanour. She could almost hear the multitude of questions bubbling under the surface.

"You must be exhausted, *cara*. Can I get you anything?"

"No thanks, I think I'd like to go for a walk while

it's still warm enough."

"*Va bene*, let me get you a wrap, in case. Would you like company or ...." Chiara allowed the question to trail off.

"Er, no. Well, yes actually, I think I would."

Chiara opened a cupboard in the hall where she collected a couple of wraps to keep them warm should the sun's rays fail them. Handing one to Lucia she thought how slight and vulnerable she looked and wondered how she could best help her with these unusual experiences. Whilst her own intuition was strong, she had not experienced any of the things of which Lucia spoke. Yes, she had heard of such things and could only imagine how frightening this all was for Lucia who had not been brought up with the old ways as she had. She remembered her sister Daniela's derision if such things were mentioned so it was unlikely she would have passed any of their mother's knowledge to her daughter. Daniela had always avoided forages into the woods for plants and had shown no interest in their mother's wisdom for healing. In fact, she had not only left home as soon as she could, she had also left the country.

"We can walk through the olives if you like. I think it will be getting chilly in the woods." Chiara suggested.

"Okay, I'd love to. It's so lovely there and the trees always seem so peaceful."

As they followed the path through the garden to the olive grove, Chiara linked her arm through Lucia's. "Come, let's enjoy the last of the sun's rays then I'll prepare a little food and find a remedy for you. What do you think?"

Lucia felt the warmth of her aunt's love seep through and her fears began to dissolve. She smiled. She didn't feel so alone now that she had spoken to her aunt and grandmother, and even though she didn't understand what was happening, she had a sense of hope.

"Sounds good to me."

As they reached the olive grove the sun could be seen nearing the horizon beyond Florence bathing the landscape in a soft peachy glow. The terraced ground here was uneven and the two women separated and pulled their wraps tighter as the cooler evening air made its presence felt. They continued their walk in a connected silence. The sky slowly travelled through shades of pink to deepest magenta as they followed the terraces to return to the garden path before the light deserted them.

"*Allora*, I think we are back just in time. Let me see what I can find for supper. Will pasta and salad be alright for you?"

"Of course, I don't think I can eat much after that lunch."

They returned to the villa and settled in the kitchen. Chiara produced a bottle of wine and two glasses.

"*Ecco*, if you can open this I will be back in a few minutes."

Chiara disappeared into the hall and through a door that led to her study. Here, she looked at the tiny bottles of remedies she had personally prepared. Each remedy was based on the qualities of a plant – some herbs, some flowers and some wild flowers that many people would think of as weeds. Intuitively, she selected a bottle and returned to the kitchen.

Lucia turned away from the window and the view of Florence that she had been contemplating when she heard her aunt's footsteps enter the kitchen. Chiara walked over to her and handed her the little bottle.

"This is to calm your fears and bring rested sleep. Put seven drops under your tongue a short time before you go to bed. I'll make a special remedy for you tomorrow."

"Thank you Chiara," and she enclosed Chiara's hands in her own before she accepted the bottle. "It's so good to be here with you."

"I am happy you are here too. Now, let's get some food. And where's that glass of wine?"

"Is that okay with the remedy?"

"It will do no harm; in fact, I think they are both a good idea right now!"

Chiara inspected the fridge for something to accompany pasta and decided on a simple *spaghetti peperoncino*. An easy dish to prepare of spaghetti with garlic, olive oil and chilli that she thought would be perfect and could be followed with a salad.

It was not long before they were seated at the table with bowls of pasta. Lucia was quiet and pensive and Chiara did not want to intrude in her thoughts. She would wait until Lucia was ready to share them which she was sure she would do soon. They made small conversations around comfortable pauses.

Lucia, feeling relaxed by another glass of wine, looked up from her food, "Chiara, I'm really sorry about today. I was going to talk to you and ask your advice, but not like this. I don't know what happened ……"

Before Lucia could finish, Chiara interjected with, "*Basta*, enough, please, you do not need to apologise and also, please know I will do whatever I can to help you. I have a friend with whom I think it would be good for you to speak. I will call him in the morning."

Lucia uttered a quiet thank you and thought how much she loved to hear her aunt's idiosyncratic version of the English language. She smiled and, adding more energy to her voice, said a louder, "thank you."

"Oh *cara, non ti preoccupare* - do not worry, we will find out what this is all about. And, no more words about it until tomorrow"

"Okay, I seem to have lost track of time, what day is it tomorrow?"

"Oh, Friday, I think. No, Saturday."

They both laughed, sharing the absurdity of the moment.

The rest of the evening passed without incident as they laughed over some shared childhood moments and mooted ideas of places they would like to visit over the next day or so. When Lucia began to yawn Chiara suggested she take her remedy and say goodnight. She was happy the mood had lightened but was also aware that Lucia needed to rest if she was going to find the strength to get through the next few days. They hugged, both saying, "*buona notte e dormi bene.*" Goodnight and sleep well.

Chiara loaded the dishwasher and when everything was cleaned and tidy she poured a final small glass of wine and sat on the sofa at the far end of the kitchen by the doors that opened onto the terrace. She loved her kitchen and the fact that she could prepare the food, eat it and relax before and after each meal all in the same room. On fine spring and autumn days she could open the doors onto the terrace and enjoy the panoramic view to Florence and beyond.

She sipped her wine and pondered on her niece's dilemma and what she might be able to do to help. She had thought earlier of calling Tom. He had helped her with the garden design when she first moved here and they had become good friends. He had a sensitive understanding of the land and the plants it supported and she had grown to trust his judgments as sound and grounded. He was widely travelled and this had led him to study other cultures and philosophies, and she hoped that somewhere in his opera of knowledge he would be able to make sense of Lucia's recent experiences.

She emptied her glass, put it in the dishwasher and resolved to call him in the morning.

As Luisa left the hospital she called Antonio and was relieved to find that he was still at the villa. She asked if there was any news of Lorenzo and was not surprised by the negative response. She asked him if he would stay the night at the villa and not go to his apartment in the city, and although Antonio was now desperate to leave, he acquiesced. As always he found it hard to refuse his mother and especially when he knew she was probably not as strong as she would have everyone believe.

Frustrated by his brother's absence, he called him again only to hear the familiar voicemail invitation to leave a message.

"Pah!" he exclaimed, throwing his arms upwards in exasperation. "Why does he do this?"

"Who does what?" Luisa asked.

"Oh, I didn't hear you arrive, *mamma*."

"I take it you were referring to Lorenzo, have you heard from him?"

"No, nothing. I called but it just goes to voicemail. How is *babbo*?"

"Irascible, so improving. They want to keep him a few more days and he wants to come home now, so you can imagine…"

"Ah, yes." He knew only too well how ill-tempered his father could be if he wasn't getting his own way.

"You said you will stay? I'll ask Maria to prepare supper for us." And, before he could answer Luisa had left the room.

Luisa returned to the room and before she could say anything the sound of wheels scrunching to a halt on the gravel in the courtyard below disturbed the silence. Antonio and Luisa looked at each other and said in unison, "Lorenzo." Their ears followed his footsteps as he took the terrace steps two at a time. He then made his usual dramatic entrance, throwing open the doors and bouncing into the room. Without stopping to catch his breath he acknowledged them each in turn, "*Mamma.* Antonio."

Luisa spoke first, in such a way it was hard to tell if she was being sincere or slightly facetious, "Lorenzo, how nice to see you."

Lorenzo displayed his disarming smile, "*Lo so,* I know. How is *babbo?*"

Luisa paused, and refraining from any admonishments or recriminations, reiterated what she had earlier explained to Antonio. "Will you stay for supper, I'll tell Maria ….."

"Thank you *mamma*, no. I have an appointment in town."

Always in a hurry, going somewhere, doing something, Luisa thought to herself. She knew it was futile to ask anything as he would just see it as prying and then she would see less of him than she did now. Still, recent events had left her concerned for his wellbeing. His irresponsible approach to life had certainly displeased and caused his father to despair.

"*Va bene.* Maybe you could call in to the hospital to see *babbo* tomorrow?"

"Yes, of course. I just need to shower and change and then I must go."

"As you wish." Luisa lost any desire to talk to him and wondered where she had gone wrong in raising such a selfish and narcissistic, young man.

During this exchange Antonio had removed himself from the room to his father's study to make a couple of phone calls. He had spent what was left of the afternoon checking his emails and catching up on some unanswered calls. He still had a business to run and the last two days had set him back enough that he could no longer ignore certain matters. When he returned to the living room, Luisa was alone.

"He has gone?"

"No, he is upstairs. He'll be leaving in a few minutes."

"What did he say?"

"*Eh,* what does he ever say? I have an appointment – I have to go …….. You know how it is. Always the same."

"*Mamma….*" Antonio began but he ran out of

words.

Luisa looked at him and smiled with affection. "Don't worry, let's leave it for now."

At that moment, Lorenzo breezed in and as he crossed the room leaving wafts of aftershave in his wake, he blew kisses saying, "*ciao, ciao, a domani!*"

Almost ignoring him, Luisa said, "I'll see if supper is ready," and went to the kitchen to see Maria.

Antonio poured a glass of wine and put on the television to watch the news, thinking he may as well see what was happening elsewhere in the world outside of the Martinelli vacuum.

SATURDAY
Sabato

Saturday morning arrived and brought with it thunder, lightning and torrential rain. It wasn't to last for long, as these storms rarely did, but the pounding of the rain on the roof and windows dragged Lucia from sleep. It took her a while to orientate herself as she traversed the bridge from sleep to wakefulness. The mists cleared and so too did her awareness of her surroundings. It was like surfacing from a deep dive, she thought, as she broke through into clear air. A crash of thunder overhead startled her. This was followed by a second less dramatic crash as the storm began to move away.

She took in her surroundings and, having reassured herself as to the time and space she occupied, swung her legs out of bed, and headed to the bathroom. By the time she had showered, and moisturised every inch of her body, the storm had passed and the sun's rays were already painting gold pockets in the landscape outside.

As they had not yet made any plans for the day, Lucia put on a pair of cotton trousers and a lightweight cotton sweater over a finely woven t-shirt. She was taken by surprise by a thought to go shopping for clothes. It wasn't a new thought as part of her original plan had been to have time to buy some stylish Italian clothes while she was in Florence. It just seemed a little frivolous right now when there were other things that needed attention. Or maybe she was being a bit too serious and needed to lighten up. In any event she was beginning to feel hungry and decided it was time for breakfast before anything else. Coffee suddenly became essential and she went down to the kitchen.

She almost skipped the last few stairs as the smell of coffee from the kitchen hit her nostrils and she took Chiara by surprise as she bounced in to the kitchen.

"Ah, there you are. You slept well?"

"Yes, yes I did, thank you. Right now though I'd love some coffee."

"Oh," Chiara said, her voice deepening in understanding. "It's just about ready. Here, sit down and I'll bring it over."

Lucia went over to the table which was already laid with cereals, fresh fruit and warm bread rolls.

"*Cara*, help yourself to what you would like and the coffee is coming."

Lucia filled a bowl with muesli, fruit and yoghurt. The coffee arrived and her need satisfied. Chiara joined her at the table.

"I spoke to Tom earlier, you know, the friend I told you about. He said he can come over this morning if you like. I said I would speak to you and let him know if that is a good time. What do you think?"

"Erm," Lucia paused to digest the fact that

something was actually being done and that she now had to face the reality of what was happening to her. "Er yes, of course, unless you have plans?"

"*Bene*, I'll call him after breakfast and arrange a time. I think you will like him."

Chiara watched her, aware of the struggle taking place within that, on the one hand wished for answers, and on the other resisted the change those answers would bring.

She had woken early and in the first, soft light of the morning prepared Lucia's remedy. She liked the silence of that time; it was a good time to work, a time when the world seemed pregnant with possibilities as it began the journey to fulfil its potential.

"More coffee?"

"Oh yes please," Lucia enthused. "It's so good. I don't know why, but it always tastes better here."

"*Eh*, I know what you mean. I think that there are as many theories as there are fish in the sea! As you know in Italy coffee is sacred."

They laughed and Chiara went on to recount how in Rome they insisted they made the best coffee as they had the best water and that wherever you went in Italy you would be met with more stories as to why that particular region had the best coffee.

Remembering the remedy, Chiara got up and walked over to the little table by the sofa. She picked up a small blue bottle and put it on the table in front of Lucia. "Here you are, *cara*. I made this for you this morning so you can begin to take it now, if you wish. Like the one last night just put a few drops under your tongue."

"How often should I take it?"

"I have written it for you," and she handed Lucia a sheet of paper containing the instructions. "To start with, every hour."

"You were up early?"

"*Si*, I find it is the best time to work. The world is more quiet. Now, I will call Tom."

The call was brief and it was arranged that Tom would be there at 11 o'clock. Chiara merely asked if he could come over and talk to her niece. It seemed that he had an appointment in the next village and could be with them after that. *Perfetto*. Chiara thought.

"I have to be in the garden for a short time, if you would like to use my computer to check your emails, or maybe you have your own, I can give you the password for the wi-fi."

The words jolted Lucia as she realised she had not contacted her editor yet about the recent developments.

"Yes, thank you, if I could have the password."

Chiara wrote it on a scrap of paper. "*Cara*, use my office if you like. It is quiet and Mariella will be here soon to clear the kitchen. I won't be long."

Lucia picked up the piece of paper with the password and went to her room to collect her laptop. How could she have been so absent-minded not to have contacted her office? On second thoughts, she had only been here two full days, although it felt as if she'd been here forever. It worried her, this loss of control of her usually ordered life.

She took the small laptop down to the study, switched it on, entered the password and accessed her email account, less than fifty so not too bad. Probably the 'out of office reply' had deterred the less important ones. As she went through them she felt a sense of order return. Maybe it was the familiarity of the one area of her life that worked efficiently and she seemed to gain strength from sorting through, replying to some and deleting others until her inbox was a manageable six.

As she looked at the time, she remembered to take her remedy. It was 10.30 and her curiosity ignited as she began to wonder about Chiara's friend who would soon be arriving. What good could he do? How on earth could he help? It was if her mind knew that possibilities for change were surrounding her and it had to find ways to maintain the familiar ground it already knew.

Lucia sighed, and before another thought could take hold Chiara's head popped round the door. Smiling she said, "It's almost 11, *cara*, more coffee?"

"Oh," taken by surprise, Lucia wondered where the last half an hour had gone. "Yes, I'll just finish off and be there in a minute."

She had been drafting an email to the editor explaining the situation with Signor Martinelli and now completed it by saying she would let her know as soon she had more news. She added her signature, pressed the send button, then disconnected from the virtual world and closed the laptop.

In the kitchen Chiara was making a fresh pot of coffee when she heard the gravel in the courtyard signal the arrival of a car. She went outside to greet her visitor.

Tom climbed down from his 4 x 4 and removed his sunglasses. Of average height he was casually dressed in jeans and t-shirt revealing a slim body with tight, well-defined muscles. His reddish brown hair was well cut but unruly and green eyes shone out from a handsome, tanned face that lit into a smile on seeing Chiara.

"*Buongiorno, come stai?*" they said in unison, hello, how are you.

"*Va bene, e te?*" Chiara was the first to say she was well and ask how he was.

"*Si, si, bene.*"

"*Vieni,* come and meet Lucia. Thank you so much for coming so quickly."

"*Niente.* I was almost here anyway. It's good to see you."

"You too."

They entered the kitchen where Lucia was overseeing the coffee that was almost bubbling in its little pot. Chiara made the introductions and Lucia and Tom exchanged the usual polite greetings. Immediately Lucia thought she would like Tom; he had an open face although she felt somewhat shy under the direct gaze of his green eyes, which soon softened when he smiled.

"Let's take the coffee outside; it's such a beautiful morning and not yet too hot." Chiara suggested.

They sat at the table under the loggia and once they were settled, Chiara explained to Tom her reason for asking him to come.

"Lucia, can you tell me what happened, from the beginning?" he asked, his voice soft and encouraging.

"Er, yes, I'll try," and she began by recounting her recurring dream and the effect it had on her. Tom listened intently as she went on to talk about the voice she had heard and the strange feelings when she saw the painting in the Martinelli gallery.

"Mmm. Thank you. I can see why this is distressing

for you but I think, before I say anything, I would like to go to this house of your dream. That is, if you think you can do that."

"Oh," was all Lucia could manage. This was not what she had expected.

"It's okay. Take your time. There are many things that could be happening here and we could spend a lot of time exploring the different possibilities. I also have a feeling that there is a timing to what is happening and going to the house may not be the easiest way forward for you but you may find some answers there. Also I don't want to influence you in any way."

Chiara watched Lucia who sat perfectly still, her eyes focused on her hands where they met on the table. She paused before speaking.

"*Cara*, I know that this might be difficult but …"

"I'll do it." Lucia interrupted before Chiara could finish her sentence. Eyes resolute, she looked up at Tom. "What do I need to do?"

"*Bene*. I am free for the rest of the day so we can go now."

"Okay, I'll just get my things," and Lucia got up and went to collect her handbag from her room.

"Are you sure about this Tom? You know she is more fragile than she appears."

"Do not worry, Chiara. I won't let any harm come to her. We will both be there to support her; that is, if you are free and will come with us?"

"*Si, si*, I can come. I'm sorry Tom. I called you because I trust you and your knowledge and abilities in these matters."

"I know."

At the sound of Lucia's approaching footsteps,

Chiara got up from the table, picked up her bag, ensuring she had her keys, then said, "*Andiamo*, let's go," as Lucia entered the room.

They crossed the Arno and took the road that headed up into the Pratomagna. It was not long before the road narrowed and, now edged with tall pines, wound its way upwards into the mountains. After a few kilometres Chiara directed Tom to turn off to the right on to a road that led to a small village of a few houses and a bar.

"I think if you go through the village there's a track on the left that you should be able to drive down and the little house is not far from there."

Tom saw the turning and following Chiara's directions drove down the track until he could go no further and turning the car to face the way out he parked so as not to block any other vehicles.

Lucia had been quiet throughout the journey, her face resolute, giving away nothing of what she was thinking or feeling. In fact, she felt numb.

Tom opened the door next to her, "Lucia, are you ready?"

Shaken from her inner world, she looked up to see a pair of clear, green eyes observing her with a strange tenderness.

"Er, yes. Let's go." And she jumped down on to the hardened mud of the track.

Chiara watched her with concern, hoping that Tom had been right in bringing her here so soon.

The track became a narrow path through woodland and they walked along in single file, Lucia leading the way.

It was not the path she had taken in her dream yet somehow she knew the way, being called along by a knowing she couldn't explain. The land to the left sloped upward into the rock of the mountain and the path curved round and gently down accompanied now by a small rivulet fed by a stream deeper in the woods. The air was fresh with a hint of pine and resin. The sun's rays picked their way through the trees, the dappled light creating glints of golden mist.

It was Chiara who broke the silence, "I'd forgotten how beautiful it is here. I used to come here with *mamma* to collect herbs and other plants. It seems so long ago now."

Tom turned to Chiara and smiled. "Yes, it is beautiful. I don't imagine many people come here now, only the animals."

"Oh, you think there are wild boar?"

"Maybe, but I was thinking more of deer and hares."

Lucia stopped as the path opened into a clearing where the ruin of a small, stone house stood derelict surrounded by nature's uninhibited overgrowth.

"Is this the house?" Tom asked.

"Er, yes I think so. It was a long time ago and now we're here ….."

"It's alright, take your time," Tom reassured her.

They stood at the edge of the clearing looking at a scene that had probably not changed for centuries; only the seasons had coloured it differently with their cycle of heat and cold, life and death. And now, life displayed its bounty in the green leaves and wild flowers that flourished in the shade of the trees.

Now that she was here, Lucia felt strangely calm.

There was none of the fear and anxiety that had become such a familiar companion.

"Right, shall we have a look?" she looked at Chiara and Tom in turn and set off towards the house.

The ground was uneven and overgrown around the house and Tom found a stick to bang the ground in case of unseen snakes. Although he thought it unlikely so early in the year, vipers were common and a bite could be fatal.

Lucia walked up the steps to the door looking along the loggia on either side where she imagined a family sitting enjoying an early spring evening. They were not wealthy in a conventional way but were rich in their love for each other and the simple life they led. They sat around a table sharing a meal of pasta and salad with a plain unlabelled bottle of wine, probably produced from their own grapes. She thought it must have been a long time since this place had been inhabited as she returned to the present, unaware of slipping between time.

"Lucia?" Tom prompted. "Lucia?"

"Oh, I was just ….."she paused, suddenly unsure of what had just taken place. "I was just thinking ………, but never mind."

"What is it, *cara*?" Chiara asked.

"Well, I was just thinking what it was like ……. Oh, I don't know," she said in a weak attempt to dismiss any concern.

"Lucia," Tom took her hand and looked into her eyes. "Where did you go?"

"I didn't go anywhere. Well, I don't think so. I was just imagining what it must have been like ……" The clarity of the green eyes looking into hers left her feeling exposed, but to what she was unable to define, only that she wasn't yet ready to see it. Freeing her hand, she tried the wooden door which opened, squeaking on aged and rusted hinges. "Shall we?"

She crossed the threshold to what would have been the *cucina*, a kitchen and living room in one, where most of daily life would have taken place. At the back of the room stairs led to the upper floor and Lucia followed these to what she thought must have been a more formal living room, then along a narrow hall to the two bedrooms and a bathroom. There was no furniture, only layers of dust that added substance to the cobwebs that filled every corner and angle. She looked quickly in each room before returning downstairs to join the others.

"Did you find anything?" Chiara asked.

"No, just lots of dust and cobwebs!"

A door in the corner of the kitchen caught her attention and she opened it to find it led through to the *cantina*. There was not much there either, apart from a few dusty empty wine bottles and a couple of rotting baskets. Tom and Chiara followed her and found her looking at where the log store would have once been stacked with logs from the nearby woods. She could smell the resin. Two dogs lived here, she thought.

"Lucia," it was Tom and this time his voice came with a slight insistence. "What's happening?"

"Oh, I don't know. I was just thinking how it would have been, and it was like …"

"You were there and not there?"

"Yes, that's exactly it!" she turned to look at Tom, shaken by the reality of his words. "What does it mean?

What's happening?"

"Well, I think you have a gift and up until now you haven't noticed it. You may have just 'known' things intuitively and not paid attention to why. Now something is happening that you're not able to ignore and probably because you have a strong connection with this place."

"What do you mean? Yes, I used to play here as a child but I only came here a few times. I can hardly remember it. In fact, I probably would have forgotten all about it if it hadn't been for that wretched dream." Agitated by her own ignorance, Lucia looked around as if searching for an answer or an escape.

Tom thought she looked like a caged bird, unable to move even though the door was open. He knew to go any further with this he must tread carefully and not push her before she was ready.

"Lucia," he said gently, "I know it's a lot to take in. Maybe we should leave it for today. We can talk later if you wish."

Lucia could feel tears welling up in her eyes and not wanting to appear even more vulnerable than she already did, took a deep breath and said, "Yes, that'd be good. Shall we go?"

She took one last look round as if trying to commit something to memory then walked through to the *cucina,* out of the door and down the steps. The warmth of the air outside surprised and comforted her.

They returned to the path that would take them back the way they came. Again, Lucia led the way. Her thoughts overwhelmed her as she tried to make sense of the visit to the house when something further along the path caught her attention. Suddenly she stopped, putting up her hand to warn the others. Whispering, she said, "Look."

Tom and Chiara followed the direction of her eyes and saw what had caused her to stop. There were two deer, one quite young; standing completely still; they looked at the trio for a full minute before leaping off in the opposite direction.

"They're so beautiful!" It was Lucia who broke the silence.

They agreed and the three stood there smiling, looking in the direction where the white tails had bounced and disappeared.

As he watched the deer, Tom thought how their gentle vulnerability reminded him of Lucia, and the need for patience in helping her find her way. He knew from personal experience how easy it was to run inside and hide away from the very thing that demanded your attention.

"I am thinking it must be time for lunch," and Chiara was met with words and nods of agreement. "We could try the little place where they make their own *gelato*? Remember, *cara?*"

"Oh yes. Tom, do you have time?" Lucia said, happy to have a focus other than herself and her dilemma,

"No plans. I'd love to. If it's the one I'm thinking of their *gelato* is famous."

"We always went there when Lucia visited and *mamma* was still living here." added Chiara.

Lucia upped the pace, and they were quickly back in the car and en route to the restaurant.

They made their way back to the main road which

they followed for about twenty minutes before reaching the restaurant. Tom parked the car and they walked through the garden to the entrance and decided to sit outside under the loggia which gave some protection from the heat of the sun. The atmosphere was rustic, the tables were covered with red checked cloths, basketware hung on the walls and upright posts and a large tree grew through and above the pergola that extended beyond the loggia. They ordered antipasti, wine and water while they decided on the rest of the meal.

Lucia began to relax as the waiter brought their order and although she wasn't sure what had taken place at the house it now seemed distant and unreal, something she could put to one side.

Tom poured the wine and for the first time she looked at him and noticed that his good looks. In fact, he had a beauty that she couldn't quite put a finger on. She had been trying so hard to avoid what was happening to her that it seemed she had also managed to avoid seeing him. His face had a symmetry that was not easy to ignore now that it had been recognised. Other feelings began to surface, familiar yet unfamiliar at the same time. She felt awkward and embarrassed by this and took a sip of wine to hide any outward manifestation of what was happening within. As if I don't have enough going on, she thought and took a piece of bread praying for someone else to break the silence of the moment.

It was Chiara who obliged, "*Allora,* Tomasso, what is your news? Tell me, what are you doing now?"

"Not much since I last saw you. I'm still working on the designs for the garden at Bagno a Ripoli and," he paused, "I've made a start on the book."

"That's fantastic!" Chiara turned to Lucia. "As long as I've known Tomasso he's been promising to write a book." Returning her attention to Tom she said, "Can you tell us something about it or is it not yet ready for telling?"

Tom smiled, mainly at her use of his full name. "Well, I can tell you that my intention is to bring together what I have learned on my travels and how I now incorporate that in my designs. I want to show it is possible to have a beautiful, ecological and harmonious garden that doesn't cost the earth, in more ways than one."

The waiter returned and they ordered the next course. Tom and Chiara continued the conversation around Tom's philosophies and how his approach to garden design had changed and evolved.

"We can learn so much from nature," he said. "Everything has its season and therefore its own timing, much as it has in life."

Lucia thought how measured and relaxed his voice was. Then, as if her thought was echoed back to her, she felt cornered by it and wondered what on earth she was doing, telling herself that this was not the time and place. Or maybe it was something to do with his words about timing. So much had happened in the last few days to unsettle her usual equilibrium that she was no longer sure of anything.

"Lucia, I hear you saw the gardens at the Villa Martinelli." Tom's voice called her back to the present.

"Yes, and very impressive they are too. Although I don't imagine they have followed your ethos. I was told they have tried to retain or copy the original design from the time of the Medici, I believe there is a link between the two families. Apparently there are more flowers now to give colour, as I understand it, it would have been mainly greenery originally. Even so, it is very beautiful though a bit too formal for me."

Amazed that she had managed to form more than one sentence, Lucia continued with her meal and was content to let Tom and Chiara discuss the merits of shrubbery versus flowers.

All three resisted the temptation of a dessert and ordered coffee. However, Chiara ordered three flavours of *gelato* to take home and invited Tom to join them to eat it on their return.

It was Saturday morning and Antonio was keen to return to life outside of the Villa Martinelli. He wondered how he had allowed himself to become so embroiled in his family's dramas again. He had managed to distance himself by spending as much time as he could at the gallery and apartment in Florence. He berated himself for thinking it was just a simple matter of finding a journalist for the interview. Of course, he wasn't to know that his father would collapse and end up in hospital. It wasn't only that. The doctor had said he was stable and should be home in a day or two, no, it wasn't just that. There was his mother and, yet again, he had allowed her to manipulate him. He couldn't even say what it was she had done, she had such a subtle way of getting what she wanted by doing or saying very little.

And the journalist, Lucia, he liked her, but the interview could not take place until his father returned home. He had done what was required of him and could see no reason why he should stay at the villa a moment longer.

Luisa was already in the kitchen when he entered the room.

"Coffee?"

"*Grazie, si.*"

"I shall go to the hospital. Will you wait here for Lorenzo?"

"*Mamma,* no I can't. I have work to do?"

"But…"

"Look, you don't even know if or when Lorenzo will be back. I have to go. There are things I have to take care of at the gallery. Let me know if there's any news"

Before Luisa could persuade him otherwise, he had drunk his coffee and walked out of the room.

Luisa followed and called after him from the terrace as he walked towards his car, "Antonio."

"*Ciao, mamma.*" He got into the car, turned on the ignition and drove off before any irrational guilt could change his mind.

Luisa, frustrated by her son's departure, returned to the kitchen and decided there was no point in calling Lorenzo as he was unlikely to answer, especially so early in the day. Damn these boys, why couldn't I have had girls!

She arrived at the hospital shortly before midday to find her husband sleeping. Deciding not to disturb him, she wandered outside where there was a small garden. Set back to one side was a chapel and she opened the door and went inside. Luisa was not used to spending time in contemplation and surprised herself by sitting down and looking towards the altar. It was a simple chapel by Italian standards and her eyes were drawn to the sculpted figurine of the Madonna that dominated the altar. She looked at the woman depicted in a pale blue robe, her eyes focused on the child in her arms and felt something stir within her. She was about to dismiss the feeling when she felt tears rise from her heart and drop one by one gently from her eyes.

"*Mamma*, there you are. The nurse said she had seen you. I've been everywhere, what are you doing here?" Lorenzo breezed in in his usual cavalier manner and walked towards her as Luisa quickly composed herself.

"Ah, Lorenzo. What a nice surprise, *amore*. Your father was asleep and I didn't want to disturb him so…..."

"Well, I don't have long. Is Antonio with you?" Lorenzo interrupted before she could finish.

"No, he had business to take care of. *Andiamo*."

As they left the chapel Luisa gave one last glance towards the Madonna and felt a sense of something disturbed and unfinished.

Turning to Lorenzo she asked, "Was your father awake?"

"No, but the doctor had just arrived so I think he will be by now."

"*Bene*, Let's go and see how he is." Luisa said, curious as to what had brought her son to the hospital of his own volition. He must want something was the first thought that crossed her mind but decided it wisdom not to ask.

As they approached Giacomo's room they met Dr Giannini who was just leaving.

"Ah, *Signora* Martinelli, *Signor, buongiorno.*" Then speaking directly to Luisa he said, "I am pleased you are here *signora*. I have been talking to your husband and I think, subject to all being well tomorrow, he will be able to go home.

"That is good news. Thank you, Dr Giannini. What time should I collect him?"

"If you call about 11 o'clock I will be able to confirm whether he is well enough."

They shook hands and Dr Giannini continued on his rounds.

"*Mamma*, I think I'll go. You go and see *babbo*. I'll see him tomorrow."

"But, Lorenzo …." And before she could finish her sentence, he was halfway down the corridor heading towards the exit. She sighed in exasperation then took a deep breath to calm herself before entering her husband's room.

His mind whirled as he strode to his car. The message had been clear. Time was of the essence. He was to deliver the order within 48 hours or they would begin to look at alternatives. Impossible, he thought, as he succumbed to fear's tight clutch. It had all seemed so simple at first but he now realised that he was way out of his depth and unable to extricate himself from this nightmare. He must find a way to play for time.

Chiara went straight to the kitchen and produced three bowls which she placed on the table with the ice cream containers.

"*Ecco*! It's hardly melted. Come, sit down, I'll get some spoons."

Lucia and Tom obeyed like children in anticipation of the treat awaiting them.

"*Allora*, there's almond, vanilla and chocolate. Enjoy."

One by one they took a spoon of each flavour followed by silence punctuated only by varying sounds of pleasure.

Lucia was the first to speak between deeply satisfied breaths. "Oh, I'd forgotten how good this is."

Tom was still lost and had not yet progressed beyond an agreeing mmmm.

Chiara watched smiling. "I think I'll take some along to *mamma*. You don't have to go yet do you, Tom? I won't be long."

"Er, sure. Yes, I can stay 'til you get back."

"Great," and Chiara put the remaining ice cream into one container, "see you soon."

"How long do you think you'll stay?" Tom enquired.

"Oh, I'm not sure. I was due back in London on Wednesday but it really depends on Signor Martinelli's recovery. I'm still hoping to be able to interview him." Lucia felt unexpectedly nervous under the clear gaze of those green eyes.

"Well, if you're free tomorrow, I am thinking of going into the hills near Panzano. There's a little church not far from the town, where they have concerts and talks. We could have lunch first?"

The invitation took Lucia by surprise and her mind raced in search of words before she could respond. All she found was, "I, yes, I'd like to," then added, "though I'd better check with Chiara that she doesn't have plans."

"*Bene.* Chiara is also welcome, if she's free." He smiled, aware of Lucia's brittle fragility. "Maybe you have been there before?"

"No, I don't think so. I've been to Panzano, but a long time ago and the only church I remember is the one on the hill."

"Ah, that would be Pieve di San Leolino. No, this is a small chapel not much bigger than this kitchen, well maybe twice this size. It's quite remote; there are just two or three brothers who live there. I think it's a very special place and I hope you will like it."

"Chiara says you have travelled a lot. What brought you to Florence?" feeling awkward, Lucia tried to deflect the conversation in another direction.

"Oh, I grew up here. Italian father and English mother – a holiday romance they say. And you? Chiara said you live in London."

"Yes, live and work there. I get to travel with my work but I don't get to Florence as often as I'd like."

"And your mother is Italian and your father English?"

"Yes, they met when my father was visiting on business."

"How do you find that?"

"What?"

"Having parents from different cultures. Do you think you are more Italian or English?"

"English, I suppose, since I've lived there all my life; though when I'm here I feel more Italian. What about you?" she asked wondering how the focus of the conversation had returned to her.

"Much the same but the other way round. I think I know what you mean though, when I'm in England there is something that's familiar and I feel part of it." Tom paused then continued. "When I was travelling it seemed to depend on the language, in that English was used more than Italian, but I think generally I feel Italian."

Lucia knew the conversation was a distraction from the 'white elephant' that was sitting clearly on the table in front of her. She breathed deeply to keep her voice even and with her eyes down said, "What do you think happened today?"

"As I said earlier it could be that you have certain sensitivities and abilities you have not been aware of until now and something has happened to trigger them. The dream, the voice, the painting and the visit to the house all seem to be connected."

"What do you mean; in what way?"

"Well….."

"I'm sorry, I didn't mean to sound so…"

"You didn't. I can only imagine how it must be for you having these things happening and not being able to understand what's going on. Some years ago I had some strange experiences myself and I felt as if I was losing my mind until I found someone who could explain it and put it in a context for me. So sure, *piano, piano*, slowly, slowly, one step at a time." He smiled and placed his hand over hers. "There's no rush, you know, whenever you're ready."

Disarmed by the physical contact and his patience, Lucia felt a flush rise within her. She coughed and gently removed her hand. "Thanks Tom." Getting up from the table she took the bowls and stacked them in the dishwasher then, turning to face him, she continued, "it's not that I don't want to talk about it, I don't know how to."

Tom got up from the table, smiled and moved towards her holding out his hand. "Let's go and sit outside and we can talk about it, or not."

Lucia gave a nervous smile and accepted his invitation. They found a seat just below the loggia where the sun's rays still gave some warmth.

Lucia thought how relaxed and at ease Tom looked and this made her more aware of her own anxiety. "Can you tell me what happened to you?"

"Sure." Tom paused as if gathering his memories then said, "but not right now. Chiara should be back soon."

Lucia began to feel the chill of the evening creeping in and as if reading her mind and thinking it may not have been a good idea to sit outside, Tom suggested they return inside.

"Can I get you coffee, a glass of wine?" she offered.

"Thanks, a small glass of wine would be good."

Lucia half-filled two wine glasses then joined Tom on the sofa. He smiled and his eyes softened as he said, "It's not that I don't want to talk about it, I'd just like to know we have time so it's not rushed. I hope you understand."

"Of course," Lucia replied, uncertain about her feelings of exposure and vulnerability.

They heard footsteps on the gravel outside as Chiara returned from visiting Isabella.

"We can talk more tomorrow if you like." Tom offered.

Before Lucia could respond, Chiara swept into the

room with an armful of dried herbs. "*Mamma* is wonderful is she not, look at all this she has dried for me."

"How is she?" asked Lucia.

"Oh, much the same – determined and frustrated by her own weakness."

"And you two, have you put the world to rights?"

"I wouldn't go that far," said Tom. "I was saying that I'm going to Panzano tomorrow, there's a talk in the little church near there and I thought we could have lunch on the way. Will you join us?"

"Oh, I'd love to but I have an appointment in the afternoon. It's good though as I now don't have to worry about leaving you here, *cara. Grazie,* Tomasso."

Feeling a little awkward Lucia offered her aunt a glass of wine which she accepted before collapsing in one of the more comfortable chairs.

Tom stood up ready to leave. "It is time I went. Thank you both for a lovely day. Lucia, will eleven o'clock be ok tomorrow?"

"Yes, of course."

"I'm sorry I won't be able to come," said Chiara, "and thank you so much for coming over, Tom."

"*Niente.* I enjoyed it. See you tomorrow, Lucia."

Chiara walked with him to the car and Lucia felt as if she was a child again being discussed by the adults out of her hearing. Of course, she didn't know whether they were discussing her or not but something told her they were and she would have been right.

"She's very fragile. I'll see how tomorrow goes but I don't want to rush her. I'll need to gain her trust and, well, let's take one step at a time."

"I really appreciate your help, Tom. Maybe see you later tomorrow when you get back."

Si, certo, a domani." Tom got into his car and drove off.

While she waited for Chiara to return, Lucia went over the day in her mind. She liked Tom even if she found him a little disconcerting. She knew that he and Chiara were giving her the space to talk about it when she was ready and this in itself caused her to feel uncomfortable. She wondered whether she should talk to Chiara tonight about what had happened at the house. It wasn't that she didn't want to, she did and she trusted Chiara more than anyone. It was strange, the words would form in her head but there they stayed unable to find expression. Her train of thought was interrupted as Chiara returned.

SUNDAY
Domenica

Lucia woke in the early hours of Sunday morning, damp sheets clinging to her trembling body. "Help me, help me," the voice pleaded, fading into the distance as she woke from a disturbed sleep and her memory dragged fragmented images into her consciousness. It was the same dream but this time there was more, not only the voice but faces, people, places, none of which she recognised. If only she could remember.

Gradually she became aware of the room and the hold of the dream loosened. Her attempts to recapture the memories now locked in the dream proved futile, and exasperated, she sat up and looked at the small clock on the table next to the bed. It was only five thirty. Too early to get up, she thought. She looked around the room and the early morning air cooled her body.

Whispered images fleetingly touched her thoughts but did not stay long enough for her to grasp. Why? She felt like screaming and fell back on to the pillows staring at the ceiling as if willing it to reveal an answer. Eventually exhaustion took over until, three hours later, rays of sunlight streaming through half opened shutters called her back to wakefulness.

Lucia made a decision. She grabbed her robe and went downstairs to the kitchen where she found Chiara sitting at the table, pen in hand, writing on an A4 pad.

"Ah, *buongiorno cara*. I have to make a list these days or I forget things. The coffee's freshly made, help yourself."

Lucia took a mug and poured the coffee, adding milk in her usual way. She then sat at the table opposite her aunt.

"Chiara ..." she began.

"*Si cara,*" she looked up and saw that her niece's face had a serious yet apprehensive expression. "What is it?"

"I...... can we talk?" she hesitated before continuing. "I don't know what to do. I had the dream again, only this time there was more. I don't remember what exactly, but there were other people and.......and a voice calling 'help me'. It feels really scary and I have no idea why. I just don't know what to do, Chiara. I can't carry on like this. Why is this happening to me?" and she buried her head in her hands.

Chiara reached across the table and gently took Lucia's hands in hers. Lucia raised her head and looking into her eyes, Chiara spoke quietly yet firmly, "*Cara*, we will find out what this is all about, I promise."

Grateful for her aunt's warmth and certainty, Lucia managed to whisper, "I hope so."

"*Allora*, let me get you some breakfast. Juice? Croissant? More coffee?"

"Oh, Chiara, I'm sorry. I feel so foolish. It just all seems so real and now ...."

"*Calma, calma.*" She interrupted and walked over to Lucia, put her arm round her shoulder and sat in the chair next to her. "*Cara*, you're not foolish. It must be so disturbing for you and we will find out what is going on. I think we take one step at a time and right now, look at me, take a deep breath," she paused as Lucia breathed, "and again. *Allora*, now, you must eat."

Lucia placed her hand over that of her aunt and, feeling a small sense of security creep in, she smiled and thanked her, "*Grazie, grazie.*"

"More coffee?" Chiara picked up the coffee pot.

"Er, no thanks. I think I'd better shower and get ready"

"Oh, of course. What time is Tom picking you up?"

"Eleven." Lucia slumped back into the chair and looked at Chiara before asking, "Do you think I'm doing the right thing? I mean going out for the day."

"Why, what else would you be doing?"

"Oh, I don't know," she said waving her arm in frustration, "I suppose I just want to get to the bottom of this so I can get on with my life."

"And if you don't go out, what will you do?" Chiara smiled. "Why not go and see what happens."

"Ok, but if you're trying some matchmaking here, Chiara, I couldn't bear that. Promise me you're not."

"Ah, *cara*, I just thought Tom might be able to help you. He has much wisdom and experience and if he can't he'll probably know someone who can. That is all

– promise!" Chiara threw up her hands in surrender. At the same time she smiled to herself thinking it would be no bad thing if they did get together.

Tom arrived at the villa at eleven. He wondered how Lucia would be this morning. She had clearly been disturbed by their outing the previous day and she had occupied a large part of his thoughts since then. He knew from experience the fear and frustration of not understanding the unusual phenomena that can happen and he hoped she had managed to have a restful night.

He parked the car and walked up the steps to the door leading into the *cucina*. He could see Chiara sitting at the table and he tapped on the door. She jumped up to greet him and they exchanged welcome kisses and '*buongiornos*'.

Before Chiara could explain what had taken place, Lucia entered the room and greeted Tom with an exchange of kisses and a "*buongiorno.*" She had black cotton cropped trousers, a simple muted green top and a short cardigan in a deeper, complimentary shade. Her hair was washed and shining and Chiara thought how beautiful she looked. In that moment she felt an unexpected pang of longing for the presence of her own children. Although she was used to them being away from home, every now and then she was acutely aware of their absence.

She also noticed the appreciation in Tom's eyes and wondered where the day would take them. However, she did not wish to get involved with their day and made her excuses saying she had work to do. "Have a wonderful time, *a dopo*." She would see them later.

"Shall we?" Tom swept his arm in the direction of the door and Lucia smiled saying, "Yes, let's." They went down the steps to where Tom had parked the car. "How are you today?"

Lucia paused on a step before answering. "Well, I could say *bene* but that wouldn't be true. I had a difficult night but let's not allow it to spoil the day."

Tom wondered how long she had rehearsed this response and rather than pursue it he offered his arm, smiled and said, *"va bene, andiamo!"*

Lucia accepted his arm and as they reached his car he opened the car door for her before walking round to get in the driver's seat. There was an awkward silence as they secured their seat belts. Tom turned towards Lucia and offered, "You know, we don't have to do as we planned. We can do whatever you like. Nothing is written in stone."

"Thanks, but to be honest, I don't know what I want to do," and added quietly, "I just don't want my problem to get in the way."

"It won't and it isn't. I'm here because Chiara thought I could help and I'm here today because I'd like to spend some time with you."

Lucia felt at odds with herself. Part of her wanted to surrender to her plight and tell him everything and another part was irritated by his reasonableness and she wanted to run away. In the few seconds it took for her to contemplate the possibilities she was shaken from her thoughts by another voice saying, "It's almost time, don't give up."

Tom patiently waited for Lucia to say something then he noticed a sudden change in her expression. He was also aware of something else, another presence.

Trembling, she looked at him with a questioning fear in her eyes. "Lucia …" he began.

"I can't do this! Tom, what is happening to me?"

"Take a deep breath," and he took one himself to encourage her, "and again. Good. Now, can you tell me what just happened?"

"I …. I was just thinking what to say and, and then I heard that voice." She spat the word out as if she was trying to get rid of it.

"Ok, what did you hear?"

"Something about it almost being time and not giving up."

"Can you remember the exact words."

She looked at him with hollow eyes, "Does it matter," she began, then realising she must sound rude continued. "Yes, of course, sorry. It was, 'it's almost time, don't give up'. I'm sorry, Tom, I feel as if I'm being torn in two. I don't understand….."

"*Calma*. Have you any idea what it means?"

"None at all."

"Ok. Let's drive into town and have a coffee. I may have an idea, if that's alright with you?"

Yes, sure, anything," she sighed and collapsed into the seat.

Shortly after eleven Luisa called the hospital and asked to speak to Dr Giannini. She was told he was not available but had left a message for her to say he had seen her husband and had told him he was free to go home subject to certain conditions. She put down the phone and wondered what these conditions could be, doubtful that her husband would take any notice of them.

She went to the kitchen to find Maria and let her know what was happening so she could organise the household accordingly. She then picked up her bag and went down the steps from the terrace to her car.

Although she was happy that Giacomo was well enough to come home there was an underlying feeling of frustration, the cause of which she couldn't quite reach.

She soon arrived at the hospital, parked the car and made her way to her husband's room.

"Ah, *cara*," Giacomo was already dressed and he looked up from putting the last of his belongings into a bag. "Good, you're here."

"Yes. What did Dr Giannini say?" It seemed that any other pleasantries were being dismissed. He must be feeling better, she thought.

"Ah, not much. You know, the usual things – take it easy for a few days etc. He wrote it down. Here," and he handed Luisa a typed list of what he should and shouldn't do.

"Hmmm," Luisa gave it a brief glance. "I'll look at it when we get home. Are you ready to go?"

"Si, andiamo." Let's go.

Luisa grabbed his bag before Giacomo could begin to pick it up. "I think maybe I should take that." She noticed he was a little unsteady on his feet and extended her arm for him to lean on which he did not accept. *"Eh,* I can manage, *ma grazie, cara."*

They walked slowly along the corridor and took the lift to the ground floor. As they left the hospital building Giacomo realised that he had been inside for almost four days and began to wonder what he had missed.

"Have you heard from Lorenzo?" he demanded.

"*Si*, I saw him yesterday. He was here but didn't stay. I think the doctor was with you so he left, you know how he is." She shrugged and pointed the remote at the car. Giacomo seemed to gain strength with each step and he opened the door and got into the passenger seat. Luisa put his bag on the back seat and wondered how she was going to restrain him from carrying on in his normal energetic way.

It didn't take long to reach the villa and as Giacomo got out of the car and surveyed the view over Florence, Luisa thought he seemed to grow in stature. She had not liked to see him so diminished as he was in the hospital and felt a wave of relief as she watched the man in front of her now. As exasperating as he could be, in that moment she knew she loved him and cared deeply for him. She then brushed the thought aside as quickly as it had arrived, picked up his bag and entered the villa.

Giacomo followed her, picked up the morning paper and settled himself in one of the more comfortable chairs on the terrace and began to catch up on the news he had missed.

Luisa called both Lorenzo and Antonio and, to her frustration, was only able to leave voicemail messages. *Always, they are never there when I want them.* She joined Giacomo on the terrace, "I'll ask Maria to prepare some lunch. About half an hour?"

"*Si, cara*, it will be good to have proper food," he replied without looking up from his newspaper.

Luisa went to her handbag where she had put the list from Dr Giannini. Whilst she knew her husband would take no notice of these instructions, she could at least do her best to avoid any serious breaches of them. In brief it seemed to advise moderation in all things and Luisa wondered how she could help him curb his ebullient, and stubborn, spirit. Rolling her eyes upwards in a partial surrender, she went to the kitchen to give Maria instructions for lunch.

As she returned to the living room she heard her mobile ringtone increasing in volume and saw Antonio's name in the screen as it stopped and went to voicemail. She called him straight back.

"*Ciao mamma*, what do you want?"

"*Allora*, don't be like that."

"I don't know what you mean, *mamma*."

"*Non importa*, Antonio. *Babbo* is home and I thought you could have lunch with us. That's all."

Antonio paused while he weighed the possible outcomes of a positive or negative response. Deciding it was probably easier to acquiesce than not, he said, "*Certo mamma*, I'm on my way." Then to protect the rest of his day he added, "But I will not be able to stay long."

"*Va bene, vederti presto.*" See you very soon.

By the time Maria served lunch, Giacomo had caught up with the latest news according to *La Republica* and was already in an animated discussion with Antonio when Luisa joined them at the table.

"Please," Luisa implored, "do not encourage him, Antonio. He is supposed to be resting, not conducting business."

"Ah, *mamma*," he said, shrugging his shoulders and gestured with upturned palms, "what can I do? You know how he is."

"Mmm... just don't encourage him, please."

"And I am not a child!" Giacomo added. "*Allora*, come, let us eat." He turned to Luisa, "*Cara*, I was just asking Antonio if the journalist was still here, for the interview."

"Giacomo," Luisa took a deep breath, obviously containing her frustration, "we can leave this for another day or two, *no*?"

"*Si, si, si* ...... I'm just asking." Then to Antonio, "Maybe you could find out when she plans to leave for London. See if you can arrange the interview while she is still here?"

"I'll ..."

"*Basta*! Enough!" Exasperated, Luisa cut in before Antonio could say more. "Can we have lunch, please, and no more talk of interviews, business, *va bene*?"

"*Va bene, mamma*."

"*Si, certo*," Giacomo sighed in surrender, "*buon appetito*," and he raised his glass in a toast. Luisa and Antonio followed his lead and joined him.

Lunch passed without further mention of business affairs and whilst Luisa kept a watchful eye on what Giacomo ate and drank, she refrained from making more chiding comments.

As they approached the residential outskirts of Florence, Tom pulled the car over and stopped on the side of the road.

"I've been thinking - I have a friend who may be able to help you. If you like, I can call her and if she's free, you can meet her."

Lucia hesitated for a moment while she sidestepped

her usual defensive, well-practised response. She knew she needed all the help she could get and Tom seemed to be someone she could trust so she smiled and said, "Yes. Thank you."

Tom made the call, speaking very quickly in Italian and then mid call he turned to Lucia and said, "She can meet us in about half an hour, is that ok with you?"

"Er, yes, of course," Lucia replied somewhat bewildered by the speed at which it was happening.

"*Si, si, va bene, a presto.*" Tom ended the call. "I think you will like her. There's a little bar and *osteria* just off Via del Corso, she'll meet us there. *Allora,* let's find somewhere to park. It shouldn't be too difficult on a Sunday."

Lucia sank down into her seat as Tom made his way to the centre of the city. Her mind raced as memories of the last few days crowded in and she shuddered with mixed feelings of dread and relief as Tom searched for a place to park the car.

They were driving alongside the River Arno when a car pulled out leaving a space for Tom to manoeuvre the car and park. "It's not too far from here and we have plenty of time. You ok?"

"Erm, sort of. A bit apprehensive I suppose."

"Don't worry. Simonetta is a gentle soul and I'm sure you'll like her. Remember, *piano, piano* – one step at a time," and he gave her an encouraging smile. Lucia saw a soft sparkle in his green eyes that seemed to lift her into a lighter place and she returned the smile with one of her own. "Good," he said, "*andiamo.*" Let's go.

It didn't take long to find the bar. They took a table in the window and ordered two *cappuccini*. Soon a small woman, who could be any age between mid-fifties and seventy, walked through the door and Tom was on his feet to greet her with the customary hugs and kisses. She wore charcoal grey trousers and a lightweight coral coloured sweater; her steel grey hair cut in a sharp bob gave her an aura of effortless chic.

Lucia and she exchanged more hugs and kisses before she sat at the table, turning to the bar and ordering an *espresso*. "Ah, I am so pleased to meet you Lucia. Tom has told me about you. You are having an interesting …er … visit, I believe."

Simonetta had a warmth that Lucia immediately responded to and feeling her defences melt, she smiled, "Yes, I'm very pleased to meet you, Simonetta, though Tom has told me very little about you, I look forward to getting to know you."

"Great," Tom said. "I just knew you would be friends."

"*Va bene*. Lucia can you tell me about this dream and what has happened since you came to Florence then we will see what is to be done." Simonetta's voice was gentle yet commanding in its clarity.

Half an hour later Lucia had concisely recounted the last two weeks and was back in the present.

"The voice is always the same voice?" asked Simonetta.

"Yes, I think so. It is always so ..er .. neutral."

"*Bene*. It may be you have a connection to this place and it relates to something and someone in the past. You say nothing has happened like this before, maybe when you were a child?"

"No, not that I can remember."

"Mmmm …. and your interview with Signor Martinelli – will this still happen?"

"I don't know. Antonio said he would let me know early this week in case I need to extend my visit."

"I think you should extend your visit in any case, if that is possible. There are things you need to do though I am not yet clear what they are. Can you do that?"

Surprising herself, Lucia responded positively to Simonetta's directness, "I can call my editor tomorrow morning. I'm sure I can arrange to take the rest of the week if necessary."

"*Bene*. In that case, I suggest you come to see me tomorrow morning and we will find out what is going on. *Va bene?*"

"Yes, of course."

"And if anything else happens before then will you please call me and let me know." She handed Lucia a business card which merely had her name, Simonetta Morelli and a mobile number. "Tom will explain where I am. *A domani*." They all exchanged hugs and kisses and Simonetta was gone.

Lucia felt a door had been opened in her mind, leaving her with an unexplainable sense of peace. She looked at Tom as she would a compass seeking help in navigating this new and unknown territory.

Simonetta's effect on people was not new to Tom and he remembered their first meeting when, for him, it was like someone excavating his very soul. There was no place to hide and although this initially filled him with fear he soon experienced a profound relaxation along with a sense of being heard at a very deep level. He believed she had a special gift that somehow circumnavigated time and space as it is generally understood and this allowed her access to what he had come to term as other dimensions. The cultures and teachings he had explored over the years had taught him that we are so much more than our physical bodies and are capable of more than we believe possible. He momentarily recalled how his mind had been stretched and pulled in unmentionable directions as he learned to see life in previously unimaginable ways.

Suddenly aware that Lucia was looking at him attentively, he smiled, "You ok? Simonetta can have quite an effect on people. All good, of course."

Lucia continued to look at him wondering if she would ever be able to speak again when she was caught by Tom's hand on hers. "Yes, thank you, though I'm not sure what happened. I feel different. Calmer somehow. Oh, and hungry."

"Ah yes, lunch. It's a bit late for Panzano but we can stay here or, if you prefer somewhere else….?"

"This is fine, Tom, thanks," relieved not to have to move.

Tom called over the waiter and said they would like to stay for lunch and would that be possible. The waiter said he would enquire and returned with a positive reply. He indicated there was an inner courtyard with tables outside and asked if they would like to move. Tom looked at Lucia who was clearly still trying to find her way and said they would prefer to stay where they were.

The waiter asked if they would like to sit at the bar while he prepared the table for them. He then laid a linen cloth and napkins and set two places ready for their meal. Tom thanked him and turning to Lucia asked, "How about a glass of Prosecco to celebrate ... to celebrate the day?"

Coming back to life, Lucia thought the world had taken on an extra vibrancy and she nodded in agreement, managing to find her feet and follow Tom to the bar. "Yes, a celebration."

Tom ordered two glasses of Prosecco and within minutes they were seated again at their table where they perused the menus. The usually extensive menu was limited to a special Sunday lunch menu and it soon became clear they had been lucky to get a table here as the restaurant began to fill with couples, families and friends. The hub of conversation grew louder and the waiters had to work quickly to keep everyone happy.

Their waiter returned with the two glasses of wine, freshly baked bread and olives. Tom and Lucia gave their orders, both choosing the shorter meal of five courses. Lucia took a sip of wine and beginning to feel more relaxed asked, "How do you know Simonetta, how did you meet?"

"It was a few years ago, just after I'd returned from my travels. It was in the bookshop in *Via de' Cerretani* and I was looking for something to read, a novel. Simonetta stood next to me. I could feel her presence and when I turned to see who it was, she smiled and said, "Can we have coffee? I have something to tell you." As you can imagine I was surprised and yet at the same time intrigued and felt I couldn't refuse. Without going into too much detail, she explained that when she saw me she had 'received a message' for me, that she is very psychic and when she came to stand next to me she felt I would understand. She gave me the message and we talked for a while and I agreed to meet her again the following week. She was interested in my travels and experiences and I was fascinated by the breadth of her wisdom and knowledge of esoteric matters. It was she who introduced me to the little church I told you about in Panzano and other special places. We met regularly for a while and then, well, you know how it is, lives change."

Tom was interrupted by the waiter bringing their first course. A platter of *antipasti*, a colourful canvas of cured meats, vegetables and *crostini* to which Lucia enthusiastically helped herself. Confirming that they had everything they needed, the waiter continued his busy opera of attending to his other customers.

Lucia, her head to one side, looked questioningly at Tom, "and….?"

"Oh, yes, well it's a long story and maybe better for its telling to wait for a quieter setting, if that's ok with you?"

"Sure, I'll look forward to hearing more," Lucia smiled, aware of an easy warmth between them and wondered if she was actually flirting with him without meaning to, then immediately dismissed the thought in self-embarrassment. She concentrated on her food appreciating the authenticity and difference to what she usually found on offer in London. "Mmm, this is good."

"Do you ever think that you might like to live in Italy?"

"Er, not really, my life has always been in London though I suppose I could work from here. No, I've never given it much thought. Why?"

"I just wondered, being half Italian, if you've ever wanted to explore and experience those roots more deeply."

"And you? You mentioned "your travels", where did you go, did you ever think of living in England?"

"No, probably like you and Italy, England was somewhere for holidays and to visit family and my travels took me to the other side of the world, to Australia and the Far East. As for living elsewhere, no, I can't imagine living anywhere else, after all I'm more than half Tuscan," Tom said with a huge smile that brought a sparkle to those deep green eyes. Again, Lucia felt relaxed in his presence yet at the same time was wary of something that touched an inner conflict within her still fragile being.

"A penny ......?" Tom began.

"What?"

"For your thoughts. Where were you?"

"Oh, I don't know," the words accompanied by something halfway between a gentle laugh and a giggle. "Probably half in London and half here ...... much as I am most of the time in a way."

Tom marvelled at what he perceived, then checked himself remembering he was there to gain her trust not seduce and challenge that trust.

"So it's true what they say then," Lucia continued, "once a Tuscan always a Tuscan and there's nowhere else you would want to live?"

"So they say, and personally, I'm not able to refute that."

"Hm, I don't think I could say that about London or even England."

The waiter arrived to clear the plates and no sooner had he done so he was back with the next course of pasta. Lucia had ordered her favourite, *spaghetti alla vongole* and Tom was presented with a shallow bowl of handmade ravioli filled with spinach and ricotta in a sage and butter sauce. Another waiter brought a small carafe of red wine.

"Oh this looks so good."

"*Buon apetito*," Tom raised his glass and Lucia mirrored his toast.

They continued their meal and by the time they came to the coffee they had covered the pros and cons of living in Italy and England and their feelings of belonging to both and to neither.

"That was a wonderful meal, Tom, though I'm not sure I can move. Could we go for a walk before we go back to the car?"

"*Si, certo.* A good idea," and he indicated to the waiter to bring the bill.

Outside the temperature had risen a few degrees and the streets were quiet, most people either still having lunch or their siesta. Lucia liked the quiet and they walked past the *duomo*, window shopping on the way.

When they came to the Piazza della Santissima Annunciata Lucia stopped and took a deep breath as she took in the beauty of the architecture. "I just love it here. There's a simplicity and harmony that …," and as her voice trailed off Tom added, "takes away your breath?"

"Yes, exactly! It's so beautiful. I remember coming here as a child with my grandmother. I would always want *gelato* and she would always say if I could count the bees on the plaque behind the bronze statue of Ferdinand 1 de Medici, I could have one. Of course, it was impossible, no matter how hard I tried. They're in concentric rings and I didn't have the required focus. One day though, when I was a bit older I did some research and found out how many bees there are. *Nonna* could not believe it when I gave her the right answer."

"And how many are there?" Tom asked teasingly.

"You mean you don't know?" Lucia laughed. "Surely you were also subjected to …"

"I think I might have been but I don't really remember."

"Well, you must count them!"

"And if I get it right?"

"Er, you can have *gelato*!"

"Oh no, please! No more food."

"Ok, I'll think of something else," she laughed and walked round to the back of the statue, "come."

Tom followed and looked at the bees then started to count. As Lucia had said, the concentric circles made it very difficult and his concentration seemed to be focused more on his digestion rather than his brain. With a mischievous smile he said, "Ninety one."

"You knew."

"Well, yes – but please don't make me eat *gelato*!"

Lucia gave his arm a friendly punch, "Ok, *andiamo*."

Tom smiled, pleased that Lucia seemed more relaxed and happier than when he had met her a few hours ago. A feather of doubt crossed his mind as to whether or not he had done the right thing introducing her to Simonetta but it was immediately brushed aside by a knowing that he recognised. He had. Still aware of her fragility he took bigger strides to catch up with her, at the same time delighting in her newfound lightness.

Lucia was having fun and felt a freedom that had eluded her for so long. Aware that Tom had caught up with her she turned to face that disarming smile. "Shall we go before the city wakes up again," she said referring to the Italian ritual of *la passeggiata* when families took to the streets in their finery as the ultimate homage to *la bella figura*. Image being everything. "Which way is it to the car?"

"Sure, probably a good idea. We need to head back towards the Piazza della Signoria and the Uffizi." He was about to comment on her newfound lightness but decided not to as it would only highlight what had been troubling her before.

They walked along the Via dei Servi towards the Duomo, then along narrow streets and alleys as Lucia revelled in the sense of having the city to themselves. In that moment she loved Florence with an emergent sense of belonging. She thought of her mother and her dislike, or was it disdain, for most things Italian and that it must be sourced in something that had caused her a great deal of pain. An unfamiliar wave of compassion flowed through her taking her by surprise and in the nanosecond that followed she saw the last few years of her life unfold before her. How she had tried to obliterate her own pain behind the façade of a successful career but only succeeded in disconnecting from herself. "Oh!" she said, unintentionally out loud.

"Lucia?"

"Oh, it's nothing. I ….er….just realised something and …."

"It took you by surprise?"

"Well, yes. How did you know?"

"I've known Simonetta a long time and she can have that effect on people."

"Why, what do you mean?" Lucia was beginning to feel a little uncomfortable and sensed her usual defences surfacing.

"It's nothing to worry about." Tom searched for the best way to explain this extraordinary woman's gifts. They had reached the Piazza della Signoria already busy with tourists taking photos of Neptune and David. "Come, the car is not far now and I will try to explain." Lucia said nothing but the look she gave Tom clearly said she hoped so.

They passed the Uffizi where long queues waited patiently to see the art treasures of Florence and artists lined the pavement displaying and hoping to sell their work. Ahead the River Arno flowed below the wall in front of them and they turned left towards the car leaving the familiar view of the Ponte Vecchio behind them.

Once in the car, Lucia looked at Tom demanding the promised explanation. *"Va bene,"* he said. "Simonetta comes from an old Florentine family, from generations of healers passed on through the female line. It has not been easy for her as this 'gift' sometimes skips generations and it passed by her mother who it seems hoped it would also not be present in Simonetta. Her mother ignored any sign that Simonetta gave of possessing healing abilities. She also hid them from the rest of the family and Simonetta became fearful of not just who she was but also of asking anyone for help. Fortunately, her *nonna*, a healer herself, noticed what was happening and took her under her wing as it were. Imagine, this was still a time when such people were either highly respected or deeply feared." Lucia felt a chill wash over her. Tom, aware of the change in her energy, continued. "You only have to look to the time of the Inquisition for evidence of persecution which, of course, continued long afterwards. Ignorance and superstition carries much pain in its wake."

Lucia felt another chill and a far distant memory nudged and then was gone. Again, Tom noticed the change in her and, again he continued.

"Anyway, it turned out that Simonetta had remarkable healing and psychic abilities and her *nonna* encouraged her to study with some of the great teachers of the time. You can imagine her mother was not happy and through love for her mother, Simonetta worked hard at her more conventional studies and eventually managed to live an academic life that embraced both worlds. She is well known and respected for the books she has written on the history of Florence, particularly at the time of the Inquisition."

"She has children?" Lucia said without thinking and as soon as the words were out, wondered why she had said them.

"Yes, two boys and one granddaughter, though she is only a baby so as yet has not shown signs of whether or not she carries the "gift. If that's what you meant?"

"Em..., I suppose so."

"Now, what was going on with you just now?" Tom asked in a gentle tone.

Lucia looked thoughtful, "I ..., er ..., it was when you were talking about how people like that used to be treated and when you mentioned the Inquisition ... I thought ... I don't know. It was as if I knew something and at the same time didn't know." She looked at Tom hoping for words of wisdom or at least a kind of explanation.

Tom thought how vulnerable she looked, and beautiful. He paused remembering how fragile her trust was, and said, "*Va bene*, it's hot in here, let's start moving. We can talk as we go."

He turned on the air conditioning enough to cool the now airless car without turning it into a fridge and they crossed over the Ponte alle Grazie and headed out of the city.

"Tom," Lucia said hesitantly, "do you think I'm going mad?"

"No, of course not," he replied and pulled the car over to the side of the road. Turning towards her, he continued quietly and evenly, "I think you have a connection to something that happened here in the past and for some reason it is, *come si dice,* how do you say, 'calling' you. I'm hoping, no, I'm sure, Simonetta will be able to tell you more and help you when you see her tomorrow."

Lucia could feel tears welling in her eyes and prayed they would not spill over. Why is it when people are nice and understanding it's so upsetting, she wondered. Looking straight ahead she managed a mumbled, "I hope so."

They continued the drive in silence, Lucia trying to contain a tumult of emotions and Tom, not wanting to push her over her own emotional barrier, breathed deeply and did his best to create a sense of calm in the restricted space of the car.

As they neared Chiara's home Lucia said, "Would you mind if we went to see *Nonna Isabella*?"

"Of course, it's not far is it? I seem to remember

it's further along that little road at the end of the estate?"

"Yes, that's it. I'd really like you to meet her, if you have time, that is?"

"Certo, volentiere, it would be a pleasure."

Lucia felt calmer now and smiled. She liked the way Tom slipped into Italian when unsure or taken by surprise.

As soon as Luisa left the room Giacomo continued with his earlier request. *"Allora,* Antonio, you think you can arrange this interview to take place within the next few days?"

"Ma……..," Antonio caught himself in time, before expleting a *Madonna,* in exasperation at his father's insistent obstinacy. "Did you not hear *mamma?"* He sighed again. "I will see what I can do but please, let it be for now."

"So be it," and Giacomo shrugged in reluctant surrender.

Luisa returned with coffee and was immediately aware of the change in atmosphere. "What now? Has he been harassing you again?" she asked, looking at Antonio.

"It's alright, *mamma….."*

"No, it's not." Luisa spoke evenly, controlling her anger at her husband. "And Giacomo, you should know better. Now, please, can we finish the day without any more talk of business."

As soon as he finished his coffee, Antonio stood, *"Mamma* I must go. Thank you for lunch and," he turned to Giacomo, "I'll be in touch."

"Oh, must you go so soon, I was hoping……,"

"*Mamma,* I already told you I could not stay. I will be in touch."

"*Va bene,*" Luisa looked down and gave a small shrug in feigned acquiescence. Antonio turned and walked towards the terrace steps before his mother could continue with her usual charade. "*Arrivederla,*" he called and waved as he disappeared towards his car.

Luisa sighed and was about to admonish Giacomo for driving her son away but thought better of it and instead suggested he take a siesta.

"*Si, si, si .....,* please, don't fuss."

She stood and walked round the table to where her husband was sitting. She knelt beside his chair and took his hand. "*Amore,* you have just come out of hospital and I love you very much. It is not fussing. So, please, let's not do too much too quickly, *eh*?" She said gently raising an eyebrow in unison with her words.

"*Eh,* you are right," he said with a submissive smile. "It's not easy, and ….,

"What?"

"Well," he paused, "I was wondering if there was any word from Lorenzo?"

"*Eh,* there you go again," Luisa stood up, moving away from the table. "Please, Giacomo, just let it go!"

"*Carissima mia, vieni qui,* my dearest, come here," pleaded Giacomo.

Luisa looked at her husband, surprised by his ameliorative response. She was used to the usual argumentative repartee they exchanged and it was rare for him to retreat. She turned and took a step towards him. He suddenly seemed small and vulnerable again despite his apparent robust physicality. Unsure, she raised an eyebrow. "And….?"

"And ….," he smiled, "let us not argue. I don't seem to have the energy for it."

Antonio returned to his apartment in Florence later that afternoon after first stopping off at his office. He needed to find space, not only between himself and his father's demands, but also between himself and his mother. In his office he was able to immerse himself in a world he not only felt part of, but had also played a major part in its creation.

Satisfied that everything was in order, he checked his appointments for the following week and decided he would leave the call to Lucia until the morning. He didn't wish to disturb her on a Sunday and he wanted to forget about anything to do with his father for what remained of the day. He checked his mobile for messages. *Niente*, nothing.

He let himself into the apartment and, relieved to have the place to himself, he poured a glass of wine and sat outside on the small terrace watching the sky deepen through shades of gold as he mulled over the last few days.

"*Nonna,* I think you already know Tom, he's a friend of Chiara."

Si, si, piacere, and please, call me Isabella."

"*Piacere,* Signora Isabella." Tom replied respectfully.

Isabella smiled, "So tell me, what have you two young people been doing?"

Lucia regaled her with details of their lunch and their walk around Florence and in particular the bees and how she remembered having to count them as a child. Isabella laughed at the memory. "And what else?" she asked knowingly, wondering if her granddaughter would share whatever it was that had lifted her spirits. Tom smiled at her astuteness and waited to hear what Lucia might say.

"Ah yes," she said, taking her time to find the words. "*Nonna,* you know I've been having these dreams and last night it was..., well.., worse. Tom very kindly arranged for me to meet a friend whom he thought may be able to help me." She paused for a moment and looked at Tom, then continued. "Anyway, we met this morning and I'm going to see her tomorrow. I like her very much, and somehow, I've felt a lot better since I met her."

Isabella looked at Tom quizzically, "Tom, who is this *signora*?"

Before Tom could reply, Lucia answered, "Her name is Simonetta Morelli, *nonna.*" Then added, "I'm sorry Tom, I didn't mean to be rude."

"*Calma, amore,*" Isabella became serious, "I'm acquainted with Simonetta, she is well known in Florence. Tell me, Tom, how is she known to you?"

In her enthusiasm Lucia was about to answer again, but managed to restrain herself when she realised her grandmother's tone had changed.

"I met her some years ago."

"Mmmm. And what do you know of her, Tom?"

"Well, I believe she is an exceptional woman with an unusual gift and I hope she will be able to help Lucia understand what is happening to her."

"*Bene. Infatti,* in fact, I have known Simonetta since we were children and, yes Tom, she does have a remarkable gift. I think if anyone can help you, Lucia, it is her." Then changing her voice to a lighter tone, "*Allora*, can I get you a drink or something to eat?"

"No, no *nonna*, we're fine, aren't we Tom?" Tom nodded in agreement as she added. "I don't think I'll eat or drink anything for a while!"

Lucia could see that her grandmother was tired and she didn't want their visit to be a strain for her. "*Nonna*, maybe I can call by tomorrow when I get back from seeing Simonetta and we can talk more."

"*Certo*, I would like that. And Tom, it's a pleasure to meet you again. Thank you for helping Lucia with this, she is precious to us."

"The pleasure is mine, Signora Isabella."

"No, no don't get up, *nonna*. We'll see ourselves out. *A domani*," and Lucia bent down and kissed her on both cheeks. When Lucia stood up, Isabella held her hands out to Tom and taking his hand in hers, she gave him a broad, wrinkled smile, "Thank you, young man. I hope to see you again soon."

"As do I, signora." Tom felt a warm and deep affection for the older woman who, despite her fragile appearance, he knew to be much more than she chose to show.

As they got back into the car Lucia confided in Tom, "I'm worried about her, Tom. She seems so frail and insists on staying there on her own. Chiara has tried to persuade her to move into the house but she just won't listen."

Tom chose his words carefully, "I think it's important to honour her wishes, she is stronger than she appears and …, well, sometimes we just have to let life run its course. She knows you both love and care for her a great deal but she has to be able to live her life the way she wants to."

"Yes, I know you're right but it's hard not to worry. She's changed so much since I was last here. I know, I know I have to accept it." Her voice became soft and quiet as she went into herself.

"Come, it's been a long day for you. Let's get you home."

"Thank you, Tom. I really mean it. You've been great."

He drove the short distance to Chiara's where her car was already in the courtyard. He switched off the engine and got out to open the door for Lucia. "I'd better be going. I have to go into town tomorrow so if you'd like a lift I can show you where to find Simonetta."

"Are you sure?"

"*Certo,* I'd be happy to. I have an appointment at 11 so I could pick you up about 10 if that's ok with you?"

"Great. Thanks. See you then. And thank you again for today."

They kissed cheeks and exchanged *ciaos*. Tom got back in the car and drove off with mixed feelings of contentment and apprehension.

Lucia found Chiara at the kitchen table focussed on her laptop screen. She looked up on hearing Lucia's footsteps. "*Ciao, cara, tutto bene?* Is everything alright?"

"*Si, si.* Tom introduced me to a friend of his and then we had lunch in town. We walked around for a while then called in to see *nonna* on the way back. How about you? You have a good day?" She thought Chiara looked tired.

"Oh, I've been working most of the day and I've just finished," she said closing her laptop with a finality that intended no further discussion. "Do you want to eat?"

"*O dio*, no. Lunch seemed to go on forever. I don't know how people can eat so much," she sighed sinking into one of the armchairs.

"A glass of wine then?"

"Er, maybe a small one."

Chiara stood and walked over to the worktop where she poured the remains of an already opened bottle of Chianti and handed one glass to Lucia. "*Ora,* now, tell me about this friend of Tom."

"Well, her name is Simonetta and I liked her very much. Tom thought she may be able to help me understand what has been happening recently."

"*Eh,* of course." Her voice became suddenly flat.

"You know her?"

"*Si,* she's a friend *di mamma.* I think they went to school together or something like that. She is, *come si dice,* how do you say, well known here?"

"You sound as if you don't like her?"

"No, no, it's not that. You know how Florence is, there are stories. People don't like what they don't understand so there is talk, though *mamma* has always thought well of her."

"What do you mean, Chiara?"

"Italians can be very superstitious and imagine ….er…. *ombra, buio* …, darkness in many things. Centuries of fear still remain today."

"What has this to do with Simonetta?"

"Lucia, *cara*, if anyone can help you I think it would be Simonetta but ….."

"That's exactly what *nonna* said."

"Yes, and she's right. All I'm saying is be careful who you talk to about this other than myself, *mamma* and Tom."

"I don't imagine there is anyone else I'd talk to, I hardly know anyone here. But, Chiara, you're making me worried…."

"*No, no, no* …, that's not my intention. It is sometimes difficult to understand the way things are here if you are not used to it, that's all. Please, do not worry and I truly hope she can give you some answers."

Lucia released the breath she'd been holding, "Yes, so do I. Oh, I almost forgot. I may need to stay a few more days, will that be ok? I'll call the magazine in the morning."

"Of course, *cara*, that would be wonderful. You know you can stay as long as you want to." They both smiled and Lucia felt the warmth and generosity in her aunt's voice, a comfort after the conversation about Simonetta. She tried to brush aside any rising doubts as they spent the remainder of the evening exchanging memories of their earlier lives until they each realised how exhausted they were. After mugs of chamomile tea they said their goodnights and went to bed.

MONDAY
Lunedi

Lucia woke from a deep and dreamless sleep, surprised to see it was already 8 o'clock. She stretched diagonally across the bed as she gathered herself, working out where she was, what day it was and any other essential information she needed to know. Italy. Monday. And, oh yes, the meeting with Simonetta was this morning. And, she must call the magazine to arrange a few more days here. What would she tell them? She didn't like to lie but, she could say she still hoped for the interview with Signor Martinelli which could be true, or maybe, she could suggest another story on an aspect of Florence's rich art collection. She was sure she could come up with something plausible.

She stood at the window looking out at the now familiar panoramic view studded with elegant cypress trees and Florence in the distance. She raised her arms and stretched again, this time as if to embrace the essence of the light and the land. A sense of peace and belonging, that was at once familiar and unfamiliar, swept over and through her.

She showered and dressed in a simple grey linen dress and darker grey jacket, before going downstairs where Chiara was already sitting at the table in front of her open laptop. "*Ciao, ciao, cara, come stai,* did you sleep well?"

"Yes, very well thanks, and you? It's such a beautiful morning."

"*Si, si, grazie.* I just have to check a few emails. Coffee is made. I won't be a minute."

Lucia was getting used to the Italian diet of endless coffee, something she had not been able to do in London. The coffee seemed to not only taste better here, but didn't have the effect of a high speed train running through her body. She poured a coffee, picked up a *cornetto*, an Italian croissant, and sat down opposite Chiara. "What are your plans today?" she asked.

Chiara closed her laptop, "There, all done. I have to check on the plants then I'll go to the shop and make sure everything is alright for the week. What time are you seeing Simonetta?"

"Oh, Tom's picking me up at 10 o'clock and taking me there. Maybe we could meet for lunch afterwards if you're free?"

"That would be lovely but see how things go with Simonetta. You can call me when you leave her and we can go from there. *Va bene?*"

"Yes, of course."

"And don't worry if you're there a long time. I can wait, there's always plenty to do at the shop."

"Ok, thanks."

Chiara went to check her plants and Lucia picked up a magazine and went outside to sit and read while she waited for Tom. She thought how peaceful it was in the haze of the morning sun and was disturbed by the distant ringing of her mobile phone. She rushed to answer it before it stopped and went to voicemail. "Pronto," she said catching her breath.

"Lucia? *Sono* Antonio."

"Ah, *buongiorno, come stai?*"

"*Bene, grazie. E lei?*"

"*Si, bene, grazie.*"

The formal greetings out of the way, Antonio started to explain the purpose of his call. "I hope I am not disturbing you, but I wondered how long you will be in Florence and if you will still be free to meet with my father."

"I'm hoping to stay until the end of the week and I'd be very happy to meet with him. When would be convenient?" Lucia thought this was working out perfectly. If she arranged to see him later in the week it would be easy to extend her stay until then.

"I was thinking Wednesday or Thursday."

"Shall we say Thursday? What time?"

"I could pick you up at noon, maybe have lunch with us and then spend a short time with him. I'm sure you understand he is still recovering but would be delighted to meet with you."

"Of course. I'll see you Thursday."

"*Perfetto.* Until then. *Arriverderla* Lucia."

"*Arrivederla.*" There was a click and the line went silent.

Lucia was suddenly transformed into business mode.

She found the number she wanted in the contacts list of her phone and pressed the 'call' button. After a brief conversation with her editor it was agreed to extend the deadline for the article and as she ended the call, Lucia held the phone to her chest, twirling in a short dance, happy it had all been so easy.

At that moment she heard Tom's car arrive. She collected her bag and herself and went to meet him.

After the usual greetings Tom looked at her and said, "You seem different. Anything I should know about?"

"Oh, well first, I slept really well. Then, just before you arrived, I had a call from Antonio Martinelli asking if I can still do the interview with his father so I'm seeing him on Thursday."

"So you can extend your visit?"

"Yes, I called the editor and it's all taken care of."

"That's great news. Shall we go?" Tom walked round to the passenger door and opened it for Lucia.

The drive into Florence slowed as they approached the centre and Tom was pleased he'd allowed enough time. Despite the restrictions on cars allowed into the city, the traffic could still be dense and frustrating. It was not only traffic that slowed their progress, it was also the tourists who seemed to be oblivious to any road sense they may have once possessed.

They followed the road along the south side of the Arno towards the Ponte Vecchio. Tom turned left towards the Boboli Gardens then slowed down before turning through an archway in a long wall that led to an internal courtyard where he stopped the car.

"*Ecco,* here we are."

"It's like entering a secret world. It's beautiful," Lucia gasped, admiring the shafts of lights from above as they touched the cascades of geraniums tumbling from ancient terracotta urns.

"Yes, it is, isn't it? Simonetta is on the first floor through that door." Tom pointed to a large polished wooden door in front of them. "I shall be in town for a few hours if you need a lift back."

"Thanks Tom, but Chiara's in the shop so I'll go over there when I leave here. I'd like to call you later though, if that's ok?"

"*Certo, certo. A doppo.* 'Til later then."

Lucia stood in front of the polished door, her breath held in feelings of apprehension and anticipation. She breathed out, then in and out again before ringing the bell. There was a loud buzz that released the lock and she pushed open the door to reveal a wide marble staircase that led to Simonetta's apartment. She felt small in the grandeur of the entrance and heard a door open above as Simonetta appeared on the landing to greet her.

"*Buongiorno,* come, it is good to see you again. *Come stai?*"

"*Va bene, e lei?*"

"*Bene, bene* but please there is no need to be formal.*"* Simonetta said, commenting on Lucia's use of the formal pronoun. "We are friends, no?"

"*Si, certo. Grazie.*"

They entered the apartment and Lucia was immediately surprised not only by its size but also by the opulence of the furnishings. High ceilings and grand chandeliers welcomed her to the inner hall and continued as Simonetta directed her through the *salatto* where tall windows were framed with sumptuous drapes, and huge oil paintings and mirrors in ornate gold frames filled the walls.

"Come, let us sit in here where it is more comfortable," and Simonetta led her through to what Lucia thought must be the library. Tall over filled bookcases lined the walls but the furnishings were less grand and the furniture less formal and therefore more comfortable. Lucia had always thought that Italian furniture hard and rigid in comparison to the soft squidgy sofas she had at home.

"Would you like coffee?"

"Yes, thank you."

"Please, make yourself comfortable, I'll just be a moment."

Simonetta went to the kitchen to organise the coffee and returned a few minutes later with a tray filled with a pot of coffee, little cups and a plate of small pastries.

"*Allora.* Please, help yourself. Now, tell me, has anything happened since I saw you yesterday?"

"No, nothing. I slept really well and, in fact, I've been feeling better than I have for a long time."

"*Bene.* I have thought about what you told me yesterday and I believe that there is a connection between the past and the present. What I mean is, something that is happening to you now has activated something in the past to which you have a connection either directly or indirectly. Do you know anything about or have you ever thought about past lives?"

"No, not really. Do you mean reincarnation?"

Lucia frowned.

"Yes, in that we may live more than one life, that this is not all there is. I think also you are experiencing that the physical world you know is only a part of who you are. *No?*"

"Er .... I suppose so. I hadn't quite thought of it like that."

"Lucia, *secondo me,* I think, you have a gift, an ability, which has been suppressed until now. *"Dimmi,* tell me, is there anything that happened around the time that the dreams began?"

"Not that I can think of."

"Think. Is there anything that may relate to Italy and in particular to Florence?"

"Well, the only thing is this trip, the interview with Signor Martinelli. Oh yes, Antonio called this morning to ask if I would still be able to meet him and we arranged for me to go on Thursday. So I've arranged to stay for the rest of the week."

"Bene, good, that gives us time. Which came first, the dream or the interview?"

"Oh," Lucia paused while she thought about it. "I think I had the call about the interview first. Then it was a couple of days before I confirmed I could do it. I'm almost sure the dream started after that."

"*Bene, bene.* It's as I thought. We need to see what this connection is and why it has activated now."

"I don't understand."

"*Come posso dire,* how can I say? When you agreed to accept this interview and come to Florence you seem to have triggered something. Maybe there was something when you were doing your research? Something unusual?"

"Not that I can think of. It is an amazing collection and quite a coup to get an interview with Signor Martinelli. He rarely gives them. Although he was quite insistent that there would be no personal questions, and that I should refer only to the art collection."

"And why do you think they approached you?"

"I'm not sure but I think it helped that I'm half Italian. I believe he wanted someone who understood not only the art world but also Italian culture. Also there has been speculation in the press recently about his younger son, Lorenzo, and his hedonistic lifestyle which must be causing his father some embarrassment."

"I see."

"Wait, there was something else. When I was in the gallery there was a painting, a portrait, it was strange, it was as if it pulled me in, and then ...... then I heard the voice again."

"Can you remember anything about it that was familiar – a certain look, the clothes, the background maybe?"

Lucia tried to recall the image but simply frowned and shook her head.

"I'm sorry, I just can't......"

"*Piano, piano,* let's try something. Close your eyes and take your time. Allow the image to surface from your memory. Do not force it ....., let it appear in its own time." Simonetta's words soothed and encouraged.

Lucia took a deep breath and, relaxed by Simonetta's voice, she saw the painting materialise in her mind's eye.

"Yes, I have it," she said in a whisper for fear of losing the image.

"*Bene,* now can you describe what you see, in

detail?"

Lucia felt her immediate environment disappear and all she was aware of was the painting. She focussed on the profile image of the man, his face, his clothes and the setting but found nothing that was familiar. It was when her eyes met his left hand where an ornate ring sat on his smallest finger that she felt a deep chill and the now familiar voice spoke to her.

'*It makes me very happy that you have come at last. Our family has known great pain and now is the time for this to be reconciled. You will understand more as your journey continues. Remember, it is time."*

Lucia spoke the words aloud as she heard them.

"*Bene,* you can open your eyes now."

"What does she mean ....., who is it and who is the man in the painting ....., and that ring ....? What's happening to me?"

"*Calma, calma.* Take a couple of deep breaths," Simonetta said also breathing deeply as she spoke. "There, that's better. *Eh,* it's possible that this has stirred something, although I sense that it touches more than we can see at the moment."

"What do you mean?"

"I'm not sure yet. There are different ways to approach this and, if you are willing, I would like to include you in the process. It will mean taking you back in time and accessing the memories that are finding their way into your present. It is quite safe but first I need to know that I have your trust."

"*Certo,* of course. What do you want me to do?" Lucia felt a mixture of fear and a desire to get it over and done with.

"First, I'd like you to be comfortable and relax and

when you're ready close your eyes and take a few deep breaths." Simonetta's voice was soft as she gently guided her into the process.

It's almost dark and I'm running, running through the woods. It's hard to breathe and I'm tired and hungry. My arms and legs are scratched from the overgrown brambles and undergrowth. I'm frightened, very frightened. I know I mustn't give up I must not be caught otherwise I will not live.

There was burning, lots of burning, people screaming ...... I don't want to remember...., my parents ...... what happened ..... why am I alone?

I have to keep going, I have to get away. I remember now, I jumped on the back of a cart that was leaving the city .... it stopped over the bridge near Pontassieve and I jumped off and ran for cover in the woods. I have to find somewhere to rest, sleep ..... find food ...., just running....., running.

I can't go on. I stop and listen. I don't hear anyone following. There's a very old tree with a fat trunk. I collapse on fallen leaves and lean against it. I'm so exhausted ...., I don't know what to do....... Lucia's voice trailed off into silence.

Simonetta spoke softly, encouraging her to continue, "and then what happened?"

Oh, I must have fallen asleep. I'm very cold. It's dark now. I have to move, find shelter. I must keep going. I can barely see ....., I smell woodsmoke, there's a house. It's so quiet, it must be late, I go into the cantina, hide in a corner, pull some straw over me ...., I think I sleep.

There's noise outside and it's light. Slowly I look

to see what is happening. A man and two boys are loading a cart. Oh no! They're coming this way ..., I run back to the corner and hold my breath. Oh, all is lost! A dog runs in and heads straight for me, it's barking and the man comes to investigate. "What is this? Alfonso, go call your mother!" I'm so scared. I barely understand what he's saying as he speaks in dialect. "It's alright. We won't harm you. Eh, Livia, come see what we have, maybe you can convince her we mean her no harm."

The woman's stooping and holding out her hand to me. I don't think they mean to harm me and I touch her hand. Slowly, she comes closer and helps me to my feet. "Come, little one, come with me." She leads me out of the cantina and into a small cottage next door. She asks me my name and I tell her it's Marinella. It's warm inside. "Here, sit by the fire." She indicates a chair and I sit in it. She covers me with an itchy blanket and leaves the small room. She comes back with hot milk and a chunk of freshly baked bread. It's so good to eat something. She doesn't say anything, just watches me and smiles now and then."

Simonetta waits for Lucia to pause before gently asking, "and how long do you stay there?" She watches carefully as Lucia considers this and there's a shift in the tone of her voice as she replies.

"Er ....,I stay with the family for some time. They give me a bed and food and I help Livia with the chores and in the garden. They don't ask questions. They tell me their daughter died. I think they see me as a replacement as it were.

One day, I hear horses and run into the house. Livia tells me not to be afraid. She goes out and speaks to the men who dismount and follow her to the house. They look around and she tells them I'm her daughter. They accept this. After they've gone she tells me that she knows I've done nothing wrong, that I'm a good person and I'm safe with them. I don't know how or why she knows this. I feel safe here.

"Why did you run away?" Simonetta asked.

"*I ...., there were men, like the ones who came to Livia's house, they came to my home and took my parents. I was outside and I followed them. The men went in all the homes taking some people and not others. They marched them like a procession to the piazza where they had built bonfires in a circle. They tied my parents and others to a pole at the centre then lit the firewood. There were screams ....., and the smell ...., I ran. One of the men knew my family and he saw me. He told the men to catch me. I'm lucky that I know the streets well and I was able to lose them. Then I jumped on this cart that was leaving the city.*

"Do you know why they took your parents?"

"*Only that it was to do with what they believed. They had taken them before and kept them locked up for a week before letting them come home. The men called them heretics.*"

"I think that is enough for now." Simonetta spoke quietly to Lucia as she brought her back to the present. "Here, when you are ready, please drink some water."

It took Lucia several minutes to familiarise herself with her surroundings. Simonetta watched patiently before speaking again.

"Welcome back. How do you feel?"

"I'm not sure, a bit strange, but in a good way."

"Well, *piano piano,* slowly. You did very well and we should not be in too much of a hurry. It's a bit like, *come si dice,* how do you say, peeling an onion, one layer at a time. Now rest awhile, and drink more water, I'll be back shortly."

Simonetta returned after a few minutes and, satisfied that Lucia was ready to continue with her day, asked, "Can you come back tomorrow at the same time?"

"Yes, of course but this is taking a lot of your time …."

"Not at all, I'm interested in what is happening to you and you are also a friend of Tom's so I'm happy to help you. Let's leave it for today and we can talk more tomorrow."

"Thank you, Simonetta, thank you very much."

"*Eh, niente,* I think you are alright now. *A domani.*"

Simonetta led the way back to the main door and the courtyard where they exchanged hugs, kisses and ciaos. Lucia then went out into the streets of the Oltrarno, the other side of the River Arno, and headed towards the Ponte Vecchio. Suddenly realising she was hungry she checked the time. It was just after one so she called Chiara hoping she was still in time for lunch.

"*Si, si,* come to the shop."

"Great, I'll see you in about ten minutes." She walked quickly through the crowds of tourists who filled the city's streets. She was surprised at how 'normal' she felt after her meeting with Simonetta. She likened it to waking from a dream and not being able to remember all the details.

Lucia entered the shop and was greeted by an enthusiastic Chiara. "Come, *cara,* let's go and eat and you can tell me how it all went with Simonetta." Chiara ushered her out of the shop, along the street and into a small *trattoria.*

"Ah, *buongiorno, Signora Chiara.* For two?"

"*Si, grazie Massimo e come stai?*"

"*Bene, e lei?*"

"*Bene, bene.*" Once the usual questions as to each other's health were out of the way, Chiara and Lucia were led to a table and handed menus." By the way, the mozarella is excellent." Chiara recommended. "And, well ……, it's all good, you choose."

"Would you mind ordering for me, Chiara, I need to go to the bathroom, I won't be long." Lucia said as she stood up and left the table. Once there she looked at her reflection in the mirror. What am I doing? In the absence of any reply she continued to search the face in front of her as if it could tell her something she did not already know. Maybe this wasn't a good idea, she thought as more doubts tumbled into her mind. *"Tutto bene,* all is well," said the voice. Lucia spun round half expecting to see someone standing behind her but she knew there was no one there. Feeling cornered, she checked her reflection in the mirror, and when she heard nothing further, composed herself and returned to the table.

"Ah, cara, tutto bene?"

Lucia stared at Chiara as she repeated the words she had heard only a few minutes earlier. "*Si,* yes, I er …., did you order?"

"Yes. Are you sure you're ok? You look very pale,

cara."

"Oh, maybe it's the lighting." Lucia realised how hollow that must have sounded as well as being dishonest. Why was she hiding what had just happened from Chiara? "I'm sorry, Chiara. It was just that when I was in the bathroom I heard the voice again saying the same words you said as I came back to the table, *tutto bene."*

"O dio. It is not a surprise that you look so pale. Was Simonetta able to help?"

"Yes, and I've arranged to see her again tomorrow. In fact, I was feeling good after seeing her; maybe that's why it came as such a shock to hear the voice again. Anyway, I'm ok, let's enjoy lunch. What did you order?"

"Oh, mixed antipasti then some fish. *Va bene?"*

"Si, si, sounds great. How was your morning?"

"Eh, the usual. Tell me about yours."

The waiter arrived at their table and poured two glasses of wine before Lucia could answer. Another waiter followed on his tail with the antipasti which he placed on the table and wished them *"Buon apetito."*

"Lucia?" Chiara prompted.

"Yes?"

"Your morning?"

"Oh. Actually, do you mind if we don't talk about it until after I've seen Simonetta again tomorrow. It somehow doesn't feel right. I don't want to disturb anything if you know what I mean."

"Certo, cara." Chiara raised her glass in a toast, *"Salute,* let's eat."

As he drove away, leaving Lucia at Simonetta's home,

Tom couldn't help wondering whether he had done the right thing introducing Lucia to Simonetta. On the one hand he had no doubts as he trusted Simonetta implicitly; yet on the other ..... , he couldn't quite put his finger on it ...., was it that he was concerned Lucia would find it all a bit strange. He followed his thoughts as he drove to his appointment near Impruneta. Was he perhaps being protective towards Lucia and if that were the case, what did it say about his feelings towards her?

He remembered the attraction he felt at their first meeting and how her seemingly fragile beauty had awakened something within him. However, he soon realised that, in the present circumstances, it was more important to gain her trust than pursue his interest in getting to know her in a romantic way.

It had been a long time since he had shown much more than a passing interest in another woman. Whilst he'd had a few short relationships, he'd known his heart was not open to fully engaging in the intimacy necessary to sustain one. Was this now changing? Maybe. He arrived at the villa and, focussing on the business to hand, put any extraneous thoughts to the back of his mind.

Antonio entered his office at the rear of the gallery relieved to return to his usual business. The drama surrounding his father and the interview had gone beyond anything he expected. What had started as a simple request had become a major undertaking and impinged far too deeply on his time.

As far as he was concerned he had fulfilled his part. Of course, it was not his father's fault that he had been taken ill but ...., probably he was more annoyed with himself for making himself so available whenever his mother called, only to later resent her demands.

And then there was Lucia, the journalist he'd selected to do the interview. What was it about her? She seemed familiar and yet he knew he had not met her prior to their meeting in London. She had occupied his mind frequently over the past few days.

Oh, she was attractive, even beautiful, just not his type. So why did she disturb his thoughts so often? Whatever the reason, he would not now see her until Thursday.

Lucia sat back in her chair, oblivious to her presence in the thoughts of the two men, Tom and Antonio. Chiara ordered coffee and asked, "*Allora,* what would you like to do now?"

"Oh, I don't know. Have you any suggestions?"

"*Eh,* depends if you want to be a tourist or not?"

Lucia gave Chiara a cheeky smile and said with a raised eyebrow, "I don't think so." After a short pause she added, "Maybe we could visit *nonna.* Do you think she would like to go out somewhere?"

"*Bene.* We can pass by and see. By the time we get there she should have had her siesta."

Chiara paid the bill and they said goodbye to Massimo and exchanged customary good wishes to each other's families.

Luisa sat on the terrace with her morning coffee waiting for Giacomo to join her. There had still been no word from Lorenzo and she felt a mixture of irritation and maternal concern for her younger son. She despaired at his lack of respect, not only for his family but for life in general and prayed that his latest disappearances were no more than high spirited rebellion.

The sun began to feel warm on her face and she moved her chair a little to take advantage of the remaining shade. It would not be long before the terrace would be flooded with light and the midday heat would force her indoors. She mused how early in the year she already seemed to be dodging the heat of the sun and hoped it wasn't a precursor to a long hot summer.

She finished her coffee and was considering whether to go in search of Giacomo when she was shaken from her thoughts by a scream followed by shouts of, "*Signora ....., Signora* Luisa!"

On her feet immediately she rushed inside where she met a breathless Maria. "*Signora, Signora ..., o dio, o dio.* It's ..., it's *Signor* Giacomo ....."

"Maria, *con calma. Dimme,* tell me, what has happened?"

Maria tried to speak between gulps for air. Luisa realising she was not able to speak coherently and fearing the worst, calmly said, "Show me, Maria, come, show me."

"Oh, *Signora* ....., he ..... he, I don't think he is breathing, *o dio, o dio!*"

Luisa remained calm as Maria led her to the study. As they entered the room she knew something was very wrong. There was a stillness and a taste in the air that she could only associate with death. Maria held back at the doorway busily crossing herself, and reluctant to enter the room again. Luisa went in alone.

Giacomo was slouched in the green leather armchair. A letter that he had been reading rested in his left hand. Even though the sun beamed through the tall windows Luisa felt there was a darkness in the room. Numbness overtook her and she forced herself to move towards him. He looked so peaceful, almost like a sleeping child. She suppressed any rising emotions as she tentatively touched his arm as if to gently wake him from a doze.

"Giacomo," she whispered without hope. When there was no response, she controlled her breathing before panic could set in and placed her hand on his neck to check for a pulse. Even though she knew there was none, the inevitability of his death sent shock waves through her.

She picked up the phone from the table beside her and pressed the quick dial button to call Dr Giannini. When he answered she explained what had happened and he assured her he would be there without delay.

Luisa walked over to the window that looked out on to the garden but her attention was pulled back into the room by Maria's repeated, "*O dio, o dio*." She turned, facing into the room once more, closed her eyes and took a deep breath to compose and prepare herself for what needed to be done.

Once outside the room she put her arm around Maria's shoulder, "Come, let's go to the kitchen, the doctor is on his way." She then steered Maria to the kitchen and sat her in a chair while she poured two glasses of *vin santo*. "*Ecco,* here, drink this."

Maria, still shaking, crumpled into the seat and accepted the glass, sipping the wine between sniffs and snivels. Luisa watched her and half wished she could just let go and freely feel the grief and fear she was holding tightly locked inside.

She heard car tyres scrunch on the gravel and went to meet Dr Giannini. There was more scrunching, this time louder, as an ambulance arrived.

"*Buongiorno, dottore.* Thank you for coming so quickly."

"*Buongiorno, Signora.* I'm so sorry …… can you show me where….?

Luisa interrupted, "Of course, please follow me."

Once again she walked the length of the hall to the study and paused in the doorway. Dr Giannini put his hand on her arm, "I'll take it from here."

"*Grazie,* thank you. I'll be, er…..," Luisa paused, feeling anchorless, she tried to decide where to go. "I'm sorry. I'll be in the kitchen with Maria. It was Maria who found Giacomo and she is terribly upset."

Dr Giannini looked momentarily at Luisa assessing her controlled demeanour. "I'll join you as soon as I can."

As Luisa retraced her steps to the kitchen her mind began to race through all the things she would have to do. She stopped to rein in such thoughts as she knew she must first speak with the doctor before doing anything, and by the time she reached the kitchen she had managed to create order in her mind once more. Maria was still clearly distressed and she did not want to send her away to be on her own. Maybe Dr Giannini could give her something, she thought. In the meantime, she poured some more *vin santo* into the two glasses and sat down to wait for the doctor.

It was not long before Dr Giannini joined her. He explained that he could not be certain about the cause of death until he had made a complete examination. As he was speaking Luisa saw Giacomo being taken on a stretcher to the ambulance but this time his head was also covered with a blanket.

Luisa thanked Dr Giannini and explained that it was Maria who had found Giacomo and asked if he could give her something for the shock.

"Of course," said Dr Giannini as he opened his case and handed her a small plastic bottle containing four capsules. "And you, Signora?"

"No, no, I'm fine. There will be a lot to do and ….."

"Signora Luisa," he interjected, "is there someone who can be with you and help you with such things?"

"*Eh,* my son will help."

Dr Giannini hoped she was not referring to Lorenzo as he remembered his recent behaviour at the hospital.

"Have you any idea what could have happened?" Lucia asked.

"Not really, no. It could have been many things and I don't wish to speculate but I will let you know as soon as I have completed the examination. So, if there is nothing else?"

"No, *dottore*. Thank you for everything." Luisa stood, shook his hand and walked with him to the main door.

"I will be in touch as soon as I can." He said as he turned to go down the steps to his car.

Luisa stood at the door for a few minutes after the car had gone. She felt as if part of her life was draining away. She knew she could not allow herself to surrender to it and snapped her mind back to the present. Garnering her will and determination she returned to the kitchen.

Maria seemed a little calmer and Luisa decided it would be a good idea if she were kept busy. "*Allora,* we must do our best for Signor Giacomo. Please, lay out the finest linen and if you need to wash or iron anything then do so, and let me know when it is ready."

Maria stood up, smoothed her apron, and left the room to follow Luisa's instructions. Luisa sighed and went to the living room to start on the calls she knew she would have to make.

O dio, where to start? Antonio's office number was the first one she punched into the phone. It seemed to ring endlessly at the other end before going to the answering service. Luisa hung up without saying anything and called his mobile and again was greeted with the recorded message of his voicemail. Frustrated at not being able to speak with him she left a message asking him to call her urgently.

Next she called Lorenzo expecting to leave a similar message but instead was greeted with, "Pronto."

"Oh, Lorenzo, where are you?"

"*Buongiorno mamma,*" he said with a touch of sarcasm.

"Lorenzo," she paused to compose herself, "Lorenzo, can you come now, please. It's your father ....."

"Why, what is it now?"

"Lorenzo, *basta!* Enough! Your father ...., he is dead."

There was a short silence, followed by the dialling tone as Lorenzo ended the call.

Luisa sighed in frustration at her son's offhanded manner and went in search of a writing pad and pen to list the other people she would have to inform of Giacomo's death. She went over to the small writing table by the window, opened the drawer and took out what she needed before sitting down to start the list.

She looked out of the window on to the garden at the familiar Florentine skyline in the distance. It all seemed so abrupt; as if her anticipated memories had been stolen. Her future dreams suddenly empty, erased from her life's canvas. Before she could reproach herself the phone rang.

"Pronto."

"*Ciao mamma, sono* Antonio."

"*Ciao amore,* something has happened, can you come now?"

"But ….,"

Before he could speak Luisa continued, "It's Giacomo, *e morto,* he is dead."

"*Arrivo subbito,* I'll be there straightaway."

"*Grazie amore.*"

Again, there was that emptiness. Her heart ached as her mind searched for memories to fill the void, but her will strained to close the door for fear she would never emerge from such reverie. She stood straight and breathed deeply as if drawing strength from an unseen source. She knew the call she must make next and picked up the address book to find the number.

Their lawyer was an old family friend and had known Giacomo for more than fifty years, almost her lifetime, and something she found hard to reconcile in that moment. She made the call and arranged for him to come to the villa that evening.

Before she had chance to reflect further she heard footsteps running from the courtyard to the terrace and a breathless Antonio entered through the terrace door.

"*Mamma, che succeda?* What happened?" he asked as he put his arms out to hold her.

Luisa held up her hand in protest, "*No,* not now. There is much to do," and she forced a smile to reassure him. "Maria found him this morning in the study. I was waiting for him to join me for coffee and ….., *allora,* it was as if he had just fallen asleep. I called Dr Giannini and we'll know more when he has done his examination."

Antonio looked at his mother. He was well aware of her need to be in control and didn't want to be the match that ignited the touch paper, he could leave that to Lorenzo. "What can I do?"

"*Eh,* I've started on a list of people to call and Signor Conti will be here this evening to discuss the legal affairs. And you, *amore,* can you check anything to do with the gallery? Oh, and there's the journalist from London ….. mmm, not to worry, I'll call Chiara myself."

"I can call the journalist, Lucia Walker, if you wish?"

"*Va bene,* I will still call Chiara."

"As you wish, *mamma,*" was all Antonio was able to say as the whirlwind that was Lorenzo rushed into the room and ran towards Luisa, breathlessly crying, "*mamma, mamma, che succeda,* what happened?"

Again Luisa held up her hand to ward off emotional contact, "*Calma, amore, basta,* enough." She straightened to her full height to reinforce her façade of imagined strength and capability. "Come, let's sit down," and she indicated towards the seating at the centre of the room.

Antonio followed her direction and sat in one of the armchairs as Luisa arranged herself on the sofa opposite. Lorenzo paused to recover from his mother's rebuttal before sitting in an armchair also opposite his mother and a few feet from Antonio.

"Mamma ....," Lorenzo began.

"Allora," Luisa cut in, "we won't know what happened until Dr Giannini has done his examination. I've already called Signor Conti and he will come over this evening. Now, there is a lot to do."

As they walked out on to the street Chiara found the warm afternoon air stifling after the air conditioned restaurant. *"O dio,* it is so warm and so early in the year!"

"Oh, I don't mind. It's been so grey and unpredictable at home, I quite like it."

"Eh, wait until the summer and see, it will be unbearable."

"You'll go to the sea though, won't you?"

"Si, certo, ma........, but, here's the car." Chiara used the remote to unlock the car and as she opened the driver's door she heard her mobile ring from the depths of her bag. She quickly slid into her seat and fished in her bag for the phone in an attempt to answer it before it went to voicemail. On finding it she pressed the OK button, *"Pronto...... si, ..., Eh,* Luisa ...., *o dio, o dio!*...I'm so sorry. Yes, of course. *Ciao."*

Lucia frowned at Chiara as she got into the car, "What is it, what's happened?"

"It was Luisa, apparently Giacomo died this morning and she asked if I would let you know."

"Oh," was all Lucia could say. She looked at Chiara as if more words might follow but they didn't.

"I know, it's strange, *no*? I mean that she should phone me, well, so soon after ….." Her voice trailed off as more words eluded her also.

"Yes, I suppose. What should I do, I mean what is the custom here?"

"Well, there's nothing we can do right now so let's go home. Will this affect your stay?"

"Er, no I don't think so but I will call the magazine and let them know. I wouldn't want them to find out from someone or somewhere else."

Chiara turned the key in the ignition and pulled out into the Florentine traffic.

The afternoon sun burned through the windscreen and Lucia watched the buildings recede as they left the city and headed south. She wondered what would happen now that Giacomo Martinelli was no longer available for an interview. It seemed to her that this trip was turning into an ever changing kaleidoscope over which she had no control.

"Do you still want to stop off and see *mamma*?"

"Yes, let's," Lucia said thinking that seeing her grandmother might bring some normality to this unpredictable world in which she now found herself. "Is it always like this, Chiara?"

"What do you mean, *cara*, like what?"

"Well, the way everything keeps changing. It seems you can't be sure or rely on anything. It's like walking on quicksand."

"*Eh,* sometimes life can be like that, *no?*"

Lucia looked up at the cypress edged skyline in search of inspiration and muttered a quiet, "mmm." She sighed and turned, smiling, towards Chiara. "I'm sorry, it's just that everything feels as if it's dissolving before my eyes and there's nothing I can do about it."

"Well, maybe there's nothing you need to do, *cara,* at least not today." Chiara kept her eyes on the road as they turned off towards the villa and Isabella's *casetta.*

"I know, you're right," Lucia surrendered with a hint of reluctance in her voice. "And thank you."

"For what?" Chiara pulled the car up outside her mother's and added, "Come, let's see how *mamma* is."

Lucia had been occupying Isabella's thoughts for most of the morning, in fact much of the time since her visit the previous day with Tom.

She had often wondered when Lucia would become aware of her 'gift' and now that was happening she was pleased she had someone like Tom to help her. Her musings turned to her daughter, Daniela, Lucia's mother, and she let out a "tsk" in frustration. Always so quick to condemn, Daniela had shied away from anything she didn't understand and had left home at the first opportunity only returning, it seemed, when she had to. Happily for Isabella the children, Lucia and James then later Gabriella, had visited often when their father's business trips coincided with school holidays. Or maybe he had arranged it that way. As for Daniela, she sometimes accompanied him when he came to collect them which meant she did not have to stay longer than a day or two.

With an image of a young Daniela in her mind, she

remembered her as an insular child, yet headstrong and impetuous. It had been some years before Chiara had been born and in that time she had been used to being an only child. Isabella struggled to find memories that might give her a hint as to why Daniela felt the need to escape, not only her family, but also Italy. Whenever she had raised the subject with the adult Daniela it had always been dismissed as her imagination and that she had moved to England because she loved her husband and for no other reason.

Isabella's thoughts returned to Lucia and how, when she visited as a child, she had encouraged her to learn the names and virtues of the herbs and plants she used in her remedies. She hoped she had inspired a curiosity of the natural world that she knew Daniela would not have encouraged. Another, "tsk" and a shake of the head followed.

And Chiara, she smiled as she remembered how different she was to Daniela, so soft and fluid in comparison. She hoped she had not favoured one more than other as that had never been her intention, but her relationship with Chiara had been so much easier. Daniela's brittle defensiveness had not made for a peaceful life.

Had it always been that way, she wondered. She searched her memories. Maybe ..., maybe, she thought, it became worse after Pietro's death. It had been a shock to the whole family. He had always been so healthy and vital and then, gone. A heart attack they said. A wave of sadness swept over her as she saw his gentle face, so loving. Yes, maybe that was part of it. Daniela had adored her father and seemed lost after he'd gone. She had tried to comfort both children as best as she could but she'd also been in the depths of grief herself.

Isabella drew herself back to the present and was again considering Lucia's situation when she heard a car stop outside. She knew it was Chiara as the sound of her car had become so familiar to her and there was no one else these days that came to visit.

"Permesso?" Chiara called out asking permission to come in as she opened the front door.

"Vieni, vieni, come, come," Isabella responded. "Here, in the kitchen."

Lucia followed Chiara to the back of the cottage where Isabella was sitting at the large, scrubbed table covered with old photos and papers.

"Buona sera, mamma, come stai? How are you?" asked Chiara. Lucia joined in the greeting.

"Bene, bene, siedi, siedi, sit, sit." Isabella replied.

Chiara and Lucia pulled out chairs that scraped on the old, terracotta tiles and sat down. "So, where have you been?" asked Isabella as she looked from one to the other.

"Well, I've been in the shop and then I had lunch with Lucia, but she's had a far more interesting day. I'll let Lucia tell you about it while I go to check on a few things in the garden, *va bene?"*

Chiara left Lucia and Isabella sitting at the table while she went outside. *"Dimme, amore,* tell me." Isabella encouraged, happy to have some time alone with her granddaughter.

Lucia was not sure how much she should share about her morning with Simonetta but soon found the words flowed from her like a stream running from the mountains. Isabella made an odd *eh* or *hm* as she listened to Lucia retell her journey.

When she had finished Isabella released a long exhale that seemed to have been held in a dark silence for years. She looked at the old photographs on the table and then at Lucia and saw an innocence born of ignorance and wondered how she would react to the truth once she found it, if in fact she did. Deciding to hold her counsel, Isabella said, "So, you will see this Simonetta again tomorrow, you say?" Lucia nodded. "And it is helpful?" Again Lucia nodded as the ability to speak momentarily escaped her.

"*Bene,* would you like a tisane? Maybe some *melissa*? It was always one of your favourites."

Finding her voice and her feet Lucia said, "Let me put the water on, *nonna,*" and before Isabella could move she had walked over to the stove where she picked up the little enamel jug and filled it with water. As she put it on the stove to heat she smiled at the way her grandmother refused to use an electric kettle, still preferring the little enamel jug she had always used.

She opened the door to the loggia as Isabella called directions as to where to find the herb. She recognised it immediately, rubbing the leaves together to release the fresh, lemon aroma as she had done as a child.

She returned to the kitchen where Isabella was preparing a tray, "I think it would be good to sit outside, *no*?"

"*Si nonna,* it's cooler now, and look, here comes Chiara."

"*Eh,*" Isabella fetched another cup. "*Ecco,* here, bring it here *amore,*" and nodded in the direction of a china teapot on the tray, a gift from Daniela that she had eventually surrendered to using.

Lucia poured the hot water over the herb and carried the tray outside where Chiara was helping to make Isabella comfortable in one of the cane chairs as she said, "It's looking wonderful *mamma,* so much is at its best at this time of year, don't you think?"

"Si, si. I agree, it all grows well now before the summer heat. And you, Lucia, how long are you staying?"

"Oh, I'm not sure now that Signor Martinelli is no longer with us, but I think until the end of the week. I have to speak to my editor; in fact, would you excuse me and I'll call them now." Lucia walked a little way into the garden to make sure she had a clear signal for her mobile and made the call to London.

Meanwhile just out of Lucia's hearing, Isabella spoke first, *"Dimme cara,* tell me, what do you think of this Simonetta – do you think it is a good thing for Lucia?"

Chiara studied her mother's face which as always was inscrutable before saying, "Who knows *mamma.* What I do know is that I trust Tom and if he thinks she can help Lucia then so do I. I know it may not be what we want but we'll just have to deal with that if, or when, the time comes."

"What do you mean? Deal with what?" This time, although she tried to sound casual, a tension in her voice betrayed her.

"Mamma, please, there's no need to continue this pretence, not with me. And, what were you doing with all the old photographs?"

"Eh, I thought Lucia would like to meet some more

of her Italian family. It's a good idea, *no?"*

"Maybe." Chiara stopped speaking as Lucia returned after making her call.

"That's settled. They'd like me to stay on anyway and see if I can still do an article about the Martinelli collection and what will happen to it following Signor Martinelli's death. So, I'll be able stay another week as planned." As she sat down, Lucia became aware of a slight tension in the air and an image of two women sitting at a similar table, but from another time, flashed across her vision. She caught hold of the table and Chiara reached towards her saying, "Are you alright?"

"Yes, I'm fine, thanks, I just felt a bit dizzy." She sipped her tea and decided not to say anything more about it. "Probably too much excitement in one day," she added.

Chiara nodded in agreement. "You must be tired also; it's been a full day for you, in many ways."

"Let's drink our tea, *e poi,* and then, how would you like to take your *nonna* for a walk round the garden?"

As usual Lorenzo had somewhere he had to rush off to and therefore stayed for little more than an hour, during which time he said very little. Antonio, on the other hand, remained to help his mother go through the papers relating to the gallery. Luisa then busied herself with checking that there was nothing she needed to do in relation to the villa and domestic matters. Giacomo had held the financial purse strings as far as the villa was concerned giving Luisa a generous allowance to cover the day to day expenses which in addition to her own significant resources gave them an indulgent and comfortable lifestyle.

And now? Luisa pondered momentarily on life without Giacomo but was interrupted by Maria confirming that she had laid out the linen and asking how many there would be for dinner. Suddenly, mindful that time was passing, she thanked Maria and asked her to prepare a simple dinner for her and Antonio.

Antonio, content that he had done all he could, wondered what his mother would do now that Giacomo had gone. He did not want to get caught up in yet another of her webs of manipulation nor did he wish to abandon her when she needed support both emotionally and with the gallery. And, of course, there was Lorenzo whom he was certain they would see more of when it involved money. He could not help having a niggling concern at the back of his mind for his mother's welfare. He prayed the whole of affair would be free of too much drama.

Signor Conti arrived shortly after six o'clock. "My condolences, Luisa. Have you heard from Dr Giannini yet?"

"Not yet, no. You remember Antonio, *no*?"

"Of course, though you were much younger then," he said turning to Antonio and shaking his hand.

Antonio nodded.

With the pleasantries out of the way, Luisa directed them to the living room where they sat around a central low table and she poured three glasses of *vin santo* before sitting down next to Antonio.

Signor Conti addressed Luisa as he spoke. "As you

know Giacomo's affairs were somewhat complicated and, under Italian law, half of his estate will go to you, Luisa and the remaining half divided equally between your children. However, as you know, he recently arranged for the majority of his art collection to be donated to the City of Florence. Many of the artworks have been in the Martinelli family for generations and, along with some pieces that Giacomo acquired himself, represent a small fortune. As a result this leaves the villa and any other business interests to be divided between you. I will need to get up to date accounts and I've also brought some forms that you will need to complete. I appreciate this is a difficult time for you but it would be most helpful if you could do this as soon as you can. I'm sure you know with legal matters the wheels can turn very slowly."

"Thank you. Antonio, maybe that's something you could help me with?"

He nodded. *"Certo, mamma."*

Lucia and Chiara returned to the villa. The air was cooling after the heat of the afternoon sun and Lucia was musing on her walk round the garden with Isabella, which had brought memories of childhood holidays flooding back of times spent in another garden. She was also aware of the difference in the Isabella then and the one who had walked beside her in the garden. It saddened her to see her grandmother so diminished. Even though she understood it to be part of the natural cycle of life, the thought of not having much time left with Isabella brought a lump to her throat. She looked at Chiara as she prepared a light supper and wondered how it must be for her seeing her mother become more fragile day by day.

She felt a sudden wave of vulnerability wash over her and shook herself in an attempt to clear it. "Is something wrong?" Chiara asked.

"Er …, no, I was just feeling a little muzzy and …., well, I suppose I was thinking about *nonna* and …," Lucia paused trying to find the best words.

Chiara turned to look at her with a compassionate smile, "I know. She has changed so since you last saw her. It is difficult, *no*?"

"Mmm. I suppose the last time I saw her she was, I don't know, so much more."

The sharp ring of the phone disturbed the stillness, "*Pronto. Ciao* Tom. *Bene. Si, certo.* It's Tom," Chiara handed the phone to Lucia.

"Oh," she said, and took the phone. "*Ciao, come stai?*…….We've just got back from seeing Isabella……. Yes, it went well, I think…... I'm seeing her again tomorrow…….. Would you mind if we talk then?……. Mmm, I'm very tired now and …… Yes, of course. *A domani.*" She put the phone back and said, "Tom said he'll pick me up in the morning. He has an appointment near here first."

"*Eh,* that's convenient."

"What do you mean, Chiara. Are you suggesting…?"

"I'm not suggesting anything!"

The two women smiled then laughed as Lucia exclaimed, "Chiara!"

"*Allora,* it is not a bad thing, *no?*"

"*Allora,*" Lucia mimicked with emphasis, "I think I have enough going on, don't you?"

"Mmm, I'm just saying ……" Chiara teased.

After a light and delicious supper of warm olive bread, *antipasti* and salad fresh from the garden, the two women relaxed with chamomile tea and mixed conversations that travelled from their childhoods to their current lives in their respective countries. Eventually Lucia's eyes would no longer stay open and she kissed Chiara goodnight and went to her room. As she stretched and curled under the duvet, a warm glow seemed to surround and protect her and she fell, smiling, into a deep and undisturbed sleep.

TUESDAY
Martedi

Sun was already pouring into the room when Lucia woke, surprised she had slept so late. She showered, dressed and went downstairs where she found the kitchen was empty and a note on the table informed her that Chiara had already left for her meeting.

She made coffee and helped herself to fresh bread and croissants that Chiara had left in a basket on the table. She found it strange to be on her own and wandered outside to enjoy her breakfast. Absorbing the light and silence she thought how different this was to her usual mornings in London, always so rushed and somehow hollow and unfulfilling.

Her thoughts were disturbed by the distant ringing of her mobile. She ran into the kitchen in time to answer it. "Hello, *pronto*," she said as she caught her breath.

"*Buongiorno, sono Antonio.*"

"Oh, *buongiorno,* Antonio," she said, surprised. "I'm so sorry to hear about your father, Chiara told me.

Please, give my condolences to your mother."

"Thank you, you are kind. The funeral will be tomorrow." He paused briefly before continuing. "When we spoke the other day, you were going to do the interview on Thursday and I think it would be good, if you would like to, to still come to the villa. I can take you through the gallery again and probably answer most of your questions about the collection."

"That's very kind of you...., if you're sure that ......"

"Of course. I am happy to do this and it would be a shame for your trip to be wasted. Shall we say, ten thirty at the villa? I can send a car for you at ten."

"Thank you, yes that will be fine." Lucia responded, feeling a little uncertain about this turn of events.

"Va bene, until Thursday then. Unless of course, you wish to attend the funeral tomorrow. *Arrivederla."*

Lucia heard the dialling tone and somewhat bewildered, she looked at the mobile as if it would answer the unvoiced questions still in her head. The arrival of Tom's car cut short any further thoughts and she picked up her bag and went to meet him.

They exchanged the usual salutations. "You seem distracted, is everything alright?"

"Yes, fine. It's just that I had a call from Antonio Martinelli before you arrived asking if I would still go to the villa on Thursday and interview him about the collection. It just felt odd so soon after Signor Martinelli's death and ....., oh, I don't know, it all seemed a bit abrupt, I suppose."

"Will you go? I suppose in one way it will mean your trip will not have been wasted as far as your work is concerned."

"Mmm, that's what he said."

Lucia got into the car and they drove into Florence, Lucia lost in her thoughts and Tom choosing not to interrupt them. As they approached Simonetta's apartment, Tom broke the silence, "Would you like me to take you back when you have finished?"

"Er, yes, that would be great, but I ….."

Tom interrupted her. "No buts, one of the joys of being my own boss – I can arrange my day as I please, within reason of course. Just give me a call when you're ready, I won't be far."

Simonetta was in the courtyard watering the plants that were still in shade. She put down the watering can to greet them. Tom made his farewells and Simonetta led Lucia to the room they had occupied the previous day.

"Allora, how are you today?"

"Good, thank you."

"I have coffee ready, would you like some?"

"Yes, thank you."

Simonetta poured two cups of coffee and placed one on the little table next to Lucia with a small jug of milk, "the English way?"

Lucia smiled and thanked her. "Is there anything that has happened since I saw you yesterday?"

"Well yes, Chiara had a call from Luisa Martinelli to tell her that her husband had died that morning and then, this morning, Antonio called to say he would do the interview as he knows the collection well and should be able answer most of my questions."

"Oh dear, will you do it?"

"I think so. I haven't really had time to think about

it."

"I'm sure it will all become clear at the right time."

Lucia drank her coffee and looked quizzically at Simonetta, wondering what she meant.

With the coffee finished Simonetta guided Lucia through the same process to take her back to where she had left off the previous day.

"How long did you stay with the family?" Simonetta prompted her.

'I'm not sure. I think two winters. There is a man. He comes to the house sometimes to help Alfonso. He looks at me strangely. I tell Livia and she says she thinks maybe he's a bit simple. I'm not so sure. He doesn't say anything but he frightens me and I stay close to Livia when he's there. The days pass and gradually I accept my new life away from the city and everything I know. My old life seems wiped out by the fear of the night I fled Florence. The men who were looking for me have not returned and I pray I am forgotten.

Sometimes Alfonso takes me to market with him. Not as far as the city but to the local village where they do not know me. I don't think Alfonso and Livia know why the men are looking for me but I think they do know the difference between good and bad and they see my innocence. I'm not able to talk to them about it. Maybe I'm scared they'll change their minds about me if they know too much so I keep quiet. I miss saying prayers with my parents and neighbours. It's hard to do it here as the house is very small with little or no privacy so I say them in my head.

I'm not sure how old I am now, maybe fourteen or fifteen. My body is changing and I have my monthly bleedings.

When I go to the market with Alfonso he likes to go to the cantina and speak with the other men. While I wait for him I meet other young people my age. There's Isabetta and her brother Gianni. Their father is a woodsman like Alfonso and they share their stories while we share our dreams for a better future. They also bring me news from the city where they sometimes go with their father. I don't tell them about my past or who I really am but it is good to hear them talk about familiar places and I sometimes have to bite my tongue for fear of giving myself away in my desire to be included. I think Gianni likes me in a different way to Isabetta. He smiles at me a lot and I have to look away to hide my blushes."

"*Dimme,* tell me," says Simonetta wanting to move Lucia's remembering forward, "why do you leave Livia and Alfonso's home?"

'*Eh, I get married. To Gianni. We live with his family now. We have a daughter Sylvana, it means from the forest, and we are happy. I miss Livia and Alfonso but when she can, Livia comes to market with Alfonso so she can see me.*

Then one day Livia arrives looking very upset. She tells me the men from Florence have been to her house again asking about me. She told them she didn't know where I was but she thinks they didn't believe her. She says they seemed to know more about me than they did before and she can't understand why they didn't believe her. Immediately I see the face of the man who helps Alfonso in my mind's eye. I don't say anything as I don't understand what it means. Livia is very worried for me. She says the men seemed angry and urgent to find me. I'm sure they won't find me where I am. How could they?

Two days later I hear news that these men have been seen in the village asking about a young girl. I pray hard that no-one will think of me as I'm now a wife and mother. Gianni knows nothing of my story and thinks that I am the daughter of Livia and Alfonso. I don't like being dishonest as it is against my beliefs but I am scared and maybe a little ashamed though I'm not sure why.

A week passes and I think it is safe once again and I go to the market with Gianni. At first I feel nervous but everything seems normal and I begin to relax. Gianni goes to the cantina and I sit with Isabetta in the piazza. She is also married and expecting a baby so we have lots to talk about. Suddenly I feel a chill rush down my spine and as I look across the piazza towards the cantina I see the man who had been helping Alfonso. I turn away and try to hide my face but I know it is too late, he has seen me. Thoughts race through my mind. Could it have been him that denounced me? Why would he do that? Who is he? Why did he go to work with Alfonso?

I try to act normal as I leave Isabetta and take a long route back to our cart hoping that I'm not followed. I'm scared, not just for myself but also for Sylvana and Gianni. I don't know what to do. What if they find me, what will happen to Sylvana? And Gianni? I can't put them in danger.

I can't sleep so I begin to form a plan. I know Sylvana will be safe with Gianni and his family and I decide the only thing I can do is to leave. I've heard there is a travelling fair coming to the village in a day or two. Maybe I could find a way to hide with them. I feel torn apart at the thought of leaving Sylvana and Gianni and my new life but I can't take the risk. I don't understand why these men are looking for me but I know that I don't want them to find me. I shiver at the thought of what might happen to me if they do.

It's difficult to get away. My daily life is so entwined with others. Two days pass and I become more and more anxious. If I wait until I go to market with Gianni, will it be too late? I will have to find another way. I don't know how I will survive but I have a few coins and a necklace that belonged to my mother and I carry these with me all the time.

My chance comes when I am working in the field near the road. A cart passes by. I can see there's a man, a woman and young child. The man stops the cart and asks for directions to the village. They are going to the fair. I offer to show them the way if they take me with them. I jump on to the cart. They say they've come from further south, near Orvieto.

There is something familiar about them though I don't know what it is. They ask me where I'm going and I say I'm also going to the fair. They tell me their names are Luigi and Rosa and the little girl is Rosella. They say they are going to visit a cousin who lives near Florence, then they heard about the fair and thought they would stop on the way. It has been a difficult journey from Orvieto in the heat. They ask about me and my life and I lie. Again, I am forced to do something that makes my very soul ache. I say that I'm alone and working my way north and thought that maybe I could find a way to travel with the fair. I notice that every now and then they exchange knowing looks *and I begin to feel scared. They seem to sense this and try to reassure me that they do not intend to cause me any harm. They say they see goodness in me and if they can help me they will. In some ways they remind me of my parents and I feel sad at the thought.*

I see them look at each other again and this time the man gives an almost imperceptible nod. Rosa asks about my parents and before I can think of another lie I tell her they are dead. Luigi pulls the reins and directs the cart to the shade of an oak tree. Rosa looks at me with kind eyes and again I feel a familiarity. She asks where my family came from and, again, I find I have to be honest and tell her they were from Florence. She sighs with a heavy knowing.

I'm not able to pretend anymore and I start to cry and then sob. Rosa puts her arm around me and she helps me to tell her what happened in Florence and how I came to be here.

When I finish I am exhausted and feel empty. Luigi and Rosella are silent throughout the telling. I'm confused. Have I done wrong by speaking the truth?

Rosa takes my hands in hers and tells me she understands and that I do not need to be afraid. She then tells me their story of how they had to flee Orvieto. She explains about the Inquisition and their obsession with killing all those whom they believe to be guilty of something they call heresy. She says her cousin had written warning them of what was happening in Florence and advising them to leave Orvieto before it was too late. She looks at Luigi and again he gives the slightest nod. She then tells me that I can travel with them if I would like to and that we can go to the fair and then to her cousin's home. I'm unable to speak and nod over and over again. Rosa takes out some bread, cheese and some fruit and we eat before we set off again.'

Simonetta spoke a few gentle words to bring Lucia back to the present. Let us stop here for today. I think it is almost time for lunch – you will stay and join me?"

Lucia gathered herself and is surprised how quickly she is able to change from one time to another. "Yes, thank you."

"*Bene.* First, please drink some water; then we can go to the *cucina* and see what there is to eat."

The kitchen was a large room with a central table. Simonetta produced antipasti, salads, bread and cheeses. "I have fresh fruit juice, will that be alright?"

Lucia nodded. "Thank you, it looks wonderful."

"*Eh,* it is a very simple lunch and what you need at this moment, I think."

Lucia smiled, "Yes, you're right."

"*Allora*, do you remember what happened this morning?"

"Yes, I think so …., well, most of it."

"Good." Simonetta swept an open hand across the table indicating that Lucia should help herself. "I think I am beginning to understand your story. Do you know anything about the Cathars?"

"Er, I don't think so," and she frowned as she searched her memory.

"What about heretics and the Inquisition?"

"Well, yes. I remember Gallileo was held as a heretic for believing Copernicus' theory that the sun was the centre of the universe."

"Yes, that was later. The Cathars were persecuted as heretics by the Inquisition in the 13th and 14th centuries. Most people think of them in relation to France but there were large Cathar communities here in Italy. They were Christians who did not follow the doctrine set by the Catholic Church. Their beliefs were rooted in the earlier church which they believed was a more pure form of Christianity. Whilst they did not have priests they did have elders whom they called *parfaits* or perfects.

For a long time the Cathars were accepted in Italy and came from all strata of society. However, much depended on the politics of the day and as these changed so did the tolerance of beliefs that did not comply with the doctrine set down by Rome.

Eventually the Inquisition hunted down all the Cathars, intent on wiping out the bloodline."

Lucia listened intently to Simonetta's words as they stirred a knowing deep within her. "And you think this is what happened to Marinella's parents? But, what has this to do with my dream?"

"Yes. I think there is more to unfold yet. And your dream, I think is, *come si dice,* how do you say, symbolic, a metaphor. It comes in a way you will recognise and come to understand."

"So, why me? Why did, do I hear and see things? And now …."

Simonetta smiled, "Simply, it is time. I think we need to make one more journey, if you are willing, and you will have some answers."

"Yes, yes. When?" Lucia said eager to find resolution.

"Well, I think you have done enough for today. I'm

busy tomorrow and you have the interview on Thursday, how about Friday morning?"

"That's fine with me," Lucia agreed feeling a little deflated that she would have to wait until Friday.

As if reading her mind, Simonetta said, "Do not worry. It will be good for you to have a day of leisure. If something should happen that worries you, just give me a call. Now, would you like coffee?"

"Thank you, yes."

Simonetta looked directly at Lucia before saying, "You know, you are doing very well. You are at the beginning of an exciting journey. I know how hard it can be. The curiosity is strong but please, be patient, *piano, piano,* one step at a time, *no*?"

Lucia felt the warmth of her words touch her anxiety and she smiled and said, "thank you."

"We can talk more on Friday. Now, shall we call Tom, he is taking you home, *no*?"

"Er, yes," said Lucia, taken back a little and wondered how Simonetta knew her plans.

As Simonetta dialled Tom's number, she reminded Lucia, "Remember, if you have any worries or something should happen and you need to talk about it, please call me. You have my mobile if it is urgent….., Ah, Tom, *buona sera* ….. *si, si* …… *grazie… ciao, ciao.* He's on his way."

After hellos, hugs, kisses and goodbyes, Tom and Lucia left Simonetta and Florence and drove south into the heat of the afternoon sun.

Tom didn't want to press Lucia with his curiosity and therefore didn't ask any questions about her morning with Simonetta.

Lucia felt more relaxed after Simonetta's encouraging words though was a little apprehensive about what she should say to Tom. He hadn't mentioned anything about her visit but she felt compelled to say something. Aware of a tension building within, she turned to Tom and said, "Thank you for driving me, Tom, and for not asking about this morning. I think it went well. Simonetta thinks I need to go once more so I'll see her again on Friday."

"Niente," he smiled, "there's no pressure. If you want to talk about it, I'm here, and if not, that's also ok."

Lucia felt the tension dissolve and she thought how lucky she was to have Tom as a friend.

"I was wondering, do you have any plans for the rest of the day because if not, and you have a swimsuit we could go to a *terme* not far from here and maybe have an early supper after."

"Oh, well, yes I have – a swimsuit, I mean," she replied, a little surprised, "and, no, I don't have plans though I'll have to pick up the swimsuit and let Chiara know."

"Great. Let's do it. We're almost at Chiara's now."

Tom pulled off the main road and five minutes later parked in the courtyard while Lucia went into the villa to collect her swimsuit and a towel. She met Chiara in the kitchen as she was leaving and explained their plans.

"Bene." Chiara said with emphasis and a knowing look.

"What?" Lucia exclaimed indignantly.

"Nothing," Chiara replied with an innocent shrug of her shoulders. "See you later. Have you all you need?"

Lucia looked at her aunt and raised one eyebrow. "Yes, I think so. *Ciao.*" And ran down the steps to the car where Tom was patiently waiting.

He headed south towards the A1, the '*Autostrada del Sole*', motorway of the sun.

"Where is the *terme*?" asked Lucia.

"Oh, it's not far from Siena. I thought maybe you have been before, with Chiara perhaps?"

"I don't think so. Is it far?"

"About an hour, but worth it, I promise."

"I believe you."

They left the motorway and drove across country to another and after a short distance they turned off into a small town. Lucia noticed how the landscape had changed to soft undulations and Tom told her this area was known as Le Crete. It felt open and boundless, less inhabited. Once through the town they took a narrow, dusty road that after a while became bumpy and tree lined before finally opening to reveal a hotel. Tom drove round to the car park where a new stone building sparkled in the sun.

Once inside they went into their separate changing rooms after arranging to meet by the bar. Lucia changed and put her belongings in a locker taking only her towel and flip flops. As she caught her reflection in the mirror she realised how vulnerable she felt, undressed as it were, in front of Tom and wondered why she had agreed to come. She instantly dismissed the thought as stupid and wondered what was wrong with her thinking.

Tom was already waiting in the bar wearing trunks

and a towel that he'd thrown over one shoulder. Lucia tried to avoid looking at his tanned and toned body as she berated herself for the conflicting feelings that ran through her.

As Tom saw her approach he caught his breath and quickly contained his feelings as he accompanied her down the steps to the lower pool where they each spread their towel on a sun lounger.

"Shall we?" Tom asked opening his arm in the direction of the pale luminescent water.

"Oh yes," responded Lucia as she left her flip flops at the pool's edge and eased herself down the steps into the warm aquamarine liquid. She pushed out towards the centre of the pool grateful that there were not too many people to share it. Bathed by the warmth of the sun's rays and the thermal water, she floated on her back and surrendered to the moment. Tom joined her then disappeared underwater. He surfaced with a handful of a white substance.

"What is it?" frowned Lucia, wrinkling her nose at the smell.

"Sulphur and calcium carbonate, I believe. Apparently good for the skin, oh and respiratory problems – here," and he offered his hand to her.

"Er, what do I do with it?"

"Oh, just rub it all over!" he teased and dived underwater in search of more. He returned with another handful and rubbed it over his arms. Lucia did the same and laughed as she saw other people in the pool looking as if they were covered in white chalk.

She went underwater in search of her own supply and surfaced in front of Tom. The reflected light from the water gave his green eyes a luminous glow and she was once again aware of feelings she had long forgotten. She swam away in search of time and distance from her own memories and what was awakening within her. As if I don't have enough going on, she thought and she swam to the far side of the pool. She rested her chin on her arms at the pool's edge and looked across the rolling landscape. Tom joined her.

"It's beautiful, isn't it?" he said.

"Yes, it is. How did you find this place?" she replied, still looking at the view.

"I think it was Simonetta who first told me of it and I know Chiara sometimes comes here. There have been a lot of improvements in the last few years. Before there was just the small pool by the hotel then they excavated the three pools that are here now and added the bar and restaurant. Would you like something to drink, a juice or an English pot of tea," he teased.

Disarmed, Lucia yielded a little, "Juice would be great, thanks."

Tom swam in the direction of the bar and she pushed off to lie back in the soothing water and contemplate the unsettling emotions she would prefer to ignore. So much had changed in her life in such a short time; from order to chaos. She thought she had found some support in Simonetta but was not prepared for the feelings facing her with Tom. She paddled her way back to the steps and as she saw Tom walking towards her with their drinks she felt an unwanted excitement radiate through her.

As she stepped out of the pool Tom also struggled to deal with his own dilemma. It had been a long time since a woman had stirred him in this way and he felt he was standing in the middle of a minefield. His mind raced through an exploration of the situation. She was only here for a few days and he had already maintained an emotional distance so as to gain her trust and support her through an experience he understood well. Before he could follow his thoughts further she met him by the sun loungers and wrapped herself in one of the towels.

She sat down and took her drink from him. "Thank you," she smiled, "this place is amazing. Thanks for bringing me here, Tom."

"It's a pleasure," and he relaxed on the adjoining sun lounger. He watched as she arranged her towel and lay back allowing the sun to dry any remaining water droplets covering her body. He couldn't remember when he had last felt so inhibited and cleared his throat hoping it would also clear his frustration at his inability to speak. He reached for his drink and his eyes searched the horizon for relief and inspiration.

Momentarily oblivious to his inner turmoil, Lucia closed her eyes and allowed the sun's rays to warm her skin. His cough and movement disturbed her and she raised her arm to shield her eyes as she squinted in his direction. She felt a tension that she claimed as her own as unspoken words filled her mouth.

It was Tom who managed to speak first. "Sorry, it must have gone down the wrong way," he explained, blaming the drink and seeking a way to diffuse the near palpable energy that sat between them. He remembered how each person is so much more than is visible and within their aura exists their past, present and future, and was aware of an unheard conversation taking place. He finished his juice, rolled over on to his stomach and rested his head on folded arms turning to look towards

Lucia. "Tell me more about what it is like living in London, " he asked hoping to find some neutral, safe ground.

"Er, well ... I suppose it's much like Florence or any city – noisy, dirty, full of tourists and yet, at the same time, it can be vibrant, exciting and inspiring." She said adjusting the lounger to a slightly more upright position. "I'm fortunate, I live in a quiet area that's fairly central."

"And your family? You live alone?" he ventured.

"My mother lives in the country, she hates London, more so I think since my father died. My brother lives in London and my sister is backpacking somewhere in Australia."

"I'm sorry, is it long since your father died?"

"Almost three years." She paused and added, "I don't think my mother is happy on her own. I imagine it is difficult for her not having someone to care for now that he's gone and we've all left home."

"Do you visit her?"

"I used to, but since ….., er, not really, my work is, well, demanding."

Tom, aware of her hesitation, said, "Forgive me, I didn't mean to pry ….. "

"No, no, you're not. It's just that …., I haven't spoken about it to anyone other than my brother and then I suppose I was selective in what I told him."

He watched her, wanting her to continue but hesitant in pursuit for fear of her retreating.

Her brow creased and looking up into the depth of those green eyes she came to a decision she had avoided for a long time. She adjusted the back of the lounger to an almost sitting position and held her drink in both hands.

"A few years ago, I was in love – with a man, Ben and with life, a life we had planned together. We met while I was at university and saw each other whenever we could, which was most weekends. He was a couple of years older and had finished his studies before me. He worked in London and when I got a job at Christies we moved in together." She paused, took a sip of juice and returned the glass to the same position between her hands. She looked up to glance at Tom then refocused on the glass.

"We were the happy, successful couple or so I thought. We worked hard and enjoyed life – you know, friends, a great social life, holidays, all those things. We had plans. Maybe move out of London, start a family. I thought we would always be ...., grow old together. Then one day, without warning, he said that it wasn't what he wanted any more. He told me there was no-one else though I've always found that difficult to believe. Within a month he'd moved out and gone to America – new job, house, the lot."

"What did you do?"

"At first I lost myself in work; I was devastated and I suppose didn't want to feel the pain. My time at Christies had enabled me to meet a lot of interesting and influential people in the art world and somehow I slid into the work I do now. So, for the last three years I've travelled and written about a lot of art."

"And now?"

"I don't know, Tom," and she slowly raised her eyes from her glass to the horizon. "Since accepting this assignment ... I ...I... don't know." She sighed, turning her face to look at him. "You know the rest."

"Yes, I suppose I do. I think … I hope you are now finding the healing you need. Distance can sometimes offer new perspectives." He said with a gentleness that she found equally reassuring and disturbing.

"Another swim before supper?" and he was already on his feet and heading towards the pool. "Coming?" he added, turning in her direction.

Lucia accepted the invitation, jumped up and followed him to the steps where she lowered herself into the warmth of the water. They swam the length of the pool to a crescent shaped corner that gave way to a view of the rolling green hills of Le Crete broken only by a faded terracotta villa and a line of cypress trees.

More people were arriving for their evening submersion in the healing waters. Momentarily she wished this moment could extend into forever where she felt safe distanced from the vagaries of what had become her life.

Tom, on the other hand, was attempting to deal with rising emotions that, while not inappropriate were, he thought, untimely.

They each gave in to the balmy water, floating, turning and absorbing the beauty of the Tuscan landscape, and the moment. Each lost in their own thoughts not realising how similar they were. As the pool became more crowded Tom suggested that maybe it was time leave and find somewhere to eat. Reluctantly Lucia swam to the far edge of the pool and climbed out, each step returning her to the reality she had managed, for a brief time, to escape.

Clean and refreshed they once again met in the bar. Tom was sitting in an armchair by the window when Lucia walked in.

"I hope I didn't keep you waiting," she said.

He stood up and, again, felt his breath tighten in his chest as he found some words. "No, no, I'd only just sat down …." He managed to swallow the words that followed his thoughts that it was worth the wait. "I was thinking that we could eat somewhere nearer home if you're not starving that is? Or …" In the silence of his mind his dream would have been to enjoy a leisurely dinner at the hotel restaurant after which they would spend the night making tender and passionate love in one of the hotel bedrooms.

"Yes, that's ok with me."

Her words caught Tom from his reverie unsure, at first, to what she was agreeing. "*Va bene,* shall we go?"

The evening air was warm as they drove back towards Florence. Their conversation was light as they each commented on the changing landscape. Tom shared stories of places he knew as they passed them; the festa at Petraviva – a friend lived there, wonderful olive oil from an estate here, a good friend with a vineyard there. Each area and town had something to offer, a famous artist, architect, history.

In less than an hour they were leaving the Valdarno and nearing the outskirts of Florence. Tom turned off the main road towards Bagno a Ripoli, not far from Chiara's home, and was soon driving through high gates into the car park of the restaurant.

"It's a bit rustic but the food is excellent and typically Tuscan."

"Great, I've just realised how hungry I am." Lucia said.

The restaurant was busy. They were seated in a

corner by the owner who greeted Tom with great enthusiasm. A waiter brought warm bread, olives and a carafe of water and they ordered wine while they perused the menus. Tom suggested the *ravioli di spinaci e ricotta al burro di salvia* followed by *trippa alla fiorentina*. Lucia, overwhelmed by the choice, surrendered to his recommendations.

"You've been here before?" she asked.

"Er, yes – a few times," he grinned.

By the time the wine arrived Lucia felt emptied and tired; not in an unpleasant way, more a relaxed and comfortable end of the day feeling. Yawning, she apologised, "It's been a long day."

"*Davvero*, indeed." Tom said, lapsing into Italian.

They picked at the bread and the olives, and Lucia was the first to break the silence. "The other day you said you had travelled a lot – where did you go?"

"Erm … well, I spent some time in Australia then I moved on to India, Japan, and Indonesia before returning to Europe."

"What took you there?" she asked as the first course arrived and was placed in front of them. They both eagerly accepted the parmesan that was offered and fell silent as they took their first mouthful.

"Oh, this is wonderful," purred Lucia, "the pasta is so …, er…., it's so light and thin, and the sauce …."

"Mmm, it's all made here, by hand. It is good."

"It's so different to what we get in England – it's like silk."

Silence once again took over as they ate. When they had finished Tom relaxed back into his chair, "Now, you were asking? Oh yes, my travels." He wondered how much he should reveal of that part of his history and decided to let it unfold as he spoke. "Well, I suppose it all started as a means of escape as these things often do." He smiled, thinking that this was the first time he had actually spoken of this to anyone other than Simonetta and felt an unexpected lightness as he began.

"I'd just finished university and was ready to enter the commercial world. I had to decide whether to stay in Italy or look elsewhere. My girlfriend had also just finished her studies and was facing the same dilemma. We'd been together since school and planned to settle somewhere, marry, raise a family, all the usual things that couples do. Anyway, it wasn't meant to be. Before we could come to any decisions Maria became ill and was diagnosed with a brain tumour. It all happened so quickly and within two months she'd gone. She had the best medical care but there was nothing they could do."

Tom continued with an ease that surprised him. "At first I was numb, then distraught and then angry. I felt as if my whole world had collapsed and any faith I had in a God I thought may have existed, vanished. I became unbearable. I drank too much, did drugs, all to escape the pain. I went to one psychic after another in hope of a message, a word from Maria that would make sense of what had happened. I thought I saw her everywhere but never long enough for me to speak to her.

Then I started to have these dreams, not just about her but other people that I didn't know. Eventually, my parents thought it would be a good idea if I visited an uncle in Australia. I went along with it as I just wanted to be far away from any memories of my life with

Maria."

Tom paused and Lucia realised she was not breathing.

"They were right, of course, my parents. It took time. My uncle and his family lived on a farm near Melbourne and I found working on the land therapeutic."

The next course arrived creating a natural interval before he carried on and Lucia absorbed each word.

"They didn't push me or rush me, just introduced me to people they thought could help. One of them was a native elder who suggested I go walkabout. He said that because of my experiences my soul was sick; that was why I was having the visions and dreams. I wasn't sure at first. I'd stopped the drugs but was still drinking though not as much and I didn't fancy the idea of no alcohol at all, let alone me as my only companion. I went to stay with Martin, the elder, for two weeks to prepare for my walkabout. I won't go into that only to say that it was a tough two weeks and there were times when I thought I couldn't take any more. Mind you, it was nothing to what I experienced in the bush and I was really thankful he'd been so hard on me. I was out there for twenty-one days and when I came back my whole perspective on life had changed. My understanding of life and death was completely different and I had come to a kind of acceptance about what had happened to Maria although I still had a long way to go.

I stayed on at the farm for a few months. My uncle needed help and paid me the same as the other workers so I was able to get some money together. I still visited Martin and he continued to teach me the ways of his ancestors. I then became curious about other cultures and decided to go to India and I spent the next few years travelling, working and learning. From India I went to Thailand then Japan. I met some wonderful people, studied with amazing teachers until one day I knew I had to come home."

"And the dreams?"

"They stopped when I was in the bush."

A comfortable silence fell between them as they finished their meal. Lucia looked at Tom thoughtfully before speaking.

"Thank you, Tom. I really appreciate you telling me."

"I hope it helps. I believe we all have our own journey and we often touch each other in unexpected ways."

"Yes, I think I see what you mean." She hesitated before asking, "Do you think my dreams will stop?"

"I think you are well on the way to healing whatever is creating them, so yes, it is likely they will." He smiled wishing he could do or say more and at the same time knowing that was not yet possible.

"Mmm ..., I think seeing Simonetta has been, is, a great help. It's odd though, I don't feel I can talk about it yet. It's sort of incomplete, not ready."

Tom remembered how long it had taken him to be able to speak about his journey and knew he must let her find her own way and timings if it was going to be of any value to her. "I'm sure you'll know when the time is right," he said in an attempt to reassure her.

"Yes, I imagine so," she shrugged and suddenly wondered how long she would be able to resist the urge to dissolve under his calm gaze. An unaccustomed feeling of warmth rose up through her body and before it could reach her face and be read in the blush of her cheeks, she excused herself from the table.

She looked at her reflection in the mirror questioning what her body was telling her. 'I'm so-o-o not ready for this,' she thought. Then immediately berated herself for thinking that he could possibly be interested in her. As she looked into her eyes she knew from somewhere deep within that was not true and just as she was about to turn away she heard a voice say, 'when the time is right.'

She looked around the room and she was alone. 'What do you mean?' she asked with her mind.

'You will know.'

'But …' she stopped knowing the conversation had come to an end. Feeling a little disconcerted by the exchange, she washed her hands and smoothed her hair before returning to the table.

"Coffee?" Tom offered.

"No thanks, but you have one."

"No, let's go," and he signalled to the waiter for the bill, mindful that she must be tired.

Outside the temperature had dropped and Lucia was pleased it was not far to Chiara's. They were there in less than ten minutes having spent that time quietly embraced by their own thoughts. Tom parked the car so that it was facing the view towards Florence. They sat for a few minutes each wondering how to end the evening.

Finally, Lucia broke the silence, half turning towards him. "Thank you so much, Tom. It was just what I needed."

"*É un piacere.* It's a pleasure," he said, again lapsing into Italian. He pulled himself from his desire to be with her and opened the car door.

"Maybe we can do it again before you return to London," he said before he got out of the car and walked round to open her door.

"Yes, I'd like that," she replied as she stepped out of the car carefully avoiding physical contact with him. Then she reached up on tiptoe and kissed his cheek as she said, "*Buona notte* and thank you again."

"*Buona notte*," he responded and had to control himself from taking her in his arms. "If you need anything, just give me a call." And he returned to the driving seat and waved to her as she turned to see him leave.

"Ah, *cara*, you have a nice evening?" Chiara greeted her from the *cucina*. "Would you like a *tisana* or something?"

"Er, maybe I will take a *tisana* to bed with me. I'm so tired and we have the funeral tomorrow." Lucia said not wanting to recount the day.

"*Va bene, camomilla?*"

"*Si, grazie.* I'm so tired," she said as she fell onto the sofa.

"Where did you go?" Chiara ventured.

"Erm …, oh, a wonderful *terme* …, it was amazing. The water, the views …., everything." She enthused. "Then we went to a restaurant not far from here. Great food. And I had tripe! Er, *trippa fiorentina*. You remember *mamma* would never cook it and I certainly thought I would never eat it, but I loved it!"

"Ah yes, I think I know the place you mean, you go through big gates …"

"Yes, that's it."

"*Si,* the food is very good, typically Tuscan. Here the *tisana* is ready."

"Oh, thank you. Will you forgive me if I take it upstairs? We can talk tomorrow. What time must we leave for the funeral?"

WEDNESDAY
Mercoledi

As Antonio woke he already wished the day was over. He rolled from his bed and staggered into the shower. Once showered and shaved, he dressed in his darkest suit then went down to the *cucina* for breakfast.

His mother was already there, elegant and austere in a black dress. He gravitated to the smell of freshly brewed coffee and poured what would become the first cup of many. He took a pastry from the table and went to sit outside where an overcast sky reflected his grey mood.

He sensed his mother's edginess as she came to join him and he tried to prepare himself for what she might ask of him. He had already made a promise to himself that he would not get involved in any family wrangling that concerned his late father's estate. It was clear after Signor Conti's visit the previous evening that Giacomo's financial affairs were anything but straightforward. Surprisingly he had pre-empted his younger son's spendthrift ways and safeguarded his precious art collection by donating it to the City of Florence. However, there was still the villa and other assets to be divided and whilst he had no worries for his mother's financial well-being, he was concerned for her emotional welfare. He wished this could all be behind him and dealt with rather than lurking in the future, yet to be approached.

"More coffee?" his mother asked as she placed the pot on the table.

"*Grazie mamma, come stai?*"

"*Bene*," she shrugged. "Any news of Lorenzo?"

"*No mamma*, I've left messages."

"Mmmmm …" was all she said.

Antonio prayed for strength to see him through what he anticipated would be a long and potentially tortuous day. His mother was already highly wired behind a fragile and brittle façade. Distraught by Giacomo's sudden demise, she now had to maintain her dignity throughout the day. Whilst he believed she was strong enough to carry this off, he was not convinced she would survive Lorenzo's absence.

People began to arrive shortly before eleven. The chapel adjoined the villa and Giacomo lie there in an open coffin awaiting everyone's last respects. Luisa had put on a black silk jacket and watched from the terrace as friends and family, colleagues and business associates filed into the small chapel. Antonio joined his mother.

"We should go."

"I know," she said in resignation.

Antonio took her arm and they walked together down the terrace steps and towards the chapel. As they reached the door a rush of air presented a breathless Lorenzo who took his mother's other arm.

"I was looking for you in the house and ......"

"*Eh,* you're here. Let us go in."

Lucia and Chiara sat at the back of the chapel. Lucia turned as Luisa and her two sons entered. Antonio, seeing her, acknowledged her with a nod and a half smile. She couldn't quite see the man the other side of Luisa until he took a step forward at which point her blood ran cold. She felt as if every ounce of energy had drained from her into the earth. She felt dizzy, nauseous, disorientated and confused all at once. Her vision blurred and the tightness in her chest made it hard to breathe.

Chiara noticed her blanched face and trembling hands.

"What is it, *cara*?" she whispered, covering Lucia's hands with her own. "*Dio,* you're frozen!"

Lucia sat rigid unable to move or speak. Then a shaft of sunlight entered the window high above the altar and shone along the aisle towards her. She felt its warmth and was aware of being uplifted from the terror that had taken hold of her.

"All is well, there is nothing to fear now," said a voice so pure and gentle its beauty was almost unbearable.

Still Lucia was unable to move. Chiara saw a change in her expression and felt a warmth now radiating from the hands she continued to hold.

"Lucia, *cara,*" she prompted.

She turned her head slowly towards Chiara and looked at her through empty eyes. Unsure as to what was actually happening to her niece, Chiara decided it would be best to take her outside, away from whatever it was that was disturbing her so deeply.

People were now forming a line to the coffin to pay their last respects and Chiara hoped they would be able to slip out unnoticed.

"Can you stand?"

Lucia continued to look at her from vacant eyes. She supported her by the elbow hoping she would be able to get her on her feet. It worked and although she was only able to move her very slowly she managed to lead her across the short distance to the door. Once outside she encouraged Lucia towards a bench where she sat expressionless seemingly unaware of her surroundings.

Chiara considered what to do, hoping she just needed a few minutes in the fresh air and she would then be able to tell her what had happened. She sat next to her waiting for a sign that she was returning to normal but none came. Deciding she did not want to still be here when the procession left the chapel for the mausoleum, she again took Lucia by the elbow and directed her to the car which fortunately was only a few yards away.

They drove back to the villa in silence. As soon as she parked the car she called Tom. He said he would be there in twenty minutes.

She sat in the car next to her niece wondering how she could pierce the veil of whatever bound her. Taking her mind back to the chapel she searched for a clue, anything that could explain Lucia's condition. *Niente*, nothing.

Tyres scrunching the gravel announced Tom's

arrival and Chiara realised she had not moved since she had called him and neither had Lucia. She got out of the car to greet him and explain. Tom opened the passenger door of Chiara's car and knelt down by Lucia. After several attempts to communicate with her he put one arm under her knees and the other under her arms and eased her from the car. He then carried her up the steps and Chiara unlocked the door to let him in. He gently lowered her on to the sofa while Chiara searched her remedies for something that may help.

"What happened?"

"I don't know. We were sitting in the chapel when I felt a change take place. She was so pale and when I touched her hands they were like ice. When I spoke to her she just stared at me ...., I don't know, Tom ....., I've searched my mind but I can't think of anything unusual ... The chapel was almost full and Luisa had just come in with her two sons ..."

Something disturbed Tom. "Did Lucia see them?"

"I don't know, I wasn't really paying attention."

"Don't worry, Chiara. I think something has triggered a memory and she is in deep shock. Let's keep her warm and, did you find a remedy?"

"Yes, *ecco*, here." She released a few drops from the small bottle into a glass of water and handed it to Tom.

He eased Lucia into a sitting position and held the glass to her mouth gently encouraging her to drink. Whilst she obliged and swallowed a little of the water, her eyes remained impassive. Once he was satisfied she had taken enough of the remedy he lowered her again on to the sofa, pulling a soft blanket over her.

"I think we should let her rest for a while and allow

the remedy to take effect. What do you think, Chiara?"

"*Si, si* ……, I wish I could remember what could have happened then …."

"Chiara, this is not your fault. I'm sure she'll be fine, she just needs time. Come, how about some coffee?"

"Of course," she replied and absentmindedly filled the little coffee pot and put it on the stove as she searched her memory for any remnant of a clue.

They sat at the table and Chiara again recounted the morning to Tom hoping to find what had caused Lucia to react so dramatically. Lucia lay on the sofa with her eyes closed. Tom listened intently but, like Chiara, could see nothing unusual in the events she described.

"*Eh,* it's after one, maybe we should eat something?" said Chiara feeling the need to do something useful. "I can do some pasta?"

"*Grazie,* that would be great." Tom smiled for the first time since his arrival.

Chiara put some olive oil in a pan, peeled a couple of cloves of garlic, added them to the oil and heated the pan over a gentle heat. Once the garlic was soft she removed it from the pan and added tomatoes. She picked some basil leaves from a plant on the window sill and chopped them ready to add to the sauce.

"Oh ….."

Both Tom and Chiara turned in unison to see Lucia try to sit up.

"Er …, what happened …. I …, I…"

"It's ok."

"*Cara…*"

"How did I get here?"

They all spoke at once. Tom took her hand as Chiara put her hand on her forehead.

Tom spoke in a soft voice as he explained that she seemed to have had a shock.

Relieved to see Lucia sitting and talking, Chiara went to check on her sauce and put on the pasta. She left Tom to deal with the explanations so she could finish what she imagined would be a much needed lunch.

Tom gently massaged her hands as he talked her through the morning's events.

"I ..., er ...., I don't really remember. I was in the chapel and then ...., well, then everything went black."

"Can you remember what happened just before?"

"Oh ..., I ..., no, I don't think so."

"Va bene, don't try to force it, you'll remember when you're ready. Right now, I think we should eat. It smells good, Chiara. Come, do you think you can stand?"

Lucia leaned on his shoulder and levered herself off the sofa. "Yes, thank you," she said with a smile. Tom stood and followed her to the table ready to catch her if she weakened but although a bit wobbly, she made it unaided.

"I'm so sorry to have caused so much trouble ...."

"Niente, it's nothing." Chiara and Tom chimed in unison.

"Cara, I'm just happy you are ok," Chiara said, "and Tom, thank you to you for coming so quickly."

Lucia sat down trying to orientate herself. Feeling weak and shaky still, she wondered what could have happened to incapacitate her in this way. She felt caught between realties; one she was trying hard to hold on to and the other was rapidly slipping away leaving only unanswered questions. She was aware of Tom and Chiara's attention and tried to smile reassuringly through a fog of disconnectedness.

Chiara served the pasta into bowls and offered grated parmesan. She hoped the remedy was helping Lucia return to the present and stay grounded in it. Like many Italians she also believed food was a great healer and encouraged Lucia to eat.

It all looked so enticing, the food, the smells, but Lucia experienced it in slow motion through a soft focus lens. Chiara and Tom spoke as normally as they could both hoping this would penetrate the layers of shock surrounding Lucia.

Gradually, the remedy effectively dissolved the veils and she gasped as clarity began to return.

"Aaah," she sighed on a deep out breath, and looked in turn at Chiara and Tom with a soft smile. "Mmm, I think I can eat now."

They ate in silence allowing Lucia to gain some strength. With her appetite satiated she looked up, this time with a wider smile.

"Thank you both for your patience. I still don't know what happened. It was as if I was suspended in a dream and couldn't find a way out."

"Don't worry, *cara*," Chiara reassured her. "I'm sure it will become clear."

"Was it like the dream you told me about?" Tom asked.

"Er, well …, yes, I suppose it was in a way. It was more the feeling of it. You know, that same feeling of inevitability …, that there's no escape."

"I wonder, maybe it would be a good idea to call Simonetta – she did say to call if anything happened, *no*?"

"Oh, I don't want to make a fuss and ...."

"I agree with Tom, maybe she can help."

"Oh, I don't know. Can I think about it for a little while?"

"Of course, *cara*."

"Of course, take your time."

At the Villa Martinelli food was also about to take centre stage as the guests returned from the internment of Giacomo in the family mausoleum.

Luisa maintained a sense of dignity and elegance throughout the whole proceedings and prepared herself to greet the mourners and accept more wishes of condolence. Antonio and Lorenzo stayed by her side and other extended family members hovered close by. It was the perfect picture and one of which Giacomo would have been proud, thought Luisa.

Friends recounted their memories, some laughed, some cried and it seemed to Luisa that Giacomo was, to her surprise, now remembered with some affection. Was memory really that selective she wondered?

Antonio, on the other hand, was wondering what had happened to Lucia. Not that it mattered to him but his curiosity would not leave him alone. He knew she had been in the chapel but when they turned to leave he could not see her anywhere. Neither could he understand why it bothered him so much. Since, he decided, there was nothing he could do about it, he joined his mother on the terrace.

"*Eh,* Antonio, you remember ……" and Luisa led her son into conversation with a couple he recognised as clients of his father.

The next hour or so passed in a similar vein until people began to leave. Luisa was showing signs of tiredness and Lorenzo, as always, was once again noticeable by his absence.

"*Mamma,* come, you should rest," Antonio suggested.

"*Si, si, si, ma ...,* but ….," she sighed, and surrendered by following him inside. "Will you stay? Tonight, that is."

"*Si mamma.*" Although it was the last thing he wanted to do, he didn't want his mother to be alone on this particular night. "And the English *signorina* is coming tomorrow morning to do the interview so I will already be here."

"Oh …., of course." Luisa's mind was already drifting to other matters. There was so much to do, to organise and yet, there was this emptiness, this chasm that she needed to cross. Even though she thought of herself as an independent woman, she was beginning to realise how much she had relied upon Giacomo and how much she would miss him. It was a sense of presence, she thought, and now it was an absence of presence: a light gone out in the world. She suddenly felt unexpectedly alone.

"*Mamma*?

"*Si, si, lo so* … I know." Luisa looked at her son, as if reading his mind, and placed her hand on his. "Don't worry, I will be fine. As for Lorenzo, well..... I understand your concern but, *eh* … it will all be fine."

Antonio hoped this was not the calm before a storm

and accepted her attempted reassurance with quiet resignation. "Why don't you lie down for a while?" he suggested.

"Mmm ...., I think I'll take a siesta," Luisa said, seeming not to have heard her son.

The sun's rays pierced through the clouds with the yellow, grey glow predictive of a brewing storm. Antonio remained on the terrace and poured a glass of wine. He was tired, physically and emotionally and wished the next 36 hours could already be in the past and his life returned to a more familiar state of equilibrium. He didn't know which was worse, his mother's manipulative nature or Lorenzo's unpredictability. Despite his mother's failings he knew her present needs were genuine, well most of them.

He sighed and wondered what she would do now that Giacomo had gone and he prayed the division of the estate would be without acrimony. He didn't doubt Lorenzo's capacity to dissipate his family's fortune; at least his father had had the foresight to preserve the art collection by donating it to the city even if it did mean his mother would have to rely more on her own means, which were in fact, considerable. So again, why the concern?

He drank his wine as he looked towards the darkening Florentine skyline, contemplating the rising disquiet he felt within.

Lucia sat alone on the terrace and looked towards a different view of Florence pondering whether or not to call Simonetta. Part of her wanted the whole thing to just go away and part of her knew she had to face it in order to understand whatever was happening. She could see the storm brewing in the chiaroscuro of the sky, reflective of the conflict she felt within.

Chiara and Tom waited patiently inside as they discussed some future landscaping to accommodate Chiara's ever-growing range of herbs.

Lucia stood in the doorway, and relenting said, "Ok, I'll call Simonetta." And she walked over to join them at the table.

Chiara covered her hand with her own saying, "*Cara,* I'm sure it's the right thing to do."

"I'm not sure …., I just don't know what else to do and, to be honest, I'm …, what happened today …., well, I'm scared." Lucia could feel tears welling up as she showed her vulnerability and quelled them with a deep breath.

Observing, Tom considered how he could best support her. "If you like, I'd be happy to take you."

"Oh, thank you, Tom. I don't know how long it will take though and I feel I've taken up so much of your time already."

He looked directly into her eyes as if to convince and reassure her, "Lucia, no worries, I'm happy to."

Aware of an almost palpable energy between them, Chiara began to clear the table.

Lucia made the call to Simonetta. It went to voicemail and she left a message. Disappointment and doubt seeped in as her courage ebbed.

Tom tried to catch her falling mood and before he could find the words Lucia's phone rang.

"Hello……." There were a few moments of silence as she listened to the caller, followed by, "Si, si. ……. *Va bene…… a presto …… ciao.*"

Chiara and Tom looked at Lucia expectantly.

"She said she'll be home in half an hour and I can go any time after that. Odd, she didn't ask why, she seemed to know."

"Yes, she has a habit of doing that. It can be a little disconcerting until you get used it." Tom said. "We can go whenever you're ready."

"Er …., ok, in about twenty minutes?" Lucia directed the words to Tom then looked over towards Chiara.

"That's fine, *cara*. I'll be here. I have some planting to do and I also need to spend some time with *mamma*."

Lucia walked over to her aunt and gave her a hug, "Thank you, thank you, for everything."

Chiara held her close and said, "*Niente*, I haven't done anything." Holding her at arm's length she looked into her eyes. "*Allora,* now let's get to the bottom of this and maybe take some more of the remedy before you go?"

Lucia nodded giving her a childlike smile. "Ok."

They arrived at Simonetta's just as the storm broke. Closing the door on torrential rain, Simonetta led the way to the study as the first crack of thunder echoed off the walls and lightning flashed high in the sky above.

"You can stay if you wish, Tom. It may be helpful, if you don't mind, Lucia? Otherwise, you can make yourself comfortable somewhere – you know your way around."

"No, of course, I don't mind," Lucia answered then immediately wondered if she had really understood what she was agreeing to.

Simonetta arranged for tea to be brought to the study and listened intently while Lucia described the morning's events as best she could.

"*Allora*, you have no memory of what triggered this reaction?"

"No. None at all."

"Mmm, I think I may have, but first let's take you to the part of your history that is relevant."

Lucia listened to Simonetta's instructions and soon forgot her self-consciousness at Tom's presence as she slipped back in time.

'*I'm at the fair. There are a lot of people. We stay close together. I'm frightened I'll lose Luigi, Rosa and Rosella in the crowd. Suddenly, Luigi stops. He turns to us and says we should stay calm, walk back to the cart and leave. My head whirls and I remember the night I fled from Florence. Rosa holds my hand and calms me as we make our way back to the road. Luigi doesn't look back until we are all safely on the cart. He tells us that he recognised one of the men and that he had seen him before in Orvieto. He believed him to be one of the inquisitors.*

I turned to look back, following the direction of Luigi's eyes, and I see a tall man dressed in black and I know I have also seen him in Florence. I think my heart will stop beating and Rosa rubs my back encouraging me to breathe.'

"Do you see this man again?" Simonetta asked. "Take your time – can you tell me when and where it is?" she encouraged.

'*I'm ... I'm not sure where I am. It's dark. I'm moving, ouch, I think I'm in a cart under a cover,* hidden. The cart stops. I can hear men talking and I recognise Luigi's voice though I can't hear the words. We're moving again. I hear Rosa's voice, she's telling me that we're almost out of the city; there's one more gate then I can come out.

It's very stuffy and I'm bruised by every bump. I pray we reach the gate soon. The cart has stopped so we must be at the gate now. Again there are muffled voices. I hold my breath and keep very still. We're moving again. I breathe again and wait for Luigi to tell me we're safe and I can come out.

The cart stops again, the cover is removed and the light is blinding. Luigi seems happy that we are safe and tells me we will head north. We climb into the hills and I hear horses approaching. As I turn round I see it is too late to hide. There are three men and one is calling for us to stop. The cart is too slow to outrun them and we have no choice.

No, no, no ....., it's the same man from the fair and this time I can see his face more clearly. I remember now, he was there when they took my parents. I'm so scared, I can't breathe.

They stop in front of us and he says that Luigi and his family can continue on their way that it is only me he is interested in. I know I can't endanger them any further and tell Luigi they must go. I thank him and Rosa and go to get down from the cart. Luigi and Rosa try to stop me and the man is shouting at us. I jump from the cart and one of the other riders whips Luigi's horse to move. I'm standing in the middle of the road and the man orders another rider to take me. He picks me up and throws me across his horse and we all ride off back towards Florence.

When they stop, they bind my hands and blindfold me. I ...,I ..., oh ....'

Lucia gasped.

"Take your time. Breathe, breathe deeply," soothes Simonetta. "It is better if you can tell me."

After a short pause and a few deep breaths, Lucia continues.

'The man, the Inquisitor, he believes I know of something or have something very valuable, a treasure. I know nothing of this. I'm no longer blindfolded and I can see his face more clearly. He has a cruel mouth and black beadlike eyes. He insists I tell him where the treasure is hidden, and hits me when I say I don't know. They do terrible things to me, I can't ....., please, no!'

"*Va bene*, it's alright." Simonetta soothed.

'There's pain ...... so much pain ...... and .... and ..... it all goes black.'

Simonetta gently brings Lucia back to the present as if singing a lullaby. Lucia blinks and opens her eyes. She looks around the room, at Tom and Simonetta, relocating herself from the shock of where she had been.

"I know him. I recognise him." she stated.

"And?" Simonetta prompted.

"I saw him today, in the chapel." Lucia fell forward holding her head in her hands, wanting it all to go away.

Simonetta was at her side holding a glass of water.

"Come, sip this. *Piano piano,* slowly." Her voice was soothing and calming and Lucia surrendered to her care.

For the second time that day, Lucia felt drained and empty, though this time was different in that she had some understanding of the cause.

Simonetta spoke, her voice quiet and even.

"I know the time you speak of and I also know of this Inquisitor. He has been many things in many lives, none of them good. It's as if his soul is searching in the darkest depths of experience ......, anyway, he turns up again. You say he is here, in the present. First, I wish you to understand that you have nothing to fear of him in this life, not now that he has been recognised. Secondly, and importantly, you have done nothing wrong, then or now.

The person you were in that life, your family and the people who helped you were, as I told you, known as Cathars. Because they challenged the church in Rome, the Inquisition wanted to either convert or annihilate all of them. I believe your parents were perfects; that is they were high up in their order and this is why they were persecuted. This man, the Inquisitor, knew they had a daughter and he would stop at nothing to make sure you did not continue that bloodline. I don't think he realised that the treasure he was seeking was you, simply because you carried the bloodline. There were many stories at that time about there being a 'treasure', even when the Medici family gained power in Florence. There have been references to their search for this 'treasure' although no evidence as to what it might have been. Didn't you say something about a property in the foothills of Pratomagna?"

"Did I? Oh, you mean the one near where *nonna* used to live, the one in my dream. Remember Tom, we went there the other day?"

"*Eh,* so there is a connection. I believe you have been called here by the past because it is time for a healing to take place for you and in turn for the others."

"I'm not sure I understand …."

"Sometimes, events from the past have an effect in the present. Old feelings arise from nowhere; they can be pleasant or not so. Something triggers a memory and …, *eccolo,* there it is. For you, Lucia, you have a special gift which has been suppressed and when you agreed to come to Italy to do this interview an opportunity was created and at the same time you were no longer able to ignore your psychic abilities. This is not something you should fear; it just takes a little getting used to.

I understand this is a lot to take in and Tom will help you, will you not?" Simonetta looked in Tom's direction and he nodded his assent. "Do your interview tomorrow and come to see me again either later tomorrow or Friday morning. Let me know which is best for you."

Lucia looked from Simonetta to Tom and back to Simonetta.

"I think you will have a lot to talk about, *no*?" Simonetta said, smiling at them both. "How are you feeling?"

"Erm, better, thank you." Lucia said, frowning. "What should I do if I see this person again?"

"Nothing. Just know that you are safe and he cannot hurt you. It is only a memory and he may know nothing of it."

"All the same, I would be happy to take you tomorrow and …."

"Oh, thank you Tom but I think I'll be alright now

and somehow I know this is something I have to do alone. I don't know why but ...."

"You are right, Lucia." Simonetta interrupted. "You will know what to do should you need to do anything at all."

"*Allora,* now, off you go and enjoy the evening."

As Lucia stood her legs still felt a little weak and shaky and she found she had to keep refocusing her eyes that now seemed to have a fresh clarity.

"And remember, drink plenty of water." were Simonetta's last words as she walked with them to the courtyard.

The storm had cleared leaving a soft golden glow as the sun began its journey towards the horizon through a misty haze. They drove in silence for a while as Lucia tried to digest Simonetta's words.

"Tom?" she began. "What did she mean by events from the past? I mean the person I was talking about lived a few hundred years ago."

"Do you believe in reincarnation?"

"What, you mean like the Buddhists and the Dalai Lama? I suppose I've not really given it much thought until now."

"Yes, but it's not just the Buddhists, there are many other cultures who also believe in reincarnation. In fact, it is said to have originally been part of Christianity but any reference was removed from the bible by councils in the fourth and fifth centuries. It was also part of the Cathar's doctrine."

"So, what you're saying is that I'm recounting events that took place in a life that I lived several hundred years ago?"

"Yes, that's right."

"And the voice I heard, that was me then calling myself now?"

"Yes, I think that is partly true."

"What do you mean?"

"Well, I seem to remember a change in the voice and I wonder …, I'm not sure that's all. Simonetta will be able to explain it better when you see her again."

"But ….."

"Here we are." Tom said as he parked the car in Chiara's courtyard. "I know it's hard but try not to think too much about it. In my experience, if you let it be the answers come in their own time."

"Mmm, as you say, easier said than done. Will you come in?"

"For a few minutes then I must get back."

"Oh Tom, I'm sorry, I ….."

"There's nothing to apologise for. I'm here because I want to be. I want to help. I think though that you need some time to take this all in before tomorrow."

"Probably," she said with a hint of resignation. "I really do appreciate all you've done, thank you."

She smiled in such a way that it pierced his heart and he quickly got out of the car to open the door for her before he overstepped a self-imposed boundary.

Chiara heard the car and came out to greet them eager to see her niece and see if she had recovered.

"*Ciao, ciao,* how did it go?"

"Oh Chiara, there's so much to tell you and so much I have yet to understand that I don't where to begin." She turned to Tom. "Can you …..?"

Chiara led the way to the *cucina*. "Wine or a

tisana?"

"Oh, no wine for me thanks."

"Nor me." added Tom.

"Why don't I make a large pot of *camomilla*? Now, Tom?"

Chiara produced some snacks and they all sat around the table with their chamomile tea. She listened intently as Tom gave his account of the visit to Simonetta after which she let out a long slow breath through her teeth.

"So you think that whatever happened all that time ago is linked to what is happening to Lucia now?"

"Yes. I have come across this before and it does explain her reaction at the chapel earlier today."

"*Eh*, I suppose. Lucia, *cara*, what do you think?"

Lucia extricated herself from her thoughts. "Well, it sort of makes sense. It's just so much to absorb and, well...., I don't know. I don't know what to do with it all and ...."

Tom looked at her with a tenderness she found totally disarming. "There's nothing you need to do. Take it gently and you will find a way with it. And now I think I'd better let you get some rest. Will you call me tomorrow and let me know how you get on?"

"Of course, Tom and thank you." she said reluctant to see him go. He had become an intrinsic part of her journey and she felt a sense of loss as he walked away.

Chiara also thanked Tom and walked with him to the terrace where they said goodnight.

Lucia was still struggling with all the new ideas when Chiara returned and sat next to her.

"*Tutto bene, cara*? I think this journey is becoming

much more than you expected, *no*?"

"Hm, you could say that," said Lucia with a weak smile. "There's so much I don't understand and yet, I know it's true. Does that make sense?"

"Of course," Chiara smiled and shrugged as if it was a simple matter. "At a deeper and intuitive level you know what is true for you, I think."

Lucia felt a moment of intimacy and safety as she and her aunt held each other's attention.

"And tomorrow? You will be alright going to the villa alone? I can take you if you would like me to?"

Lucia began to dissemble at the thought of the challenge ahead of her. "Oh Chiara, I don't know. As I said, I believe it is something I should do on my own, but …. Can we see how I feel in the morning?"

"Of course. Tomorrow is another day."

Once in her room, Lucia could not settle. She had a hot shower and got ready for bed but still her mind would not let go of the day. She switched on her laptop and typed 'Cathars Italy' into Google and spent the next hour or so reading through several of the links that reinforced and verified, not only her own experience, but also Simonetta's words. Finally, exhausted, mentally and emotionally, she closed the laptop and went to bed.

THURSDAY
Giovedi

A mist of low lying cloud obscured Florence from the surrounding hills.

Antonio, to the north of the city, woke with a strange sense of apprehension.

To the south of the city, Lucia stirred from a deep yet troubled sleep as tendrils of miasmic dreams teased her waking mind.

In the city itself, Simonetta contemplated the meanings of her own dream-filled sleep and acknowledged an unfamiliar feeling of unease.

Elsewhere in the city someone also woke from a fitful sleep, his usual bravado weakened as the grip of fear tightened and panic became an unwelcome companion.

Chiara had woken early and already walked round the gardens checking on the herbs and plants and watering where necessary. She had just made a second pot of coffee when Lucia joined her in the *cucina*.

"*Buongiorno, cara, come stai?* Did you sleep well?"

"*Mmmm, cosi cosi.* So so. Yes, I think so, sort of. *Come stai?*"

"*Bene, bene.* Come, have some breakfast."

Lucia joined her at the table, still warm with memories of the previous evening's conversations, and helped herself to a croissant. She poured her first cup of coffee and wondered if maybe it would be a better idea to avoid any further intake of caffeine.

Chiara avoided the question that hung in the air between them. "I saw *mamma* yesterday, she sends a big hug and kisses."

Lucia smiled and relaxed a little at the mention of Isabella. "How is she, maybe we can see her later?"

"She's fine," replied Chiara, deciding not to tell Lucia of her concerns for Isabella's failing health. Firstly, her mother would not have wished it and secondly, she did not wish to cause Lucia any more stress. "Yes, she would love to see you. Have you decided yet about today?"

"What, whether I should go alone or not?"

"*Si.*"

Lucia paused for a moment before saying, "I'll be ok. I just feel I have to do it."

"In that case, will you take my car?"

"Oh Chiara, thank you, but I don't have insurance."

"*Eh,* you don't drive in London?"

"No, I don't need to. Don't worry Chiara, I'm sure it will be fine," she said, forcing a smile.

"*Va bene,* but promise you will call me if there is the smallest problem. Promise?"

"*Si, si, si.* Now, I must make sure I have everything

I need. It seems ages since I've had anything to do with work, it's strange."

The car arrived to collect Lucia promptly at ten thirty. She felt her adrenals release a surge of cortisol as the tyres scrunched on the gravel, and she momentarily froze like a deer caught in headlights. Chiara gave her a hug she hoped would transmit calm and strength.

"Now, promise you'll call if you need anything, though I'm sure it will go perfectly."

Lucia, freed from the temporary paralysis, smiled. "Yes, don't worry, I'm sure you're right, see you later," she said trying to convince herself as much as her aunt.

Antonio was feeling a little more relaxed when Lucia arrived and after the usual salutations he led her to the gallery.

"I thought it better to do the interview here, amongst the treasures before they are removed. Also, we won't be disturbed."

"Removed?" Lucia queried with a frown.

"Yes. My father donated them to the City of Florence, well most of them."

"Oh, I didn't realise," she said, hoping this was not general knowledge and therefore exclusive to her interview.

They spent the next hour or so discussing the pieces of art that had been passed down through the Martinelli family from as far back as the Renaissance, their connection to the Medici and Giacomo's later additions to the collection.

When asked about the donation Antonio was evasive and merely said his father had believed they belonged to the city, to the people, not in a private collection where only a select few could appreciate them.

They each conducted themselves through their professional personas yet were aware of something intangible that neither could explain nor indeed wanted to.

"I think that covers it, don't you?" Antonio said, stretching back in his chair. "My mother has asked if you will stay for lunch; are you able to?"

Oh, thank you, yes," replied Lucia, taken a little by surprise, and torn between courtesy and apprehension.

"Good, let us go."

"Ah Lucia, *buongiorno, come stai*, it is good to see you again."

"*Buongiorno, bene grazie, e lei,* and you?" Lucia replied.

"*Bene*. Please there is no need to be formal. You have finished with my son?"

"Yes, and thank you for your kind invitation to join you for lunch."

"It's a pleasure. How is Chiara?"

"She's well. Busy as usual." Lucia suddenly felt detached and present at the same time. It all seemed surreal; the polite exchange of pleasantries riding above other darker issues which she had yet to understand. Feeling stretched across different worlds she wondered if her sanity would ever be the same again.

"Come, let us sit outside while there is still shade. Antonio, please pour some wine."

The table was already prepared and Maria emerged with a large plate of antipasti and freshly baked breads.

The smell awakened Lucia's appetite.

"Only a little for me, please," Lucia said before Antonio could fill her glass. She wanted to keep her head clear.

Luisa was an entertaining host as always. As they finished their coffees Lucia was thinking how well it had all gone when she felt an unexpected chill creep over her. Before she could process the feeling to a thought she heard footsteps running up the steps followed by a *"Ciao, mamma,"* and the man she had seen in the chapel emerged on to the terrace.

"Mamma, ciao. Ciao Antonio. Mi scusi, Signorina ..."

As their eyes met Lucia remembered Simonetta's words and, controlling the terror that threatened her breath, she held her hand out in greeting.

Before she could introduce herself, Luisa was already saying, *"Ciao, ciao.* Lorenzo this is Lucia Walker. Lucia, my son Lorenzo."

"Piacere." Lucia's pulse raced as her face smiled and she repeated to herself that she was safe.

"Piacere Signorina. I don't think we have met before."

"No, I don't think we have."

"Mamma, can we talk?"

Luisa excused herself and followed Lorenzo inside. Lucia watched as they walked through the terrace doors, surprised at how quickly her fear had subsided and was now replaced by a quiet calm and knowing. Was that it, she thought, as the fear and drama of voices and visions seemed to belong to a distant reality? It was like moving from one place to another, or closing one door to open another. Her mind tried to grasp her knowing unable to find the words.

She realised Antonio was speaking, "…… I hope you do not think him rude."

"Oh …, of course not," she said, recovering to the present. "I think, though, I must get back. I have to get the interview ready to send off tomorrow. Please thank your mother for a lovely lunch. And thank you, Antonio, for your time and …."

"*Niente*," he interrupted. "I'm only happy that your trip has not been wasted and that news of the collection will reach a wider audience. It is what my father would have wanted. Now, I'll organise the car to take you back."

"Thank you," she said as a feeling of warmth swept over her. Whatever she had previously found disconcerting about this man had suddenly dissolved and it was almost as if she had found a long lost friend. Maybe Simonetta would be able to explain, she thought. They said their goodbyes and Antonio accompanied her down the steps to the car.

Well, that was not at all what I had expected, she said to herself, as the car skirted around Florence. She couldn't keep up with her thoughts as she retraced the last two or three hours. It was not as if many words had actually been exchanged yet at the same time so much seemed to have happened, and indeed, changed. It was not long before the car pulled into the courtyard where Chiara was there to meet her as she thanked the driver and walked up the steps.

"*Ciao, cara,* how did it go?" Chiara asked with an eagerness she had hoped to subdue.

As Lucia reached the top of the steps they hugged and went inside out of the heat of the afternoon sun.

"Well, surprisingly well, actually. Chiara, I don't know what happened and I can't begin to understand it, but it was fine. Something happened that I can't explain, a bit like passing through the eye of a needle."

Chiara looked at her and tried to make sense of her words. "*Dimme,* tell me."

"Well, I don't know if I can, but I'll try."

Lucia explained that the interview had gone well and how surprised she had been to learn that Signor Martinelli had donated most of the collection to the City of Florence.

"*Eh,* probably wanted to stop that wayward son of his from selling it off and squandering the proceeds." Chiara was quick to interject.

Lucia continued to tell her of Luisa's hospitality and the sudden arrival of the 'wayward son' and how she had managed to deal with that, thanks to Simonetta's advice.

"It was amazing, now I come to think about it. It seemed that once I knew who he was, or should I say, had been, he no longer had any power over me. In fact, in a strange way I almost felt sorry for him."

"You have come a long way, *cara.* What will you do now?"

"Hm, I don't know. I think first I should phone Simonetta, and then I'd like to see *nonna.*"

She pulled her mobile from her bag and called Simonetta. After the usual greetings Simonetta merely said, "If you can come now I think that would be best."

Lucia agreed and ended the call. "She asked if I

could go over there now."

"*Va bene*, come, I'll take you, then I can go over to the shop and do a few things while you talk with Simonetta."

"Oh thank you, that would be great."

"So, how do you feel now?" asked Simonetta after hearing Lucia's account of her visit to the Villa Martinelli.

"Well, different …, it's hard to put into words."

"Take your time," "she said in a quiet and gentle voice.

"*Grazie*," and, encouraged by Simonetta's tone, she continued. "I think when he first walked in, that is Lorenzo, I felt breathless with fear but I remembered what you said and kept telling myself over and over that I was safe. And it worked. The strange thing was that I felt stretched somehow through time; as if I was neither here nor in the past or maybe I was in both, I don't know." She frowned, still trying to make sense of it.

"*Si, si,* you are right. As you changed your response to him you were able to release the energy that bound you in the past and held you in that fear. So, yes, in a way you were there and here, and yet at the same time you were neither – you were in *come si dice,* how do you say, a neutral space, in another dimension you might say."

"You mean like an observer, sort of detached?"

"Yes, you could say that."

"But why did this happen now?"

"Probably because the circumstances are so and the time is right. And, that you are ready."

"Well, I didn't feel ready."

"Ah, is it not the unreadiness that creates, or changes the awareness?"

"Mm, maybe, I don't know."

"There is much that happens in life that we are not aware of and we need a catalyst to alert us to what is needed. In that moment we often feel we have no choice, *no*?"

"In a way, I suppose so. But there's one thing I don't understand. Why did Antonio seem familiar – I've not met him before."

"*Eh,* you know. If you relax and close your eyes as I have shown you, see his face and look into his eyes, you will recognise him."

"Now?"

"*Si,* now."

Lucia did as Simonetta had told her, and was amazed at how easily the answer came to her.

"But," she said as she opened her eyes, "he's, no was, *Gianni,* my husband in that life."

"Yes, and now you understand why …."

"Of course, no wonder …., that's why he seemed familiar even though it made no sense ….and so,… does that mean because of what happened then, because I left Gianni and Silvana …… is that why ……. ? Lucia's words petered out as she tried to make sense of it all.

"These things don't always make sense. We have feelings that we do not understand and sometimes these can be very strong, as you know, but once recognised they can lose their power. I think, Lucia, when you return to London, maybe you find someone to help you better understand this gift you have. Do you know anyone who can help you with this?"

"No," she said, shaking her head. "This is the first time I've come across anything like this."

"*Eh,* it is a shame you were not helped with this when you were younger. When these energies are suppressed they have a habit of bursting free eventually."

"So, it would seem."

"Your mother – she never spoke to you about this?"

"No! I've always wondered though why my mother avoided coming to Italy. Do you think it could have something to do with this?"

"Not necessarily this but I suspect something happened. What about the rest of the family?"

"Yes, my aunt has *un' erboristeria* in Florence. It was opened by my *nonna*, then my aunt took over when she could no longer manage. Before that I think my *nonna* grew and foraged for herbs and local people would come to her for remedies."

"*Eh,* of course, I know of your aunt's shop, she is renowned in Florence for her skills and products. I understood she comes from a long line of healers."

"Yes, so I believe."

"*Allora,* this explains a little."

"How do you mean?"

"You say your mother didn't speak to you of this but what about your *nonna*?"

"Well, yes I suppose so. When I came to visit, she would take me with her to collect herbs and plants and I would help her make things. Mostly though, when I was young, I would be with my brother and sister and we would explore and play in the woods."

"You have a sister? Does she also show signs of

this gift?"

"Er, not that I know of. She's never mentioned anything. Why?"

"These things usually follow the female line. Maybe your mother's fear inhibited any development in you and your sister. Whatever the case, I hope you will find someone to help you when you return to London. When do you go?"

"At the weekend, whenever I can get a flight."

"*Va bene,* you have my phone number and I will give you my email. If you need help then please, you will contact me?"

"Yes, and thank you. In fact, I don't know how to thank you."

"There is no need. I have been where you are now and I am happy to help you. It is a lot to assimilate and I can assure you that as time passes the sense of it will deepen. Just remember you have nothing to fear. This gift, it is a positive thing. Now, enjoy the rest of your time in Florence. Is Tom coming for you?"

"No, ... er, my aunt is at the shop so I can go back with her."

"He is a special friend. I believe he can help you. See him before you go."

"Oh," said Lucia still taken back by Simonetta's directness, "I will, I'll call him later." She looked at Simonetta as she tried to voice the thoughts rushing through her mind.

"You are wondering about him, eh?" Simonetta asked before Lucia was able to find the words.

"Well, yes ..... I mean ....., was he ....., is he ...?

"Ah, that is another story, another journey for you to take when the time is right."

"But ....."

"You will know." Simonetta smiled and Lucia felt a moment of total trust in a different inevitability.

Simonetta accompanied Lucia to the courtyard where they said their goodbyes. As she set off towards Chiara's shop Lucia thought about what Simonetta had said about Tom and made a mental note to call him. It was almost seven o'clock and she realised it would be too late to see her grandmother by the time they got back and determined to see her in the morning. Her thoughts meandered across her family and Simonetta's words echoed in her mind. There was still so much she didn't know about her mother and her family; and her sister, Gabriella, had she had similar experiences and kept them to herself. She thought how distant she had been, so enveloped in her own world. Memories came and went as she walked. She knew she must speak with her mother when she returned to England.

She arrived at the shop as Chiara was turning the sign on the door to *chiuso*, closed.

"Perfect timing," Chiara smiled. I'll just lock up and we can go. We could stop to eat on the way home if you like."

"Yes, that sounds good. I'll just give Tom a call while you finish."

"Maybe he would like to join us?"

She called Tom's number and was greeted by his soft, resonant voice explaining that he was not available and requesting she leave a message. A little disappointed she said she had seen Simonetta, was now with Chiara and they were going to eat somewhere on the way home – maybe he would like to join them.

As Chiara joined her on the street she said, "He didn't answer so I left a message."

"We could stop in Bagno a Ripoli and if Tom calls we can tell him where we are. *Va bene?*"

"Ok." Lucia agreed amid conflicting feelings about the day and Tom joining them for supper.

They drove south east out of the city as Lucia told Chiara some of her earlier conversation with Simonetta. There was still so much she didn't yet understand and she hoped Chiara might be able to fill in some of the gaps.

"Did *mamma* ever say anything to you?"

"*Cara,* to be honest, we were not that close. There were many years between us as you know, and by the time I was old enough to hear her she was already grown and getting ready to leave home."

"What about *nonna*?"

"*Eh,* maybe she can tell you more."

A silence fell between them as Lucia continued to search her memories and Chiara quietly wondered how best she could help her. Before Lucia could formulate any cohesive thoughts, her mobile rang.

"It's Tom," she said to Chiara, then, "*Ciao,* Tom."

"Tell him we'll be at the restaurant on the hill, he'll know the one."

Lucia echoed Chiara's words to Tom who said he could be there in about twenty minutes.

"He's on his way."

"*Bene.*" Chiara said with an almost satisfied smile, all the time keeping her eyes on the road.

Lucia cast a suspicious look in her direction and added, "What do you mean?"

"*Niente,* nothing," she said, still smiling.

"Chiara, please ....."

"*Eh,* here we are," she interrupted as she pulled off the road and parked the car. As they walked towards the entrance Chiara linked arms with Lucia and said, "Don't worry, I am only teasing. Come, let's relax."

Lucia put her hand over Chiara's. "You're right," she sighed as she surrendered to the moment.

As they entered the restaurant Chiara was greeted as if she was a long lost relation and they were shown to a table with what they were promised was the best view of the setting sun. Lucia was instantly included in the familial welcome and once they were seated, the table was soon covered with fresh breads and dishes of olives, along with a bottle of their own wine, again with the promise of it being the very best.

Lucia found the last vestiges of tension soon dissolve in the warmth and enthusiasm of the restaurant owner and his family.

"They seem to know you," said Lucia with a touch of irony.

"*Eh,* Franco and I have been coming here for years. They've seen our children grow with theirs."

Lucia reflected momentarily on how that sense of continuity and community was lacking in her own life and how present it always seemed to be here, in Italy. Her relationships with Chiara and her *nonna* were so different from those with her immediate family, apart from James, of course. An "oh" escaped audibly.

"What is it, *cara*?"

"Oh, I was just thinking and ..... oh dear, with all that's been happening, I've forgotten to call James."

"Isn't he going to be here next week?"

"Well, yes, but I really should have been in touch ...."

"I think you worry too much, *cara*. You have heard from him?" Chiara asked with that rising inflection that distinguished it from a statement.

"Er no, but ...."

"*Basta*," she said as she placed her hand over Lucia's, "you can call him tomorrow, but now let us relax."

Lucia smiled in acquiescence.

"Ok, ok."

"*Bene*. What will you order?"

"Hm, some antipasti? Then I think I'd like some fish – or what would you recommend?"

"*Allora*, I think the fish is a good choice – let's see what the special of the day is." Chiara signalled to the waiter to catch his attention and in quickly spoken Italian ascertained that the special was *sogliola*, dover sole.

At the same time Tom arrived and after another effusive welcome from the owners, joined them at their table.

They ordered antipasti to start and unanimously agreed on a main course of the *sogliola* accompanied by a bottle of *Vernaccia di San Gimignano*.

With the essentials of food decisions and ordering out of the way Tom turned his attention to Lucia, unable to contain his curiosity any longer.

"May I ask, how did it go today?"

"Well, I think it went well," she said casting a glance in Chiara's direction as if seeking confirmation. "The interview was great. In fact, I'm quite excited about writing it up now. Then, Luisa asked me to stay for lunch and, as always, was entertaining. Even when Lorenzo arrived unexpectedly it was … well…. it was ok. I remembered what Simonetta had told me about being safe and it worked!"

They each picked at the antipasti that were now served with more fresh warm breads.

"I then went to see Simonetta and it all began to make sense. She's been amazing and I can't thank you enough Tom for introducing me to her."

Tom's heart skipped a beat and he recovered enough to stutter, "*Eh,* it … it … *niente.*"

"Well, I really appreciate all you've done but I won't go into the details now as Chiara has heard it all already. Maybe tomorrow if you're free? I'd love to talk to you more about it."

"Er, yes … erm, I'm free tomorrow afternoon if that's ok."

"Perfect. I can do my writing in the morning and book my flight etc. what would be a good time?"

"Shall we say 3.30?"

The main course arrived and their conversation flitted from London to Florence and Chiara's garden to the excellence of the fish and the wine.

As they drank their coffee Chiara asked, "Tom, would you mind taking Lucia home, I just need to run an errand."

"Chiara ….," Lucia began.

"I won't be long and I'm sure Tom won't mind, will you?" she said turning towards him in askance.

"Of course, *volentieri,* willingly."

"*Bene.* I'll just get the bill and, no Tom, this is my

treat," she said and left the table before anyone could raise an objection.

Lucia felt a wave of tiredness sweep over her. She felt emptied as the day took its toll. Tom, aware of the change in her energy, suggested that if she was ready, they should leave. She nodded, grateful for his unspoken understanding as they left the restaurant and walked towards his car.

"It has been a long day for you, *no?*" Tom asked and Lucia smiled, charmed by the inflection in his voice so typical in Italian.

"Yes, I suppose it has. It's suddenly hit me, or maybe it's the wine."

"Come, let's get you home," and he held open the car door for her. Again his proximity disturbed her but, already overwhelmed by the day's emotions, she pushed her feelings to one side and collapsed into the seat.

Tom was also having to deal with his own disturbing emotions. He took a few deep breaths as he walked round to the driver's door attempting to contain rising desires to protect, caress and much more.

It was only a short drive to Chiara's and Lucia wondered about her motives for leaving the restaurant on her own.

Before she could voice her thoughts Tom was asking when she would be returning to London.

"I'm not sure yet. Saturday or Sunday, depending on flights."

As they arrived at the villa, Lucia was surprised to see lights on in many of the rooms and the main door wide open, but there was no sign of Chiara's car.

"Tom ..." she began.

"Stay here."

"But, Tom ...."

"Please stay here. I'll just take a look."

"Tom ... be careful."

Tom entered the cantina through a door on the ground floor beneath the terrace. An old wooden staircase led to a door that opened into the hall. He listened at the door before slowly turning the handle. He eased it open an inch or two and scanned what he could see of the hall. Silence. His mind raced over various possible scenarios and how he could deal with them when he heard footsteps running down the stairs from the floor above. He pulled the door back leaving just a crack so he had only a narrow view of the hall and froze, hardly daring to breathe.

He heard muffled voices and footsteps moving towards the back of the villa. They must have heard or seen the car. Lucia! He had to get to her. He was close to the main door and assessed whether he could leave without being seen. It was a risk he would have to take. Again, he eased the door a few inches and was met with silence. Where had they gone? He pushed the door far enough to allow him to exit and tiptoed along the hall. Once outside he released his held breath and ran down the terrace steps, jumped in the car, started the engine and drove away from the villa as fast as he could.

Startled by the speed of events, Lucia demanded, "What happened!"

Satisfied they were not being followed he pulled over to the side of the road and stopped the car.

"I don't know. I couldn't see. It sounded like two

men but I can't be sure. It seemed a good idea to get away as quickly as ...." He was interrupted by the distant squeal of tyres as a fast approaching car passed them causing their car to vibrate in its wake.

"I think we can go back now."

"But .... what ....."

"I don't know. First, I'd better call Chiara. Do you know where she went?"

"No idea, no."

Adrenaline was still surging through his body as he took out his mobile and made the call. Lucia was quiet. When Chiara answered he spoke quickly in Italian and arranged to meet her at the villa. As he finished the call he turned towards Lucia, "Are you alright?"

"Yes, what about you?"

"*Si, si*, I'm fine, thanks."

"What on earth was all that about?"

"I don't know but we'd better get back. Chiara's on her way."

"Tom?"

"*Si?*" He paused and turned to look at her.

"Oh, nothing ...I ...., I don't know ..."

Tom, feeling calmer, sighed. "Look, let's go back, see what the situation is and take it one step at a time."

"Mmm .. ok."

Too exhausted to make sense of what was happening, Lucia sank back into the seat as Tom drove the short distance back to the villa. Chiara arrived as they were getting out of the car and came running over to them.

"*O dio mia,* what happened?" she said as she earnestly searched Tom's face for answers.

"*Eh, non lo so*, I don't know. When we arrived the

lights were on and the main door was open so I went in by the cantina. I heard voices upstairs and realised that they must have heard or seen the car so I went back to the car and drove away. I stopped just down the road and heard a car skid and drive past very fast. I …"

"But why? What did they want?"

"I've no idea. Let's go and see if anything is missing." And Tom led the way up the steps to the main door.

Everything seemed as it should be. Chiara maintained an orderly and uncluttered home and it was clear that the main rooms had not been touched.

"I'll check the study, Lucia, *cara*, would you see if your room is ok?" Chiara asked and was walking down the hall to the study before Lucia could respond. She looked at Tom who nodded then offered to accompany her.

Lucia walked around the room while Tom waited in the doorway. Everything seemed as it should be, then she remembered she had left her laptop on the small table and the table was now bare save for a couple of pens. Lucia turned to Tom, "My laptop – it's gone."

"Anything else?"

She looked around just to make sure before answering, "no that's all. …., but why?"

"Come, let's find Chiara." She nodded and followed him to the study where Chiara stood in the middle of the room looking puzzled.

"*Allora*, I can't see that there's anything missing and ……"

"Lucia's laptop is missing."

"But why would anyone want to take my …"

"Oh no, I'm sorry *cara*, does that mean you've lost all your work?"

"Er no. Actually it's all backed up on a memory stick. But I don't understand, why would anyone want to take it?"

"Come, let's go and sit down – we can decide what to do over a nightcap, *no*?" And Chiara led the way back to the *cucina* where she made a pot of chamomile tea and they each returned to their usual places around the table.

"I don't know what to make of all this," began Chiara. "I should call the police but, well …. I don't know – they sometimes just make things more complicated. But there is the fact that it is Lucia's laptop that's missing …"

"And you are worried that if this was aimed at her, she may be in danger?" Tom continued her thought with his own.

"Well, I wasn't going to say that, but …"

"Wait, wait!" Lucia looked at them both, her eyes wide with yet unspoken questions. "Could it just be that we disturbed them before they could take anything else?"

"Yes, of course, but they were not exactly subtle. I mean an ordinary burglar would not normally leave the main door open and all the lights on!" Tom was beginning to feel uncomfortable as he considered their blatant arrogance or was it more a warning. "Maybe, Chiara, it would be wise to call the police. If Lucia was the target …."

"But why …?" Lucia's voice became thin as fear seeped in and tightened her throat.

"I think Tom is right, we should not take any risks

here."

"*Bene.*" Tom gave a small sigh of relief as he also wondered why Lucia's laptop would be of use to anyone. His thoughts led him to her connection to the Martinelli family and in particular, to Lorenzo.

Lucia's thoughts took her along the same road and she looked from one to the other but had lost the will to speak as the shock began to set in.

"What was on your laptop?" Tom asked.

"Oh, just the research and some notes for the interview. I don't store much on it – usually just what I'm working on. It's only a small one that I use when I'm travelling."

"Why, do you think this has something to do with the interview?" Chiara was suddenly alert as she remembered some of the rumours she had heard about the young Lorenzo Martinelli. "I'll call the police."

A police officer arrived within ten minutes and Lucia was not surprised that he, Gianluca, and Chiara had known each other since they were at school together. Again, she noted, there was this continuity she sensed was lacking in her life. Chiara related the sequence of events and Lucia and Tom answered Gianluca's questions.

"Do you think they will come back?" asked Chiara.

"*Eh,* I think it is unlikely, but you should be careful. Please, if you cannot disturb the room, someone will come to see for fingerprints in the morning though I am not hopeful. These people were not hiding so I think they were not fearful. Be careful. I will call again in the morning."

"Tom, would it be too much of an imposition to

ask you to stay the night? Lucia can sleep in one of the girls' rooms and you in the other one, that way there is no need to touch anything in Lucia's room before the police arrive tomorrow."

"*Certo, certo.*" Tom agreed. "But I would rather sleep here on the sofa where I can hear anyone trying to get in."

"*Va bene.*" Chiara agreed. "Gianluca, thank you. We'll see you in the morning."

"*Si, si* but please call me if there should be anything at all." he turned to address Lucia. "*Signorina*, it may be best, and more safe for you, if you leave for London as soon as you can."

Chiara deflected his attention from Lucia, "Of course, we will do what we can tomorrow." She walked with him to the car, reassured him that she would ensure the villa was secure and would call him with the smallest need. Chiara then double checked all the windows and doors were locked and the alarm set, which it hadn't been for some time, before joining Lucia and Tom in the *cucina*.

"I'll get you some blankets Tom. Are you sure you will be comfortable here. I do not imagine they will come back, do you?"

"I doubt it very much but I think it better to be here than fast asleep in bed where I won't hear anything." he said with a tired smile.

"Oh Chiara, I'm so sorry if this is all because of that bloody interview!" blurted Lucia.

"*Cara, cara, calma, calma.* We don't know that and even if that is so, it is not your fault. Now drink your tea and let us all try to get some sleep."

FRIDAY
Venerdi

It was already past midnight. Chiara satisfied herself that Tom had everything he needed, then showed Lucia to her bed where they hugged each other goodnight. It was all Lucia could do to remove her clothes and slide into bed. As her head touched the pillow, she descended into a deep and peaceful sleep, only waking when Chiara entered the room with a mug of hot water and lemon.

Chiara sat on the bed. "You slept well?"

Lucia rubbed her eyes and squinted at her aunt as she tried to find the time between falling asleep and the present moment. "Er, yes, it would seem so. Is it really morning?"

"*Si cara.* Here, I brought a robe for you. Come and join us for breakfast."

"Mmm, thanks," was all she could manage as she looked around the room and memories of the previous evening came flooding back. "Oh, ok. I'll be there in a minute."

Despite sleeping so well, Lucia felt every muscle straining to co-operate with her desired movements, the exhaustion and tension of the last few days having set deeper in her being. She passed the hall where Chiara was talking to two police officers who had just arrived to search for any forensic evidence that may help them identify the previous evening's perpetrators. Tom stood as she entered the *cucina* and offered coffee. Nodding, she sat down at the table and helped herself to a croissant. She sensed an aura of unreality as she accepted the cup from Tom and thanked him.

"Did you sleep? I hope you weren't too uncomfortable." she hoped that was what she said though she wasn't sure whether or not she had actually formed the words.

Tom's affirmative reply seemed to confirm that her speech faculties were working normally and she smiled before raising the cup to her mouth. She drank the coffee and her body bristled into life, as the caffeine surged through her cells. "Aaah," she gave a deep sigh, "that's better."

Tom smiled, his green eyes crinkling at the corners and Lucia could not avoid meeting them momentarily before returning her attention to her coffee.

"The police have arrived to see if they can find any clues …."

"Yes, I saw Chiara talking to them as I came down the stairs. Do you think they'll find anything?"

"I doubt it." Tom said, unhopeful. "Have you thought what you might do?"

"Oh," she said, taken by surprise at having to deal with the reality of decision making. "No, not really. I suppose ......"

Chiara entered the room before she could finish and explained that the police would need to take their fingerprints by way of elimination. "They say it will only take a few minutes. I told them they could use the study."

About half an hour and a few questions and fingerprints later, they had said goodbye to the police officers and were once again sitting at the table debating what to do next.

Chiara spoke first.

"*Allora*, I spoke with Gianluca this morning and I have been thinking what is the best thing to do. *Cara*," she turned to Lucia, "you know I would love for you to stay always, but I think Gianluca is right and you should return to London as soon as possible."

"But ....." Lucia began and was interrupted by Tom.

"Chiara is right. We do not know who these people are or what they want and you will be safer in England. Maybe you could stay with your mother for a few days until we know more?"

"But this is all a bit melodramatic, don't you think?"

"Not really, *cara*. If it does have something to do with Lorenzo then you should be careful. According to Gianluca he knows some very unsavoury people and is completely unpredictable. Please, Tom's idea is good, stay with *mamma* for a few days, at least until we have a better idea what this is about."

Lucia looked at them in turn, and exasperated by the limitations in which she found herself, lifted her eyes to the ceiling and gave a big sigh in capitulation. "Ok, ok ... I give in."

"*Bene. Allora,* let's see if we can get you on a flight later today. *In fatti,* in fact, it is only a day or two earlier than you planned." Chiara brought her laptop to the table and opened it.

"*Eh,* there's a flight at 18.05. Do you want to call and see if you can transfer your ticket?" Chiara was already in organisation mode, leaving Lucia overwhelmed and panicked by the need to make a spontaneous decision.

"Oh Chiara, I know you mean well but please slow down and give me time to make sense of things, to myself that is." Lucia was reminded of the fairground rides from her childhood and in particular the waltzers where you were spun round and round with no way of getting off until the ride stopped. How she wished she could get off this particular ride.

"Of course, *cara,*" she said her eyes filled with love and compassion for her niece and her situation.

"I'd be happy to take you to the airport if that would help," offered Tom.

Chiara and Lucia thanked him in unison and Chiara added, "Gianluca said he will call later this morning to let us know how their investigations are going, so take as long as you need, *cara.*"

It was already 11 o'clock and Lucia was aware of time racing and pressing her into an unasked for corner. Chiara had gone to her study to deal with some urgent matters and she looked to Tom for reassurance.

"Do you really think there is any danger, to me or anyone else for that matter?"

"I don't know but Gianluca seems to think there may be and the fact they did not try to hide what they were doing indicates a certain fearlessness. I think it better to err on the side of caution though, don't you?"

"I suppose so. It just seems a shame for my visit to end so abruptly like this."

"*Eh,* sometimes life turns us in unexpected directions and to resist only causes more problems."

"You sound as if you speak from experience."

"Probably." He paused, contemplating how much he should say, then continued. "Whilst I am sorry to see you leave like this, I believe it is for the best. It sounds like these are not the kind of people to take any chances with."

"But Tom, I don't understand ….., what do they think they will find. It is only my notes on Signor Martinelli and his collection – nothing you can't find on the internet."

"Was there anything unusual you noticed in the gallery or maybe something Antonio said?"

"No, not that I can think of. I was surprised though to learn that, before he died, Signor Martinelli had already donated most of the collection to the City of Florence."

"Very wise on his part I should think, considering his son's reputation."

They sat in silence for a few minutes each with their own thoughts. Lucia spoke first.

"Do you think they were hoping to find the finished interview, not knowing that I still had the recording with me?"

"It's possible." Tom shrugged his shoulders.

In a distant room a phone rang. A few minutes later Chiara returned to the *cucina*.

"That was Gianluca. As he thought they did not find any fingerprints. It seems they picked the lock, he says the tools they use now are very sophisticated. He doesn't seem hopeful that they'll find them. I must start using the alarm again. I'm sorry, *cara,* this is not much help for you, I know."

"I don't know what to think anymore. I can't imagine a day or two will make much difference but I'll see if there's a seat on today's flight and I'll call *mamma*, though I don't want to worry her."

Lucia's automatic thought was to get her laptop then immediately realised that wasn't possible. "Chiara, may I use your laptop?"

"Certo, certo. I think it's still on the page for Meridiana."

Lucia opened it, logged on to her account and went through the necessary motions to change her flight. She let out a long breath and leaned back into her chair.

"All done." Strange, now that it was done she was relieved. A choice had been made, a step taken.

"Bene."

"I'd like to see *nonna* before I go."

"Of course, but I think it better not to mention what has happened here – I don't want her to worry."

"I won't." Lucia confirmed. "Do you mind if I go now? I can pack when I get back. I won't need to be at the airport 'til about 4.30 or 5."

"Go, go – I'll get some lunch ready. Tom, you will stay for lunch?"

As she walked along the path to Isabella's, Lucia

began to organise the rest of the day in her mind. Before she left she would call James and see if she could stay with him tonight then she would call her mother from London. It seemed odd to be returning to England so suddenly even though she was only curtailing her trip by a day or two. She felt cheated in some way, as if more than her laptop had been stolen.

She found Isabella sitting on the loggia, herbs spread on the table in front of her.

"*Eh, amore, vieni, vieni!*"

Lucia gave Isabella a hug and sat at the table next to her.

"What would you like, *amore*? *Una tisana*?"

"*Si, grazie.*"

She followed Isabella to the kitchen and chose a *tisana* of *Melissa,* lemon balm.

"A good choice – refreshing and calming at the same time. I will make a pot and join you."

Isabella added some lemon biscuits she had baked to the tray and Lucia carried it out to the loggia.

"*Allora, dimme,* tell me, what have you been doing?"

Lucia had already rehearsed in her mind how much, or how little, she would tell her grandmother and told her about the interview with Antonio followed by the lunch with him and his mother. "Sadly, I have to leave this evening so I can get the article in to the magazine in time."

"And the dream …. *amore*, have you had more?"

Surprised by her grandmother's question, she shook her head before saying, "No …., no, I haven't."

"And this Simonetta, she helped with that? You understand what happened?"

"Yes, *nonna*, she was wonderful. It seems it was all to do with a life several hundred years ago, to do with a group of people called Cathars. Have you heard of them?"

"Ah," Isabella sighed back into her chair and into her memory, "the 'old people' is what we used to call them. How interesting."

"Yes, it seems there was a large community here in Florence before they were wiped out by the Inquisition."

"*Eh,* this is true, though it is said that some survived and despite the efforts of the Inquisition to eradicate them, the bloodline survives today."

"Oh," Lucia paused in a moment of realisation, "Sylvana ……."

"What's that, *amore*?"

"Er, I was just remembering ……., oh *nonna*, in that life I had a daughter, Sylvana. Do you think she could have survived and carried on the bloodline?"

"It's possible, *amore*. It may explain some of the stories and that business with the little cottage. I wonder?"

"Oh, you mean …."

"*Si, si,* there have been stories about it from the Medici to the Martinelli. "Hmm," Isabella swallowed a laugh." If only they had known …., the treasure had been you, well you then, and the bloodline you carried."

"I like to think that it may still continue, somewhere," Lucia said with a wistful look in her eyes.

"*Eh,* and now?" Isabella asked wondering whether to say more or just leave it be.

"Simonetta thinks I should find someone to help me when I get back to London. And you, *nonna*, did you ever have any strange experiences?"

"*Eh, amore,* where to start! It is good you get some help. You know, you come from a long line of healers; always passed down the female line. Maybe it is possible, in that other life you were a healer and were trying to awaken you to your abilities in this life?" The inflection in Isabella's voice rose leaving the ambiguity of a question.

"Mmm …., maybe *nonna.*"

They chatted for a while until Lucia reluctantly prised herself away from her desire to spend more precious moments with her grandmother. They held each other, sharing unspoken words and feelings of love.

"You will come back soon, *no*?"

"Yes, as soon as I can, *nonna.*" She walked away, frequently turning to wave. A lump rose in her throat and a tear escaped from the corner of her eye as she tried to memorise an image of the frail yet beautiful woman with whom she wished she could spend more time.

As Lucia walked back to the villa she was grateful to have the time to ponder on the conversation with her grandmother. She felt something settle inside her, cogs falling into place yet a light wave of sadness passed through her at the thought of leaving Florence. She arrived to find Chiara preparing lunch and Tom hunched over her laptop, intent on the screen.

"Ah, you're here. *Bene.* How was *mamma?*"

"She seems well. We had a *tisana* and some of her wonderful lemon biscuits. I just feel so sad leaving and not spending more time with her."

"I know, I know, *cara,* but you will be able to come back soon, *no*?"

Tom looked up from the computer screen in anticipation of her answer.

"Yes, of course. I don't know ... I suppose I'm more aware of how time is running out to spend with her."

"Mmm," Chiara nodded in empathy. *"Allora,* lunch will be ready soon – would you like to pack first? Then you can relax before you have to leave."

"Ok, I won't be long."

It didn't take her long to pack and before she went downstairs Lucia called her brother, James. She briefly told him she was returning that evening, asked if she could stay with him and would explain everything when she saw him.

James knew his sister well enough to know she would not ask without a good reason and said he would pick her up at the airport. She was shaking as she disconnected the call and the reality of recent events once again began to sink in. She walked over to the window absorbing the beauty of the landscape. She felt as if her world had been turned upside down and inside out since arriving here. She was a different person to the one that had stepped on to the plane at Gatwick just over a week ago. Then there was Tom. He'd been so kind and supportive and... she stopped the thought there unable to follow it for fear of where it might lead her. Instead she reflected on the last few days and wondered how it would be when she returned to London. It seemed so far away and unrelated to her present circumstances and she wondered if she had done the right thing by involving James. Well, it was done now, she thought and went downstairs to join Chiara and Tom for lunch.

Back at the table, Chiara produced antipasti and warmed bread, followed with artichoke *frittata*, salad and some *patatine frite,* all washed down with some wine from her own vines.

By the time small cups of *espresso* were in front of them they had exhausted all possible explanations they could think of for the burglary. It was already after two o'clock and Lucia was feeling the pressure of her remaining time in Italy disappearing faster than she wished.

"You know, the more we talk about it, the more unreal it all seems." Lucia said. "Anyway, I'll get the article together over the weekend and hopefully that will be the end of it."

"I do hope so, *cara."*

"Chiara, I'm just thinking …., will you be alright here on your own? I mean, what if they come back?" said Lucia, suddenly concerned for her aunt.

"Don't worry, I'll be fine. I'll make sure I set the alarm and Franco will be back tomorrow."

"Oh, I'm sorry I won't see him …."

"*Eh,* next time, *cara.*"

The muffled sound of a mobile phone caught them all by surprise as they each tried to recognise the ringtone as their own. Lucia jumped up and ran over to her bag and pulled out the phone, answering it just in time.

"*Pronto ….. si……… si ……….., certo ……,"* Lucia walked out on to the terrace and returned with a puzzled expression as she finished the call, "*grazie mille ……. ciao, ciao.*" "Strange, that was Simonetta. She said she had sensed something was wrong and wanted to check that I was alright. When I told her what had happened she said it was something to do with a hole in time and that it is best I return to London, but should not worry. I don't see what that has to do with the burglary but I do trust her. Anyway, I said I would call her on Sunday – she'll apparently be able to tell me more then." Lucia sat down and shrugged her shoulders.

"I think I know what she means, "Tom said. "Sometimes when something in the past is disturbed the energy, or the memory, if you like, can cause things to happen in the present. Maybe when you met Lorenzo, even if he didn't recognise you consciously, it may have triggered something in his deeper memory which caused him to react in the present."

"Oh," Lucia sighed, "I think I understand, well a little anyway." She frowned then added, "So, are you saying that even though he doesn't know it consciously, Lorenzo is reacting to his experience and feelings when we met in the past."

"Yes, that's it. Of course, he won't know that and that's why these things often seem irrational."

"*Eh*, that would make sense," agreed Chiara. "Didn't you say that he was obsessed with finding you because he believed you had something valuable?"

"Well yes, but I don't, not now anyway."

"Yes, but he doesn't know that. There must be something that happened when you met, or something he believes you know that triggered the memory." Tom's eyes met Lucia's. "Is there anything you can think of?"

She looked into her empty coffee cup, avoiding his gaze, as she went over their meeting in her mind. "No, I've been over and over it – there's nothing."

"And your conversations with Antonio?"

"I don't know. There's nothing I can think of but maybe when I listen to the tape …., I can't imagine what though. We just talked about the paintings and sculptures in the collection, their provenance and which ones had been bequeathed to the city. He was very clear about his father's wishes that we would not discuss anything that personally pertained to the family."

"Cara," Chiara interrupted, "time is passing and you will soon need to leave. Have you everything ready?"

"Yes," she replied, getting up from the table, "I'll get my things."

After copious hugs and kisses goodbye and promises to call as soon as she got back to London, Lucia gave Chiara a final wave as Tom drove away from the villa and towards Florence and the airport.

Being Friday, he wanted to avoid getting caught up in the ever lengthening traffic that inched along the *autostrada*, and therefore took a shorter, more direct route through the city.

Lucia watched the streets of Florence retreat from view with a sadness and quiet resignation.

"Calma, tutto bene." she heard a voice say and automatically responded. "Pardon?"

"I didn't say anything." It was Tom's voice and she immediately realised that the voice she heard had been that of a female. She looked at Tom not knowing if she should say anything about it and was surprised by his acute sensitivity as he said with great gentleness, "You hearing voices again?"

"Er…., yes," she said reluctant to give it any credibility and repeated the words she'd heard.

"Sounds like you're being looked after," he said smiling.

"Mmm …, I hadn't quite thought of it like it."

"Do you mind?"

"What – the voices or being looked after?"

"Either."

"I suppose not. I've sort of got used to the voice – I just didn't expect to hear it again."

"Ah," Tom said knowingly, "I don't think these things just go away."

"What do you mean?"

"*Allora,* you have opened a door Lucia and trying to close it is a bit like trying to put the genie back in the bottle."

"Oh."

"Don't worry, you have a wonderful gift and once you are able to accept it you can begin to enjoy it. Needless to say, your life will not be same." He said with a smile that disarmed Lucia from making any immediate response. She looked out at the passing urban landscape considering his words and avoiding the emotions his smile had nudged closer to the surface.

"Here we are," he said as they pulled off the main road. "I'll drop you at 'Departures' and park the car. I'll meet you at the check-in desk."

"Thanks Tom, but you don't have to ….."

"It's ok – I want to see you safely on your flight."

By the time Tom returned from parking the car, Lucia

was just coming away from the check-in desk.

"A last cup of coffee?" Tom suggested.

Lucia relented despite it being late afternoon and walked with Tom across the concourse to the café.

She sat at a small table while Tom went to the bar to order. She felt awkward as she waited; her mind at odds with her emotions as she tried to understand the effect Tom was having on her. What should she do? Was there anything to do? She watched his back as he paid and picked up the coffees. She knew she didn't want this to be the last time she saw him. He turned and walked towards the table, putting the cup and saucer down in front of her. She looked at it finding it difficult to raise her eyes to meet his.

"Sugar?"

"No, no thanks," she said finding the courage to slowly raise her head.

"Is there someone you can talk to in London?"

"What, you mean about all this stuff that has happened?"

"Yes. I was just thinking that it's a lot to take in and it can be easier if you have someone you can share it with."

"There's my brother, but I don't know how understanding he will be."

"I'm sure you will find someone, but if you need to talk you can always give me a call if you think it will help."

Lucia shifted in her seat. "Thank you, I may take you up on that," she said with a cheerfulness that belied her growing discomfort. She kept her eye on the boarding information by way of a distraction, eager to go yet yearning to stay. Her gate number flashed on the screen. "I'd better go."

Tom walked with her to the security control where they said goodbye. Lucia felt as if she would burst. She could resist no longer and, reaching on tiptoes, she embraced his face in her hands and kissed him gently on the mouth. His instant response soon became a mutual urgency as they opened to each other. Their arms wrapped around the other's body and any distance between them dissolved. A nearby tannoy loudly announced her flight and with reluctance and slight embarrassment they moved apart.

Amidst, 'I'll call you', 'call me' and other pleas about emails and staying in touch, Lucia walked through to the security checks turning round for a final glimpse and wave as she disappeared to the departure lounge.

As she sat down she wondered what had come over her. She looked around with new eyes. Her world seemed brighter as shadows receded, chased away by a growing light as veils dissolved. The feeling reminded her of the dream that had haunted her, and she now remembered quite clearly the part when she walked through the wall. And, as in the dream, she felt she had stepped into a new landscape full of promise.

Smiling inwardly at her newfound sense of wellbeing, she was oblivious to the movement of people going through the boarding gate. It wasn't until someone rushed past her that she once again became aware of her surroundings and, gathering her hand luggage, made her way to the plane.

Tom returned to his car where he sat for some time while he also tried to make sense of what had just happened. Had he been wrong to hold back all this time? No, he didn't think so. But now ….., all that had changed in an instant. His ordered world turned on its head. Joy and fear vied for his attention as he put the key into the ignition and set off on to the *autostrada*, forgetting it was Friday as he joined the long queue of traffic.

London, ENGLAND

The sun was setting as the plane taxied along the runway at Gatwick. Lucia's thoughts were still with Tom as she contemplated what would happen now, if anything. Fears surfaced and subsided as she revisited those last few moments. She decided she would text him to say she had arrived safely.

She remembered that James would be there to meet her and further thoughts of Tom were eclipsed by what she was going to tell James.

She didn't have to wait long. James was at the arrivals gate as she walked through, ready to take her case and lead her to the car.

"Luci, *ciao*," he said as they hugged and kissed. Holding her at arm's length, he added, "You ok? You must be tired."

"Hi, James thanks for coming. Yes, it's been a long day."

They walked to the car exchanging questions and answers on family and Florence and they were soon leaving the airport behind and heading towards James' home in Wimbledon.

James took Lucia's case upstairs to the spare room in his small two bedroom cottage in a quiet backwater in the village.

"What's it to be tea or wine?"

"Oh, a glass of wine would be great," she replied and collapsed into a large armchair.

James returned with two glasses of wine and sat on the sofa.

"Look, don't worry; you don't have to explain anything tonight, not unless you want to of course. Just take your time, ok?"

Relieved not to have to go through it all straightaway, she sighed, "Thanks James. Maybe it can wait 'til tomorrow."

Lucia asked about his business and his coming trip to Florence. "They're so looking forward to seeing you."

"Are you sure you can't take some time off and come with me, or is that now not a good idea?" As the words came out James wondered if he'd said the wrong thing; he didn't want to pressure his sister into talking about why she'd left Florence and why she needed to stay with him. He quickly added, "Sorry, Luci, I didn't mean to pry."

"I know you don't and I will tell you, just not now, if that's ok?"

"Of course it is. Have you any plans for tomorrow?"

"Well, I have to write this article. I'd like to get that done. I've done most of the work but it needs to be written up. Apart from that, no."

"Ok. If there's anything I can do, you know you only have to ask."

"Thanks, James." She emptied her wine glass. "I think I'll say goodnight if that's ok." She prised herself from the comfort of the armchair. "See you in the morning."

Lucia went upstairs and as she opened her suitcase her days in Italy seemed to spill out before her. So much had happened so quickly and now she was alone she felt overwhelmed by the changes she knew were irreversible.

She took out her mobile and sent two texts confirming her safe arrival. One to Chiara, the easy one, and another to Tom, the not so easy one. She managed the wording but agonised over how to end it. Finally she put an X and a smiley face.

Exhaustion took over as she undressed and fell into bed. She tumbled into sleep among thoughts of Tom, of Florence, unable to make sense of any of them as Morpheus held her until morning.

She was woken by rays of sunlight escaping at the edge of the curtains to settle on her eyes. Blinking, she looked around as her memory worked its way from the past to the present to explain where she found herself. She sat up as she pieced together the previous 24 hours. She blushed, remembering with embarrassment how she and Tom had parted at the airport. Then there were the dreams – oh no, she thought, what have I done? Fractured images flooded in like a kaleidoscope that she was unable to stop long enough to view or comprehend. She shook her head, got out of bed and grabbed a robe before heading downstairs to the kitchen.

"Ah, Luci, good morning," James greeted her with

his ever cheerful smile. "Sleep well?"

"Morning. Thanks ...., er, yes, seem to have."

"Well, coffee's freshly made – help yourself to toast etc."

Lucia poured herself a mug of coffee with a copious amount of milk and sat down opposite James at the kitchen table. It all seemed so enclosed after Chiara's expansive *cucina*.

James thought how small and vulnerable his sister looked, so different to the capable, controlled woman who was so familiar to him. He decided to tread carefully.

"I've got a couple of things to take care of first thing but then I'm all yours. That's if there's anything you'd like to do, of course."

"Er, yes ..., that would be good. I just have to make a couple of calls and make a start on this article. Can I use your computer, my laptop was stolen."

"Sure, use mine – it's here." He pointed to a chair in the corner where the laptop nestled into the cushioned seat.

"Thanks. Maybe we could go for a walk and have lunch somewhere later......, catch up properly."

"Ok, how about we meet back here about 11.30? Will that give you enough time?"

Relieved that she wouldn't have to deal with the events in Italy straight away, she happily agreed. "Now, where's the toast?"

Showered and dressed, Lucia called her editor and discussed the finer points of the article and when she would have it ready for her to read through. They agreed that she would email a draft to her by 11 a.m. on

Monday and they would then meet later in the afternoon to discuss it and any other work.

Satisfied that she had some structure at last, she settled at the kitchen table with James' laptop, made a fresh pot of coffee and set to work. She listened to the interview with Antonio and made a start on weaving it into the notes she had already made. It felt good to be writing and after she had been working solidly for a couple of hours she heard James let himself in the front door. Jarred from her self-contained bubble, she ensured she saved her work to her memory stick and leaned back in her chair, happy with the start she had made.

"Hi, how's it going?"

"Great," she replied. "I've made a good start and I don't have to have it ready 'til Monday so I'm free to play, for a while anyway."

"Ok. How about a walk across the common and then we could have lunch at one of the pubs or Cannizaro House?"

"Sounds good to me." Lucia said, picking up on her brother's cheerful optimism. "Ready when you are."

It was a beautiful sun-filled morning as they walked under a clear cobalt sky the short distance to the common. Lucia thought that life felt almost normal and if it hadn't been for an occasional nagging beneath the surface, she could have convinced herself that was so. It was good to be outside and the familiarity of the common and her brother's presence were reassuring, even if only temporarily.

Her mobile announced the arrival of a text and

immediately apprehension filled her as adrenaline flowed offering the opportunity of fight or flight. Taking the mobile from her bag, she saw that it was from Chiara. Relief dissolved any concerns until she saw that she had missed a previous message from Tom. She opened it, emotions rising to her throat threatening to cut off her breath. Again she felt relief and berated herself for her stupidity as she read his words thanking her for her text, happy to hear from her, hoping they could talk soon.

"Everything ok, Luci?" James said, concerned.

"Yes, it's all good, thanks," she beamed causing James to wonder what on earth was going on and hoping he would find out soon. "It's just Chiara answering my text from last night."

Previously adept at hiding her feelings, Lucia was now finding it more difficult. Whilst she felt safe with James and was probably more open with him than anyone else, she still tried to hold on to established boundaries. One of these was her love life. She neither shared details of hers nor asked about his. She had always maintained this area of her life as private and, she suddenly realised, she not only kept the truth from others, but also from herself.

Since the arrival of the dream and her experiences in Italy, the tight rein of control she kept on her emotions had loosened and was no longer effective. As she thought of Tom she was aware of a mixture of fear and excitement that she could no longer deflect and ignore, it was too visceral. She saw his face, his green eyes crinkling in a smile, his warm voice reassuring her that all was as it should be, and she momentarily surrendered. Blinking to clear the image she determined to enjoy the walk and the rest of the day.

They walked across the common, circling the pond and exchanging news on their mother, their sister, Gabi, and the state of the world in general. The walk had stimulated their appetites and James asked Lucia where she would like to eat.

"Being a Saturday I suppose most places will be busy. Let's go to the pub, I don't want a huge lunch – what about you?"

"Suits me."

They retraced their steps to the edge of the common and decided on The Crooked Billet, a pub, Lucia thought, that seemed to have been there forever.

"Do you mind if we eat inside – it might be quieter." Lucia suggested seeing the mass of people in the garden and on the grass in front.

"Good idea." James agreed and they found a table tucked away in a quiet corner. As Lucia had hoped, most people were coming in to order at the bar then going outside.

The menu offered traditional pub fare for which it had maintained a good reputation over the years. She made her choice and James joined the queue at the bar to place their order. After a few minutes he returned with a glass of wine for Lucia and a pint of Young's Special for himself.

"Well, I suppose I'd better explain myself." Lucia said once James had sat down.

"Only if you want to, Luci. No pressure, you know that."

Lucia took her time and related the events of the last ten days. She chose carefully how much she divulged, only giving brief details of her sessions with Simonetta, most of which she decided to keep to herself for the time being, and pausing now and then to gauge James' response. He sat, relaxed yet attentive, and occasionally raised his glass to his mouth to drink his beer.

"So, here I am. Odd really, in some way ...., I don't know ...., it seems so normal here and it all sounds so melodramatic."

"Hm. I don't think so, Luci. You did the right thing. So you think it was this Lorenzo who took your laptop?"

"I don't know. I don't know what to think – it all seems a bit ridiculous now."

"Well, I'm not saying I understand it all but I think you are right to be careful. You know I'm going there on Monday, why don't you stay here 'til I get back? No-one need know where you are unless you want them to."

"Oh James – that would be great."

"Look, just make yourself at home and enjoy it. I'll be gone at least a week. Shame you can't come with me." He looked at her with his head slightly tilted on one side questioning the possibility in an attempt to diffuse the intensity that now sat between them.

"Er, no. I don't think that would be good idea." She said with a frown, looking at him through knitted eyebrows.

Their food arrived and their attention was directed to consuming their respective dishes as they each acknowledged a well earned hunger.

Once the initial pangs had been satiated, James resumed their conversation. "And, this guy who's been so helpful, what's his name? Oh yes, Tom – how does he fit in all this?"

Lucia felt the colour rise in her cheeks at the mention of Tom's name and the prospect of talking about him.

"Erm, what do you mean? Like I said, he's a friend of Chiara's and ….."

Oh Luci, come on, this is me you're speaking to." He looked at her with a knowing smile. "Look, you're blushing," he added with a gentle yet quietly teasing laugh.

"There's nothing to say!" she said raising her hands in exasperation. "I only met him a few times and …."

"And he seems to have had quite an effect on you."

"I wouldn't put it like that," she said as she narrowed her eyes and held his gaze.

"Sure you don't want to come with me?" he teased her further.

"You know I can't."

James picked up on the change in her voice and backtracked. "Alright, I'll leave it be. Peace."

"Ok. Peace." Lucia echoed. Since childhood they had always ended any arguments or simple teasings with the word 'peace' which meant that was the end of the matter and there were no bad feelings.

They finished their meal and walked into the village. In agreement that they would spend a relaxed evening at home, they went in search of something for supper and a DVD for later.

After visiting the delicatessen and patisserie in the high street, they returned home laden with bags filled with cold meats, cheeses, breads, salads, pastries and desserts. Wine, of course, there was no need to buy as James always had a constant supply of quality Italian wines from his business.

As they carefully put the bags down on the kitchen table, James pronounced, "Well that should keep us from going hungry."

"Yes. You know, you're incorrigible – how much do you think we can eat?"

"I know, I know. Anyway, you'll be here for a few days and you'll need to eat."

Lucia raised an eyebrow in askance, and then began to find a home in the fridge for it all.

It was now mid-afternoon and Lucia knew she had to get on with the article if she was to have it finished in time without too much pressure. She also wanted to be alone with her thoughts, in particular those that related to Tom.

"Ok if I take this into the garden?" asked Lucia pointing to the laptop.

"Sure. Actually, I've got one I hardly use in the office – I'll get it for you."

"Thanks, but ..."

"It's ok, I need to check on a couple of things anyway. I won't be long." James grabbed his car keys from the worktop and was gone.

Lucia took the laptop and found a shaded corner under the wisteria laden pergola where she could see the screen without too much reflection and returned to the last words of her article. She found it hard to settle as her mind swung to and fro between past events and future possibilities. She tried to focus on the article, wanting to get it finished, submitted and over with, as if her life would return to what she considered to be normal once it was out of the way. Frustrated by her inability to compartmentalise and create order she looked out into the garden in search of inspiration. She remembered Tom's words about her life not being the same again and felt overwhelmed by the weight of change yet to be assimilated.

She could almost feel his presence as she thought of him – his smile, his voice, his smell, that kiss – and an earthiness and quiet strength that had sustained her without intrusion. She longed for that reassurance and wondered if she should call him. An irrational fear of rejection caused her to reconsider and she retreated to the safety of sending a text instead.

Picking up her mobile she carefully worded her thanks, confirmed that she would be staying at her brother's for a few days and hoped to speak to him soon. She pressed send as she released her held breath in a huge sigh of relief.

She decided another coffee was needed. When she sat down again replete with coffee, she noticed she had received a text message. With her heart beating a little faster she opened it to see Tom's words. '*Ciao*. Happy to hear all's well and you're being looked after. Let's speak soon. X Tom.' She read it and re-read it until there was no room left for more interpretation. She wondered if she should call him but decided against it. It was enough that he had replied so quickly.

She returned her attention to the screen and her focus finally clicked in and she began to type. By the time she heard James' footsteps in the hall she had almost finished her first draft. She leaned back in the chair, satisfied with her work, and with her continued connection to Tom.

James walked through to the garden. "Hey, here you are," he said putting a small netbook down on the table. "Will this be ok?"

"Oh, that's perfect. Thank you," she said with a big smile.

"Did I miss something?"

"What do you mean?"

"Oh, only that you seem happier."

"Hm, I've almost finished the first draft, so yes, I suppose I am happy about that."

"Mmm," James said with a dubious tone. "Sorry I was so long, there was more to do than I thought. You know how it is."

"It's fine. What time is it anyway?"

"Er," he looked at his watch, "nearly seven."

"Oh, it's later than I thought."

"How about we celebrate your efforts with a glass of Prosecco?"

"Ooo, yes – good idea," Lucia agreed as she allowed herself to relax into the warmth and safety of new thoughts and feelings.

By 7.30 the temperature had dropped and they moved to the kitchen where they set out the food they'd bought earlier on the table.

James handed Lucia a plate, "Just help ourselves, ok?"

"Thanks," she said, happy to enjoy the informality.

They made space at one end of the table and sat down. James offered Lucia the choice of a red or white wine and, choosing the red, she began to wonder if the events of the last ten days had actually taken place as they seemed dreamlike in comparison to the normality of her brother and his home.

"I thought I might go over to see *mamma* tomorrow – want to come?"

Taken aback by James' suggestion she swallowed too quickly and coughed to hide any upset. "I,... er, ... I don't know James. I still have work to do and ..."

"It was just a thought, no worries."

"What time were you thinking of going?"

"Not early, maybe in time for tea – that way I don't have to stay too long. I just worry how she is out there on her own now that Gabi's gone, but you don't have to come."

Lucia relented and reluctantly agreed that, if she finished the article by lunchtime, she would go. She had wanted to talk to her mother and here was an opportunity to do so.

After finishing their meal they shared the clearing up before settling down to watch a DVD. Only just managing to stay awake to the end, Lucia surrendered to her need to sleep and said goodnight.

She woke from a fitful sleep later than she would have liked. The calm of the previous evening now a distant memory, usurped by disturbing dreams that remained only as fragments. She felt apprehensive yet could think of no rational reason for it.

She looked around the room, and satisfied that she was in London, in James' house and that it was Sunday, she contemplated her intended plans for the day hoping to find stability from the fractured images pervading her mind.

As she sat up in bed and leaned back against the pillows something within her let go and she realised the futility of carrying on with the pretence of glossing over her true feelings as if they didn't exist. She felt a weight lift from her, leaving her almost winded. At the same time as seeing her fears and doubts she became aware of a strong knowing, that she could no longer deny what had, and was, happening to her.

She remembered her conversation with James and whilst she'd told him what had happened in Italy, she had been selective, fearful he wouldn't understand. She felt divided, split somehow between two worlds, unsure of her footing in either. There was so much she had yet to understand. She stretched on a long out-breath releasing herself from her thoughts and the bed.

Showered and dressed, determined to get on with the day, she joined James in the kitchen for breakfast. After the usual exchange of good mornings and coffee and toast, James said he was going to play tennis and would leave her in peace to finish her article. Relieved, Lucia thanked him and, with the little laptop James had given her, set herself up at the garden table. She inserted the memory stick and, happy that everything was there, continued with her writing.

The morning passed quickly as she edited and re-wrote, and re-checked her research and recording of the interview until she reached the point where she knew it was time to let it be. Whilst she knew from experience that any further tinkering could spoil it, she saved it and decided to give it one last read through before she submitted it.

Leaning back, she breathed in the delicate fragrance of nearby roses and hoped that now the article was finished she would be able to get on with her life. However, relaxation eluded her, sublimated by the disquiet that rumbled round her solar plexus.

Simonetta, that was it, she'd promised to call her today. She picked up her phone and made the call.

"*Pronto.*"

"*Buongiorno, sono* Lucia."

"*Eh, buongiorno, come stai?*"

After the initial formalities, Lucia explained that she was staying with her brother, that she had finished the article and hoped to be able to go home soon.

"I think this will be alright in a day or so, but for now I would stay where you are if you are able to. I do not like to repeat rumours, for that is all they might be, but my knowing also tells me that matters concerning Lorenzo are changing and I think you will hear more very soon. Please, you will call me if anything happens?"

"Of course, and thank you."

"*Niente.* Have a lovely afternoon with your mother. This is a healing time for you now. We will speak soon. *A presto.*"

Before Lucia could ask how Simonetta knew she was going to see her mother she had ended the call. Was this the world she was entering, this knowing? So far, her abilities had only related to the past and the distant past at that. Before she could consider it further she heard James open the front door.

"Hi, good game?" she greeted him.

Collapsing in the chair next to her, he said, "Yeah, but I'm so out of condition – I really need to do something about it."

"Mmm, lunch then?" she said raising an eyebrow in irony.

She dodged his faux attempt to catch her as she skipped into the kitchen to redeem the leftovers from the previous evening's supper.

They arrived at their mother's home mid afternoon after a drive under a clear blue sky, and warmed by the accumulated heat of the sun. Lucia was still apprehensive despite reassurances from her brother. She knew there were questions she wanted to ask her mother and she also knew how unapproachable her mother could be, particularly on matters that had anything to do with Italy and the past.

The house was tucked away at the end of a long narrow lane edged by woodland on one side and flat open fields on the other. As they parked the car her mother was walking along the lavender lined path to greet them.

As she and James exchanged hugs with her in turn, Lucia realised it had been several months since she had seen her mother and she thought she looked tired and worn.

"Come, I'll make tea. We can sit in the garden and you can tell me all your news."

They followed Daniela into the house, through to the kitchen and out the other side into the garden.

"You've been busy, *mamma*, it looks lovely, so much colour." enthused Lucia.

"Thank you, darling," she smiled." Now will you have Earl Grey or British Rail?"

"Oh, Earl Grey, please." Lucia answered.

"Me too, thanks," followed James.

"I'll make a pot. Sit, I won't be long," and she disappeared back into the kitchen.

"She looks tired, don't you think?" Lucia asked.

"Yes, do you think she's alright?"

"How should I know?" snapped Lucia, taking herself by surprise, and immediately apologised. "I'm sorry James, I didn't mean to …."

"It's fine, don't worry. I know it's not easy."

Lucia sighed, unhappy at how quickly old feelings found their way, unbidden, to the surface.

Daniela walked towards them carrying a tray on which she had arranged a china tea set, a large teapot and what looked like home made scones with bowls of jam and clotted cream.

James jumped up to help her and placed the tray on the table.

"Wow, you have been busy!" he said.

"It looks wonderful," added Lucia.

"It's nothing, just a few scones," said Daniela, waving her hand dismissively. "Now shall I pour? Help yourselves to everything else."

"So, what have you been doing? Lucia, haven't you just been to see Chiara – how is she? How is *mamma*?" The questions tumbled from Daniela's mouth as Lucia wondered if she would be able to answer before the next one arrived.

"She's very well and sends her love, *mamma*, though *nonna* is not so good."

"Why, what do you mean? Is she ill?"

"Chiara didn't say, only that she is not as strong as she was and tires easily. She's still gathering and drying her herbs …"

"Ah, probably making her ill."

"I don't know, *mamma*. Will you go to see her this year?"

"Hm, I doubt it." she said and quickly turned to James. "And you, James what have you been doing? How is business?"

James, deciding not to mention his upcoming trip to Italy, merely confirmed that the business was doing well and waxed lyrical about some new products he would be adding, knowing his mother would quickly lose interest.

Daniela's eyes glazed over as she fulfilled his prophecy. "More tea?" she asked.

"What about you, *mamma,* what have you been up to?"

"Oh, not much. Now that Gabriella's gone ….." her voice trailed off.

James and Lucia exchanged the merest of glances as James was the first to try and rescue the conversation.

"Are you still painting?"

"Oh sometimes, though I haven't been inspired of late."

"I thought you were doing well with your watercolours, don't you have an exhibition coming up soon?"

"Oh that," she said with another dismissive wave of her hand," it's just a small exhibition of local artists, nothing grand."

It was becoming hard work and Lucia was losing hope of any possibility of talking to her mother about growing up in Italy. Maybe there would be another way, she thought.

By the time they had finished tea and looked at some of Daniela's latest paintings, James said it was time for them to be getting back and that he would visit again very soon.

Lucia was relieved to be heading back to London.

"You ok?" asked James

"Yes," she sighed. "I don't know what happens – I seem to become this other person and, well ….., she's impossible!"

"I suppose you two haven't got on for years. It wasn't always like that though."

"Wasn't it?"

"Hey, this is me. You know it wasn't."

"Ok, but can we talk about something else, please?"

"Sure, peace?"

"Yes, peace."

James avoided mentioning family and Italy and they covered a pot pourri of subjects from the latest films to the Higgs Boson. As they approached Wimbledon village, they were lost in the world of quasars and quarks. The conversation followed them into the cottage where they both collapsed in the living room.

"Fancy a pizza a bit later?" James suggested. "We can order one in or go out – up to you."

"Ooo, I can't think about food just yet, not after those scones!" Lucia said puffing out her cheeks.

"Ok, let me know when you're ready."

"I will."

They settled down to read the Sunday papers that

James had brought in earlier that day. Time dissolved in news and magazine articles until James broke the silence.

"Do you want to use the car while I'm away?" he asked.

"No, thanks, I don't have insurance."

"I can put you on mine if you want ..."

"No, it's ok, I've got used to not having one. What time's your flight?"

"It's the 9.45 from Gatwick. I'd better book a taxi to take me to the station." James picked up his mobile and arranged a taxi to collect him at 7. "Here's the spare key," he said, putting a key ring with two keys on the table. "Now, you know where everything is – can you think of anything else?"

"No, don't think so. I'm ready to eat though, shall we order that pizza – don't think I want to go out, do you?"

"No," he handed her a menu. "Choose your toppings and I'll phone through an order."

By the time they had eaten and dissected the contents of the Sunday papers, they were both ready to call it a day.

"Look, if I don't see you in the morning, take care and let me know if you need anything." James offered.

"Thanks. I'll be fine, though I probably won't see you in the morning. When are you back?"

"Not sure, depends how things go, probably by the weekend. I'll let you know."

They each said goodnight.

She'd been falling and even though she had woken in time, she felt shaken by the sensation and fear of what could have happened. Again, she looked around the room in order to get her bearings. This was becoming tiresome, she thought, and considered the possibility of going home to her flat.

First she had to do a final read through of the article and submit it, then get ready to go into town for the afternoon meeting with her editor.

It was strange being alone in the house. A sort of belonging yet not belonging, she thought, a bit like still being on holiday.

Granted another warm, sun-filled morning, Lucia decided to make the most of it by walking to the station and spending a couple of hours in town before going to the meeting. Now the article was on its way she felt freed from any expectations until mid afternoon.

She enjoyed the walk along the village high street and down the hill to Wimbledon Station. After a couple of changes she soon arrived at Bond Street and walked along Oxford Street to Selfridges where she intended to take her time and escape into a couple of hours of self indulgence.

Her intention quickly weakened as her thoughts were drawn to the last few days. She felt she was being pulled backwards and forward simultaneously and the inner tension overlaid any enjoyment she had hoped to find in shopping. There was now only an empty futility instead.

Leaving Selfridges she walked along to St Christopher's Place and headed for Carluccio's where she had agreed to meet Sarah, her editor. She decided to have lunch there and wait for Sarah to arrive at 3 o'clock, that way she could consider her next article and start making some notes. Thinking she had gathered some of her fragmented self into a kind of order, she soon found her distracted mind running elsewhere, this time in the direction of Tom and accompanied by a new hollow feeling in her stomach that was not related to hunger. Again she could feel the strength of his presence and could easily have turned to confide in him, but in awareness of his absence, she felt only an empty vacuum. She resolved to call him that evening.

The small square in front of Carluccio's was already busy and Lucia decided to sit inside. It was quieter there and she settled in a corner and looked over the menu. Memories of meals with Tom infused her being as she read the Italian menu and was surprised when the waiter arrived and spoke to her in English. She gave her order and tried to push Tom and Italy to the back of her mind.

Odd, she thought, after two weeks of being looked after, she was now back in London, single and self-sufficient and she wanted to return to her flat and her life to get back to normal, whatever that was. Still trying to integrate everything that had happened she knew her life had changed beyond recognition and there was no going back to how things were. Her thoughts returned to Tom and her stomach turned somersaults as she imagined his face, his smile, his presence. Why, oh why, had she kissed him? It was not like her to be so impetuous. What was she thinking of? Oh god, what a mess, she thought. It all seemed so simple when she left for Florence to do the interview and spend a few days with Chiara. Now look at it – chaos! She closed her eyes, sighed and ate her lunch.

Sarah arrived on time, they both ordered tea and she handed Lucia a copy of how the article would look.

"It's good, you've done a great job. I especially like the bit about Mr Martinelli leaving the bulk of the collection to the city – that was a bolt out of the blue. I'd like to use that in the promotional material, if that's ok?"

"Sure." Lucia shrugged her shoulders. "When will it go to press?"

"I'm hoping we can catch the next run, so it will be in the next issue. Now, what have you got lined up for me?"

"Oh, I don't know, Sarah."

"What! This isn't like you – you've always got irons in the fire. What is it, a man?" she asked, raising both eyebrows.

"What?" Lucia frowned indignantly. "Of course not."

"Well, there must be something – just saying."

"I'm fine, Sarah," she said trying to regain some ground. "Maybe I just need a holiday."

"And where might that be – Florence?"

"Sarah!"

"Ok, ok, I won't say another word about it." Sarah put her hands up in feigned submission. "Let me know when you have something, ok?"

"Of course, and thanks."

They chatted for another ten minutes about general events and gossip in the art world before saying goodbye and going their separate ways.

Oxford Street was already busy as she headed to the underground for the return journey to Wimbledon. She didn't enjoy the pushing, jostling and having to stand most of the way and, disconcerted and uncomfortable, she was glad to reach the end of the line and retreat to the cottage by taxi.

Once inside the cottage she took her mobile from her bag and found she had a missed call from Chiara. She pressed call, too impatient to listen to the voicemail she had left.

"*Pronto.*" Lucia felt relief at the sound of her aunt's familiar voice. "*Eh,* Lucia, *cara.* You have my message?"

"Oh, no I didn't see it. Has something …..?"

"I had a visit this morning from Gianluca and I wanted to tell you straightaway."

"What?"

"Lorenzo has been arrested. Something to do with drugs and fraud. It seems he has taken paintings from the collection and replaced them with forgeries. Gianluca thinks he was worried that you might have noticed something and that was why either he, or an accomplice, stole your laptop."

"He flatters me," laughed Lucia, "if he thinks I could tell a forgery at a glance."

"It's good news for you though, *cara.* It is now safe for you to return."

Chiara's words echoed loudly in Lucia's head as their meaning slowly found home.

"Yes, yes…, I suppose I can." she said in a quiet voice.

"*Va bene, cara?* I do not hear you well."

"Oh, yes, I'm fine – it's just a bit of a shock. Do you know what happened?"

"Only that the *Guardia di Finanzia* had been

watching him for some time and he and some others were arrested this morning. Poor Luisa, first Giacomo and now this."

"Oh dear, I wonder what will happen now?"

"I don't know, *cara*. Gianluca thinks that Lorenzo will go to prison for a very long time."

"Oh, that means I can go home now." Lucia said as her energy began to rise at the thought.

"*Si, cara,* I think you can. Will you come back to visit soon? I can see no reason why you shouldn't be able to now and Gianluca seemed to think that you would be safe."

"I'd love to but I have a few things to sort out here before I can think about it."

"You know you can come anytime. Franco's back and the girl's will be home for the summer soon - we'd all love to see you and, of course, *mamma* would be delighted."

The warmth of Chiara's words encircled Lucia and released some of her anxiety. "Ok, I'll see what I can do."

"*Bene*. Have you heard from Tom?"

"A text …."

"Will you give him the good news?"

,"Er yes, ok." she said with some hesitation and suspicion as to Chiara's motives.

"*Allora,* I have a man to feed. We'll speak soon, *no*?"

"Yes Chiara, very soon. *Ciao*."

"*Ciao, cara*."

Lucia put together a plate of food from the remaining contents of the fridge, poured a glass of wine and curled up on the sofa in the living room. She went over Chiara's words as she picked at the food, her appetite eclipsed by apprehension and excitement at the news and being able to go home. She planned to return the next day, but first she would call Tom. The thought of speaking to him caused her appetite to vanish completely and she put down the plate thinking she could return to it later if she was hungry.

Maybe he would be eating. He could be with someone else. What if he didn't want to speak to her? Her thoughts flew from one negative thought to another until she could bear it no longer and finally took a deep breath, found his number and pressed call.

"*Ciao*, Lucia, *come stai?*" said the deep resonant voice and she smiled.

"*Ciao*, Tom. I'm ok, and you?"

"*Si, si, bene.*" he continued in Italian.

"Er, I've just had a call from Chiara. She says that Lorenzo has been arrested – something to do with drugs and fraud. Had you heard anything?"

"No, but that's great news. You must be relieved."

"Yes, yes, I am. I'm still at James' but I'll go home tomorrow."

"Lucia…?"

"Yes?"

"I miss you."

"Oh, Tom ….," she paused as a torrent of feelings flooded her being. "I miss you too. Only this afternoon, I could almost feel your presence, and …"

"*Lo so,* I know."

"Tom …?"

"We must talk, but not like this, I want to see you. Will you come back to Florence now that you can?"

"Oh Tom, I don't know there's still so much I don't understand and …., yes!" The word flew from her mouth and she immediately wondered where it had come from.

"You will?"

She relaxed into her own knowing and said, "Yes, Tom. I just need to sort a few things out here. Can I call you tomorrow when I get home?"

"*Certo,* of course. But come soon."

"I will."

They said goodbye, each left with the thoughts of so many words unsaid yet happy with the ones already spoken.

Lucia stretched the length of the bed, happy to wake from a deep and uneventful sleep. A new feeling embraced her as she remembered Tom's words from the previous evening's call; contentment. She rolled in the delight, curling into a ball and hugging the duvet. It had been a long time since her heart had softened and she liked the way it felt. She opened her eyes, looked at the clock and, remembering the day ahead of her, leapt out of bed and into the shower.

A new lightness touched everything she did and, again, she was reminded of the sensation at the end of her dream when she had walked through the wall.

She beamed at her reflection in the mirror and resisted the impulse to book the next flight to Florence, and Tom. As she organised the day in her mind small shadows of doubt crept in weaving their fear. Maybe she was over-reacting, had she read more into his words, was she being foolish, and … so on. Such thoughts were short lived as her new found exuberance stopped them taking hold.

There was an air of efficiency as she prepared to leave and by nine o'clock her suitcase was packed and in the hall, ready for her return home. The ringing of her mobile jerked her back to the present. It was Sarah, her editor.

"Hi Lucia, I was wondering if you'd had any thoughts for the next issue?"

"Er no, not yet. I …."

"I know, you wanted some time but I thought a new focus might, you know…?"

"Thanks Sarah," Lucia said, unsure whether she was grateful or not. Then remembering what had happened the previous evening, she added, "Actually, I may have. I heard last night that Lorenzo Martinelli has been arrested – sounds serious, drugs and forgery."

"Well, that could be interesting. Do you want to go and find out more? It could be a great follow up. What do you think?"

Lucia's heart leapt at a legitimate reason to go to Florence. "Ok, I could stay with my aunt and see what I can find out if you like."

"Great. How soon can you leave?"

"Probably tomorrow, I'll check the flights." she said as her heart beat even faster.

"Fabulous. Keep in touch now."

"Yes I will, and thanks Sarah."

"Bye."

"Bye."

Decisively she ordered a taxi to take her home.

Strange, she thought, as she opened the front door against the pile of post on the doormat, it seems familiar and yet unfamiliar. She left her suitcase in the hall and took the post through to the kitchen. She felt the echo of emptiness left by her absence of the last two weeks.

Taking the laptop from her bag, she turned it on and waited until she heard the familiar start up tones. The icons came on one by one and she checked the availability of flights for the next day.

She took the phone from the hall and called Chiara who was delighted to hear she wanted to visit so soon and satisfied those arrangements were in place, she booked her flight.

It was now midday and she wondered if she should wait to call Tom. She took out her mobile to find his number and write it down for later but when it showed on the screen she was unable to stop herself from pressing the call button.

"*Ciao,* Lucia."

"*Ciao,*" she said and smiled as she dissolved in the warm tones of his voice. "I've just booked my flight...."

"When?" he interrupted.

"Tomorrow. My editor rang this morning and wants me to do a follow up article and I've just spoken to Chiara and ..." she stopped, realising she was babbling.

"I can pick you up from airport if you like."

"I like."

She opened her suitcase and assessed its contents debating what to leave in, take out and add. Deciding there was no time to do a wash she replaced one or two items and left the rest on the basis that she could put them in the laundry at Chiara's.

She looked around the flat to see if there was anything that needed her attention before sitting down to go through her post. Fortunately, she could deal with most things online and once she had disposed of any junk mail, she filed the remainder in a drawer.

The only thing left to consider now was food as she realised she had missed lunch so she went to the kitchen to investigate. The fridge was empty save for odd jars of jam and sauces, and the contents of the freezer sparse. She grabbed her bag and went out into the warmth of the late afternoon sun. She walked down to Holland Park Avenue, bought a small French boule from Paul, the French bakery, and some ripe brie, olives and sun ripened tomatoes from the nearby delicatessen. Satisfied she would not starve she retraced her steps home.

Lucia's newfound happiness ebbed and flowed as grey tentacles of doubt crept in, but found no hold. Despite attempts to undermine her decision to return to Florence, they became diaphanous as she wrapped herself in the memory of Tom's rich voice and the knowing that she was doing the right thing.

Eventually, she made her ritual chamomile tea and went to bed. She looked around her bedroom as she turned out the light, and smiled in gratitude before falling into a contented sleep.

Themah Carolle-Casey

Florence, ITALY

The flight had been full and the airport busy as Lucia walked free of customs and out through the Arrivals gate on to the concourse.

Tom stood to one side and she walked straight into his open arms. They stayed held, each by the other, before moving apart to confirm each other's presence. Lucia thought he looked taller. Tom thought she looked smaller. She longed to be held. He longed to hold her close.

Both unwilling to let go from a desire to maintain physical contact, they walked towards the exit, his arm round her shoulder and hers round his waist. Speechless until they reached the car, Tom broke the silence as he put her suitcase in the boot. He took her hand and pulled her towards him and looking into her eyes said, "It's so good to see you."

"I know," were the only words Lucia could find as he drew her closer and leaned down to kiss her gently, restraining any urgency. It was she who pulled him closer, accepting his kiss unreservedly.

With reluctance they separated and he opened the car door for her before going round to the driver's side.

"We'd better get going, Chiara says she'll have lunch ready for us," he said, reluctantly peeling his eyes from her to focus on the road.

Lucia secured her seatbelt. "Oh, ok."

Tom paused before starting the engine.

"There is so much I want to say Lucia, and to just be with you but ….," he paused. "Let's do this first, and then later maybe we can …"

They left the airport and took the route along the *autostrada* before turning off at *Firenze Sud* and heading towards Chiara's villa. Tom asked her to fill in all the minutes that they'd been apart. He wanted to know everything and by the time they arrived at the villa she had brought him up to date.

Chiara heard the car and ran down the steps to greet her niece. After exchanging effusive hugs and kisses she led the way up to the main door and Tom followed with Lucia's suitcase.

"Come, lunch is almost ready. It is just me, Franco has gone to Milan with James and they should be back tomorrow."

Lucia was disappointed not to see her brother but pushed it to the back of her mind as they followed Chiara through to the *cucina* where, only last week, they had shared so many meals.

"*Eh,* here we are again. A celebration, I think!" and she took a bottle of Prosecco from the fridge and passed it to Tom.

"Would you mind, Tom? I just have to see to this." This was a sauté pan filled with small potatoes in garlic and rosemary. "I thought you might be hungry after such an early start, *cara*, so there is a sort of Italian version of fish and chips." She said with a flourish. Before Lucia could say anything, Chiara continued almost in the same breath, "*Allora, dimme tutto,* tell me all."

They sat at the table as Tom filled the glasses. Chiara put the fish and potatoes into serving dishes and placed them on the table along with a large bowl of mixed salad and Lucia began to recite the events of the last few days.

Tom's eyes followed and absorbed every word, captivated even in repetition.

"So, that's it really. Have you heard any more of Lorenzo?" she asked, turning to Chiara.

"No, but I thought we might invite Luisa to lunch."

"Ok. What about your friend, Gianluca, can I speak to him?"

"*Eh,* I don't see why not. I'll call him later."

As the conversation moved on to other topics, Chiara became aware of a frisson in the air between Lucia and Tom as each caught or sometimes avoided the other's eyes. She had teased her about him before but Lucia had always denied any feelings for him and Chiara wondered what had happened to change this. The energy between them was almost palpable and she smiled inwardly at imagined possibilities.

"Chiara, that was wonderful, thank you, it was just what I needed," Lucia enthused as she placed her fork across an empty plate.

"*Bene.* Some fruit, coffee?"

"Yes, please, both."

"Tom?"

"Just coffee, please, then I must go – work."

"Oh," Lucia looked at him, disappointed at being deprived of his company.

"We could go for supper later, if you're not too tired?"

Chiara returned to the table with the fruit for Lucia and a large pot of coffee. "That would be perfect Tom. I have a meeting in town this evening. I'd hoped to change it but ...."

"Ok," interrupted Lucia, "what time are you thinking ...?"

"I could pick you up about seven if that's ok. And now, I must go."

"So, tell me," Chiara demanded as soon as Tom had left.

"Tell you what?"

"About Tom, what's ..."

"Nothing, I don't know what you mean," Lucia said a little too quickly.

"*Cara,* you are like a couple of lovebirds even if you think you are hiding it."

"I ..., I ..."

"Lucia," she said, slowly pronouncing each syllable. "Your eyes say it all; you can hardly keep your hands off each other. If you want to stay at his place, I understand and ..."

"Chiara!" Lucia exclaimed.

"*Eh,* I think it is wonderful, so enjoy it. Just text me and let me know whether you will be back or not."

Lucia stared at her aunt, for once speechless.

Chiara smiled, "Come, help me clear the table and we should have time to see *mamma,* she'd love to see you."

Lucia returned the smile and surrendered to her aunt's delight in her embryonic love life. "Mmm, I'd like that."

Isabella's smile grew wider at the sight of her granddaughter.

"*Amore, amore,* you have come back to us," she said, making it sound like a song. Lucia gave her a gentle hug. "And, I see you are in love."

Lucia stood back and looked at Isabella with a wary eye. "What do you mean, *nonna*?" she said with indignant humour.

"*Eh*, I know that look. You can't hide it you know."

"Obviously not," and she looked to Chiara who was pursing her lips to suppress a laugh.

"It is the young man you brought to see me?" The inflection in Isabella's voice was so slight that Lucia couldn't tell if it was a question or a statement. "He is very nice, *amore*."

"Yes, I think so." Lucia said finally relinquishing her guard.

"*Bene, bene*, I'll make some tea." And Isabella disappeared into the kitchen. "Go sit outside, in the shade."

Lucia spent the next hour delighting in their company as they laughed and reminisced about summer's long since passed. Eventually Chiara said they must go. They helped Isabella clear the tea things and reluctantly said goodbye.

"You will come again soon," she said as she gave Lucia a hug and touched her cheek.

"Yes, *nonna*, I will," she said and promised to visit

again very soon.

As they walked back to the villa, Chiara said, "It is good you have come back, *cara*. It means a lot to *mamma* to have you here."

"Yes, I know." Lucia said as a fleeting sadness passed through her. "How ill is she?"

"*Eh,* you know *mamma*, she won't talk of these things. She may mention a little thing here and another thing there and we work with the herbs and she says she feels better. She won't see a doctor and you can see, she's not so strong anymore …."

"Do you think it's serious?"

"I don't know *cara,* I don't know." Chiara linked her arm in Lucia's. "*Peró,* we have to accept and honour her wishes and, ….. and, make the most of the time we have with her."

Lucia nodded as her aunt squeezed her arm, pulling her closer and she felt the cool breeze of sadness pass by once again.

Lucia was tired after her early start and, after unpacking her suitcase, decided to lie down before getting ready for her evening with Tom. She drifted in and out of sleep and wisps of dreams came and went, too diaphanous to hold or recall. It was the last dream that caused her to wake with alarm as she tried to call out but could make no sound. At the same time the alarm clock by her bed began beeping and she looked around the room as she remembered where she was, trying to bring her dream to consciousness but, like the others, it had already dissolved beyond her reach.

Annoyed by its loss, she closed her eyes hoping to

pick up a thread, but it was no use, there was nothing, it had gone. She hadn't had any disturbing dreams since the other one had stopped and she felt unsettled and apprehensive at the thought of it happening again.

She didn't want it to spoil her evening with Tom and took a long hot shower, hoping the water would cleanse and wash away her fears and doubts. Weak from the heat and steam she stepped out of the shower, wrapped herself in a towel and opened the door to the balcony and took some deep breaths.

Her apprehension slowly transformed to anticipation and, if she'd allowed it, may have become excitement. She looked over the clothes she had brought with her and, limited by what was clean, chose a simple linen dress in coral and a short cotton cardigan in a pattern of muted greens, coral and cream that she lay out on the bed.

As she dried her hair, anxious butterflies filled her abdomen. Even though she had been out with Tom before, this was different. Whereas before he had been there to help her, take her here or there or introduce her to Simonetta, this felt like a date, something she had not done for a long time. She could sense something almost tangible in the air, tantalising, but as yet inexpressible.

She dressed and went downstairs where Chiara was having a quick snack before going to her meeting.

"*Eh*, look at you, *sei bellissima!*"

"Thank you," Lucia said as she gave a playful curtsy and tried to hide a blushed embarrassment.

Chiara's eyes twinkled with mischief as she gathered her things and said, "Maybe see you later then."

Lucia declined to respond and merely raised an

eyebrow in Chiara's direction.

The restaurant was busy for so early in the evening and Tom was pleased he had phoned ahead and booked. After the usual effusive greetings they were shown to the same table they had occupied the week before.

"I hope you don't mind coming here again, it's just...," Tom began.

"No, of course I don't. It's great." Lucia said, happy to be in familiar surroundings and not having had to travel far.

The short journey had been undemanding as they exchanged details of each other's day. There was an initial awkwardness between them that had not previously existed, more akin to a couple who had just met and were finding their way.

Both were aware of the shift that had taken place in their relationship as soon as they had acknowledged their feelings for each other. Still in the embryonic stage, there was anticipation and trepidation on both sides. Slowly they were each opening to a new possibility.

Tom remembered how vulnerable she was when he first saw her. He had withheld acting on his wish to seduce and protect her, knowing she had to find her own way first. Now, he saw a new strength and sensuality in her and he was no longer able to resist.

Lucia had gained a quiet confidence since the kiss at the airport and liked Tom's sudden vulnerability. She could feel his desire for her and, although it made her nervous, she also wanted to be enveloped by it.

Relaxed by the wine and conviviality of the

environment, they chatted amicably and enjoyed an excellent meal. They shared more of what had happened during their brief separation, and hypothesised on Lorenzo's arrest and the effect this might have on his inheritance.

As they ordered coffee and knowing their evening was drawing to a close, they each struggled to hide feelings of exhilaration and foreboding. Tom made the first move when he reached his hand across the table to cover hers.

"I'm so happy you were able to come back so soon, and," he paused as he cleared his throat, "and, I think this is a little awkward for both of us, *no*?"

Lucia, relieved that he had been the first to say something, was disarmed by the Italian inflection that transformed it into a shared dilemma.

"Mmm, "she nodded, "yes. It has been a long time."

"For me also," he said as he squeezed her hand a little.

As she looked into emotive green eyes Lucia felt as if she would burst for wanting him and slowly turned her hand to accept and hold his. At the same time she was aware of the social mores and conditioning that tried to override her longing and smiled in empathy.

Her smile lit desire in every fibre of Tom's being and he yearned to be alone with her and signalled for the bill.

Once outside, the air between them was alive with anticipated passion. As Tom opened the door for Lucia, she looked up and before she could speak their arms and mouths found each other and their bodies melded in search of an intimacy beyond words.

Tom pulled away, "I'm sorry, I, er …"

"Don't be."

"I don't want to rush you and …"

"You're not," Lucia said, feeling suddenly calm.

"You mean…?"

"Yes," she said as she kissed his cheek and slid into the car.

Tom walked round and got into the car. He turned the key in the ignition and said with a theatrically raised eyebrow, "My place for a nightcap?"

Lucia beamed and nodded.

She had not been to Tom's home before and was curious. Unlike most single Italian men he did not live with his parents but rented a small *casetta* nearby. The front door opened into an open plan living room that was simply furnished in earthy colours of rusts and ochres that Lucia found warm and welcoming. A large sofa and two armchairs sat around a large low table littered with newspapers, magazines and the odd sketched plan, in front of an open fireplace similar to an inglenook. At the far end, beyond a rectangular pine, table and chairs, an archway led to a modern kitchen. To one side of the archway, open stairs climbed along the wall to the next floor.

She looked around the room, seeking insights into the man who she was opening to. Tom indicated towards the sofa and said, "A *vin santo* maybe, or you would prefer tea?"

"Er, *vin santo* please," she replied, unsure whether or not he was serious about the tea, and sat down on the large sofa which seemed to swallow her.

Tom returned with two glasses and a bottle of *vin*

santo which he placed on the low table before joining her on the sofa.

He poured the amber liquid into the two glasses and handed one to Lucia.

They looked at each other as they sipped from their glass in knowing of the irrevocable step they were about to take. As Tom put his glass down on the table he reached out his arm in invitation and said, "*Tesoro, vieni qui,* come here."

Lucia responded by putting down her glass next to his and sliding along the sofa into his arms. He turned and cradled her head in his hand then looking into her eyes, said, "I'm so happy you're here."

Lucia reached her hand gently to the side of his face, "So am I."

They slowly moved closer and as they kissed Lucia was sure she heard a sigh and a familiar voice whisper, *"Bene,"* but she was beyond caring as she surrendered to the moment.

The morning came too quickly for Lucia as she lay in the crook of Tom's arm. He woke and, turning towards her, stroked her hair from her eyes and gently kissed them.

"Good morning, *amore*."

"Mmm, morning," she murmured, not wanting the magic of the night to end. She looked up into a pair of soft green eyes that mirrored her emergent love and trust, and began to say, "Tom, I …"

"Sssh ," he whispered as he put one finger over her lips before leaning towards her and kissing her gently. Lucia responded by pulling him closer and their now familiar bodies answered each other as they made love with ease and tenderness.

It was Tom who was the first to move as he leaned away to check the time. "I have to go soon ..., a meeting ... and ..." he said as he leaned in to kiss her again before adding, "breakfast?"

"Mmm, yes please," she beamed. "Oh no!" she cried, suddenly sitting up, "I didn't let Chiara know that ..., excuse me, I must text her."

"Ah, I'll put coffee on. You know where the bathroom is, there's a spare robe on the back of the door. Help yourself to anything else you need."

Lucia wrapped his robe around her, immersing herself in his smell, and wandered downstairs to find her mobile. With profuse apologies she confirmed she was with Tom and would be back soon, then joined Tom in the kitchen where he was waiting for the little coffee pot to bubble.

She walked into his outstretched arm as he looked at her apologetically and explained a lack of fresh pastries and suggested they stop on the way to Chiara's.

"Coffee's fine." And she stood behind him, encircling his waist as he poured the dark liquid into two small cups.

"You have milk?" Lucia asked.

"*Eh*, I forget, you like it the English way," he teased. "Yes, in the fridge."

She punched him playfully in the back before opening the fridge and saying, "Thanks."

Not wanting to lose physical contact with her, Tom took her hand and pulled her on to his lap. "What will you do today?"

"Oh," she responded, not wanting to think about it

but forcing herself to do so, then continued. "I suppose I'll see if I can speak to Gianluca about Lorenzo and Chiara said something about inviting Luisa to lunch but I don't know when."

He held her closer, "Ah, *tesoro,* I don't want to be away from you for a moment longer than I have to, will you let me know if you're free for lunch?"

"Yes, of course," she said and kissed him before tearing herself from his arms. "I'd better shower," she added as their fingertips lingered.

Tom grabbed her hand and said, "Mmm, maybe I'll join you." And they ran upstairs to the bathroom.

When they eventually left the house, Lucia was elated as joy and happiness flowed through her. After a brief stop at a bar for more coffee and a croissant, Tom dropped Lucia at her aunt's villa and she promised to call and let him know about lunch.

She found Chiara in the kitchen.

"So, look at the cat who has the cream." Chiara said with a grin that almost matched Lucia's.

"Chiara, I'm sorry …"

"Cara, non ti preoccupare, don't worry. At least I knew where you were."

"I .."

"Allora, I spoke with Gianluca this morning and he said if you pass by about eleven he will be able to see you. And, I also called Luisa and she is free for lunch tomorrow if that is alright with you."

"Ok, I'll just go and change and then …."

"Then you can tell me all about last night." Chiara said with a mischievous grin.

"Not all, Chiara." Lucia said with a raised eyebrow

and ran upstairs to get ready for the day.

Themah Carolle-Casey

ACNOWLEDGEMENTS

So many people have been part of bringing this book from inspiration to print, and I thank you all for your patience, support, encouragement and friendship. I have loved nearly every minute of the journey and could not have done it without you, Special thanks to those who held my hand through all the edits and rewrites and also the agents and publishers that did not take me on but were encouraging in their rejections. And, not least, my daughter, whose belief in me is always an inspiration.

Themah Carolle-Casey

ABOUT THE AUTHOR

Themah is a writer and artist who lived in Italy for several years. She now lives in Somerset where she is working on her second novel.

Visit her website at *www.essentially-art.com*

Made in the USA
Charleston, SC
09 June 2016